A Premonition of Evil...

That night, I had a most unpleasant dream, the first of what was to become a series of recurring nightmares. I was floating through space looking down at the earth, which metamorphosed into some kind of snakelike creature. The creature rose up as I flew over, and engulfed me. I began to fall through black space, and in the darkness I could hear angry voices. In my dream I knew what had happened. I had entered the maw of Xibalba, and the voices I heard were the Lords of the Underworld.

In retrospect, if I'd paid attention to that night's dream and those that were to follow, at a minimum I might have avoided some poor personal choices. At best, at least one death might have been averted.

The XIBALBA MURDERS

AN ARCHAEOLOGICAL MYSTERY

The XIBALBA MURDERS

AN ARCHAEOLOGICAL MYSTERY

Lyn Hamilton

BERKLEY PRIME CRIME, NEW YORK

This is a work of fiction. Names, characters, places, and incidents either are the product of the author's imagination or are used fictitiously, and any resemblance to actual persons, living or dead, business establishments, events, or locales is entirely coincidental.

THE XIBALBA MURDERS

A Berkley Prime Crime Book / published by arrangement with the author

PRINTING HISTORY
Berkley Prime Crime edition / April 1997

The Penguin Putnam Inc. World Wide Web site address is http://www.penguinputnam.com

ISBN: 0-425-15722-9

Berkley Prime Crime Books are published by The Berkley Publishing Group, a division of Penguin Putnam Inc., 375 Hudson Street, New York, New York 10014.
The name BERKLEY PRIME CRIME and the BERKLEY PRIME CRIME design are trademarks belonging to Penguin Putnam Inc.

PRINTED IN THE UNITED STATES OF AMERICA

10 9 8 7 6 5 4

For my parents

ACKNOWLEDGMENTS

Those wishing to learn more about the Maya might consider four of the many fine books on the Maya that I found particularly helpful: *The Maya*, by Michael D. Coe; Linda Schele and David Freidel's *A Forest of Kings, the Untold Story of the Ancient Maya*; Dennis Tedlock's translation of the *Popol Vuh*; and, for its explanation of the Maya calendar and the Maya of today, Ronald Wright's *Time among the Maya*. All of these books have provided invaluable information. Any errors and literary liberties are, of course, my own.

The XIBALBA MURDERS

PROLOGUE

I AM CALLED SMOKING FROG, named for one of the greatest warriors in the annals of my people, the conqueror of Uaxactún.

I am not a warrior, I am only a scribe, and many, many transits of Venus separate my time from his. But perhaps it is fitting that I bear his name. For while the great Smoking Frog's brave exploits ushered in the most glorious age of our people, I believe that I may be witness to its end.

The pale bearded men from across the waters are not gods, as we first believed. They are instead human emissaries of the Lords of Xibalba, the Lords of Death.

Soon they will have conquered us not by arms, not by their terrible diseases, but by eliminating our words, our history, and our gods, and replacing them with theirs.

I have seen how they throw down our *kulché*, the images of our gods, and only four nights ago I watched from my great canoe as a glow lit the sky over Ix Chel's island, fueled by the pyre on which they threw our sacred texts.

But the Ancient Word is eternal. I carry it with me, though it means death if I am found. I will travel to the sacred rivers of the Itzá, even to the jaws of Xibalba, and hide it there. If I survive this time, I will return for it, and remind my people of its teachings. If I do not, then I pray that in a better time it will be found, and the power of our words will once again ring across the land.

IMIX

A LOT OF PEOPLE HAVE asked me—and I suppose the next to do so may well be a Mexican judge and prosecutor—why I flew thousands of miles to help someone I didn't know all that well look for a small furry creature with big ears, a pink nose, and literary aspirations.

A more pointed question would actually be why did I persist in the search when people kept turning up dead around me?

I blame my ex-husband, Clive, ex-spouses being convenient scapegoats for almost everything, since it was because of him that I had so much time on my hands.

The real reason, of course, is rather more complicated. In retrospect, I think it was because, having lost all that I thought really mattered—a business that I had built up over several years, and a painful marriage I had clung to—I felt I had nothing left to lose.

In the end it took a spiritual journey into darkness, and a personal encounter with people I have come to associate with the Lords of Death, to restore my sense of wonder at what the world has to offer.

The beginning of this journey was a phone call from Dr. Hernan Castillo Rivas, a scholarly gentleman whose enthusiasm and knowledge of the ancient civilizations of Mexico have inspired in me a lifelong interest in that part of the world. He had been the executive director of a private museum in Mérida, Mexico, that specialized in Maya antiquities, and after his retirement, the Mexican agent for my company—former company, I should say—a shop that sold objets d'art, furnishings, and accessories, really wonderful stuff, from all over the world.

"Lara," he began, "I understand from the Ortizes that you are studying hard and that you have chosen as your subject an area of great interest to me," he said. The Ortiz family were longtime friends, and it had been they who had first introduced me to Dr. Castillo—Don Hernan, as I liked to call him.

"I have what I hope is an interesting proposition. If I am correct, your school term is ending, and you have a break for a month. I would like you to join me here in Mexico to assist me with a project I am working on. I need a partner.

"I cannot tell you more about it right now, but I can assure you that it is—what is that American expression?— right up your alley, and that it will interest and possibly even excite you?"

"You'll have to tell me more than that!" I laughed.

"This is not a subject for discussion over the telephone," he replied. "The risk is too great."

4

And then, perhaps fearing I wouldn't come on the strength of so little information, he relented a little.

"I will give you a hint, then, since you are a student of the Maya. We seek what the rabbit writes." And that was all he would say.

It was a ludicrous request, so of course I went.

As I have already mentioned, I had the time. Several months earlier, finding myself in a period of forced inactivity, I went back to university to begin to study the Maya, an ancient Mesoamerican civilization that reached its peak in the fourth to tenth centuries in what is now Guatemala, Belize, Honduras, and Mexico's Yucatán peninsula.

Before that I had been one of two proprietors, my husband, Clive Swain, being the other, of a very successful shop called McClintoch and Swain located in Toronto's fashionable Yorkville area.

Clive, whose interest in working for a living could most charitably be called, in my opinion, desultory, had unaccountably become most enthusiastic about the business in the dying days of our marriage.

The price of my freedom was half the proceeds of the sale of McClintoch and Swain, and the admonition from my lawyer to stay away from that, or any business, for at least a year.

"If you start a new business right away, Lara, he'll be back for more," she had warned. "He is trying to take you for everything you have!"

There was no question I could afford a year off. Half the proceeds of the sale would not make me rich, but with care I could survive a year or so. But it galled me to give Clive half the money for what I saw to be considerably less than half the work, and I was still smarting from the acrimony of the split-up and the embarrassment of admitting I had been wrong about him.

The one consolation was that the woman to whom I had sold the business, Sarah Greenhalgh, seemed to love it as much as I had.

I tried the life of leisure for a while, but the less I had to do, the more time I had to dwell on my situation. Hence the return to university. I found, though, that the academic life, as interesting as it might be, had not really served its purpose of keeping my mind off the emotional and financial wreckage of my life. I'll admit the call from Don Hernan came as something of a relief. Within minutes of talking to him, I called my travel agent and bought a ticket to Mérida.

It was on the day the Maya would have called Imix, the day of the Earth Being, that I locked the door of my little Victorian cottage, handed the keys to Alex Stewart, my neighbor, who promised to care for my house and my cat, an orange tabby who went by the name of Diesel. He had been the official "shop cat," and was essentially, in my mind at least, all I had to show for twelve years of work.

The journey took me first to Miami, then on to Mérida. It was a trip I used to do three or four times a year for business, but also because, for many reasons, I loved the place. This time, I suppose because of my studies, I found myself searching below me for signs of the enormous empire the Spanish conquistadores had found when they first arrived in the New World.

How surprised these early visitors must have been to find cities bigger than anything they had ever seen in Spain, or elsewhere in Europe, for that matter, since there were huge Maya cities when Paris was still a muddy village. Now the cities are largely gone, green mounds rising from the floor of the forest the only hint of their former existence.

If I could not find many physical remains of their culture, I was able to appreciate, from the vantage point of the aircraft, the imaginative way the Maya were able to describe their world. The Maya saw the earth as Imix, a water-lily monster, a reptilian kind of creature, sometimes a turtle, more usually a monstrous crocodile, lying in an immense pool of water, the earth resting on its curved back.

Under this creature is Xibalba, the underworld, the place of fear, its atmosphere the water in which the earth being, Imix, lies. Through this watery region, the sun has to pass during its nocturnal journey, becoming, in its passage through the underworld, the fearsome Jaguar God. Above the earth curves a double-headed serpent, the sky serpent whose markings are the signs of the celestial bodies.

Looking down from twenty thousand feet, it is not difficult to imagine the water-lily monster resting in the waters of the Gulf of Mexico, the sky serpent arching over it from horizon to horizon. In a way, I was disappointed when the aircraft left the forests of the Maya world behind and began the descent into Mérida.

I deplaned rapidly, clearing customs without incident. Having done this several times before, on buying trips, I was quickly able to negotiate my way through the throngs of hawkers and hustlers promising everything from cheap lodgings to a good time, then was pleased to see Isabella, the Ortiz's daughter, waiting for me. She must have flown down from Mexico City when she heard I was coming.

Isabella, Isa for short, and I have been friends for twenty-five years, ever since my father, who had spent his career with the United Nations, was posted into Mexico. We, my parents and I, spent two years there, and Isa and I, growing up together through a couple of awkward teen years, became fast friends.

Isa has built a highly successful business in Mexico City by adapting the classic women's attire of her native Yucatán, the embroidered *huipil,* to more modern tastes. Her beautifully designed women's clothing has struck a chord with Mexican women and her face and her fashions now regularly grace the covers and pages of haute couture magazines. She has a new partner in life, Jean Pierre, a French banker posted to Mexico, who is also her unofficial business manager.

"*Bienvenidos,* welcome, Lara." She smiled, giving me a big hug and handing me a bouquet of birds of paradise. "We're all so pleased you've come to visit."

I dumped my ugly duffel bag into the back of her Mercedes convertible—clearly business was good—and we headed for her family's little inn, the Casa de las Buganvillas, literally the house of the bougainvilleas. It is on a quiet little side street off the Paseo de Montejo, and the place I always stay when I'm in Mérida.

One enters by way of a curved stone staircase lined

8

with colorful tiles in blue and white, then through handcarved wooden doors into a cool and dark domed entranceway. The floors are tiled in terra-cotta, the walls textured plaster in the colonial style. Wooden ceilings are hand-painted in traditional designs and the halls and entranceway lit by large wrought-iron and blown-glass candelabras.

The inn is the ancestral home of the Ortiz family. Burdened by a house far too large to be practical, and with Santiago Ortiz Menendez away for much of the time for his work in the Mexican diplomatic corps, Francesca Ortiz began first to take in the odd lodger, then gradually to transform the house into the wonderful inn that it is today.

There are still reminders of the grander times. The reception desk is just that—a huge old carved desk that had been brought by the Ortiz ancestors on a Spanish sailing ship. Santiago Ortiz Menendez sat there now, smiling his welcome. He retired early from the diplomatic corps, felled by a debilitating degenerative muscular disease. He was now in a wheelchair, still managing to run the hotel from this post.

I leaned over to kiss him on both cheeks, European style. His many years in the diplomatic corps still clung to him with a kind of formality that he used in speaking with everyone, including his two small grandchildren.

"We are very honored to have you here with us again," he said gravely, "and we look forward to catching up on news of your family and your work.

"No doubt, however, you have had a long day, and would like some time to rest and refresh yourself. I do hope we will have the pleasure of serving you in the hotel dining room? Yes? About nine we will expect you. Dr. Castillo has said that he will, with your permission, join you for the evening meal. The family would also be most pleased if you would join us for a late coffee in our private quarters. My wife is eager to see you and hear news of your parents."

He handed me the key to my room. I was pleased to see that it was my favorite, the end room on the second floor overlooking the back courtyard. A young man I had not seen before, possibly one of the Ortiz extended family who get their start in the business world by helping out at the hotel, took my duffel bag and led the way up the stone staircase to the second floor.

Once the door had closed behind him, I crossed to the window and pushed the shutters back. The room overlooks a courtyard in the center of which is a small pool, presided over by a terra-cotta statue of a Maya god. Even in the fading light of early evening, I could see the glorious purple bougainvilleas after which the inn had been named climbing up the whitewashed walls of the courtyard.

Over to one side I could see the roof of the veranda, bleached oak trellis supported by columns of local cantera stone. The tables on the veranda were already set for *cena,* the evening meal, and Norberto, the Ortiz's older son, was already there, checking every detail, even though dinner, in the Spanish style of eating late, was at least two or three hours away.

Sitting on airplanes and in airports must qualify as one of the most tiring activities one can undertake. In any event, knowing that dinner was a few hours away, I stretched out on the bed, and soon fell into a heavy sleep.

As I drifted off, however, I thought I heard an argument, two or possibly three men in the courtyard beneath my window, speaking in a language I didn't understand. It was neither English nor Spanish, but probably one of the Mayan languages, of which there are many. It sounded like a serious argument, but I had no idea what it was about.

I awoke with a start, the phone ringing beside me. It was Dr. Castillo, telling me that he had been delayed and regrettably would be unable to meet me for dinner. He was heading out of town, he said, but would be in touch on his return to reschedule our meeting.

"I regret I must postpone our meeting this evening, *amiga,* but I assure you it is for a good purpose," he said.

"I know that you will pass a pleasant evening with the Ortiz family, however.

"Let us just say the plot thickens!"

And with that he quickly rang off.

I had a shower to try to chase the cobwebs and the gloom away. My afternoon nap had not exactly been restful. I was depressed at the thought of having to eat alone, and annoyed to think I had dropped everything to fly thousands of miles to chase a writing rabbit!

I finished unpacking. One downside to having a successful fashion designer as a friend is that it does remind you, from time to time, of the inadequacy of your wardrobe. Mine these days relied rather heavily on denim, black, and khaki. I call it my student uniform. My neighbor Alex insists I dress like that to keep men away, and perhaps I do. I pulled out an off-white silk blouse and a pair of taupe gabardine trousers. They would have to do.

As I reached the top of the stairs leading down to the lobby, I saw Isa and her father, deep in quiet conversation, her dark head bent toward his. There was an air of tension about them both, somehow, but as I started down the stairs they broke off the conversation. She was smiling, but I could not help feeling something was not quite right with my friends.

Norberto led me to the candlelit veranda and a table overlooking the courtyard. It was the table, he told me, that Dr. Castillo had reserved for the evening, and that he had asked that I be brought a bottle of wine of my choosing, as an apology for his delay.

Sipping a glass of white wine, Calafia from Mexico's west coast, I looked around at my fellow guests.

Despite my earlier gloom on the subject, I actually enjoy eating in restaurants by myself from time to time. I often amuse myself by speculating on the lives of the other diners.

There were a number of Mexicans in the dining room, many of them probably from the neighborhood, and a few of them possibly permanent hotel guests. Dr. Castillo was himself a permanent hotel resident, having moved there after his wife of forty-five years had died some two years earlier.

While the hotel is not well known to tourists from the north, it is something of a local legend. Doña Francesca is of Maya descent—married to Don Santiago, ex-diplomat of Spanish descent. Both are gracious hosts, perhaps because of the aristocratic upbringing of Don Santiago, or their many years in the diplomatic service.

But contrary to the usual custom in Mexico, where wives of the well-to-do do not learn to cook, and indeed would be horrified to do so, Doña Francesca is an accomplished chef. Her kitchen combines the traditions of Spanish cuisine with her own Maya culinary arts and is justly famous. One of her specialties is called *pescado borracho,* literally drunken fish, another, her *faisan en pipian verde de Yucatán,* pheasant in a green Yucatán-style sauce, draws not only hotel guests, but also people from the neighborhood.

This evening the pheasant was on the menu and word had clearly spread, because the dining room was filling up rapidly.

The permanent residents were easy to spot. Inclined to be older, as Dr. Castillo was, they each had a table in the dining room they considered their own. Each was greeted by name as they arrived, and acknowledged each other as they were led to their tables, which were set out to meet their particular requirements, sometimes with a bottle of wine uncorked and ready.

One in particular looked very interesting. Seated alone at the table next to mine, she was in her mid-eighties, I would guess. Aristocratic of bearing, she was clearly the product of a more formal time. She was dressed all in black, a widow most likely, and she wore a black mantilla over her white hair.

Her eyes, which fixed on me from time to time, were very bright blue, unusual enough in this part of the world, and on the table beside her she had carefully placed a black lace fan and a pair of black lace gloves. She appeared to be graciousness personified, but I had a sense of iron will there. I noticed the busboys in the dining room were especially careful when they were waiting on her table. She apparently had exacting standards. She was too close to allow me to ask Norberto who she was.

Other than her and me, only two other people in the dining room seemed out of place in this old-world setting—two men at a table in the corner.

Both of them were quite attractive, although in very different ways. One was Mexican, dark, mid-forties, with fairly long dark hair and dark eyes. What set him apart from the rest of the crowd was his attire—black jeans and a black T-shirt, rather out of place in the elegant surroundings of the hotel dining room.

The other was fiftyish, well dressed in a sort of Ivy League way. Gray flannels, blue double-breasted blazer, white shirt, burgundy tie, and neatly trimmed hair streaked with gray and just a hint of a curl over the ears. I had a sense that I was as much the subject of their scrutiny as they were of mine, but after a few minutes the dark one left.

After surreptitiously observing the remaining man over the top of my wineglass and then my menu for a while, I tried to get a grip on myself and give the pheasant the attention it deserved. Inevitably, though, I looked his way again, and this time, rather than pretending that he had not been looking at me, too, he smiled.

Shortly thereafter he left the dining room, taking a slight detour to go by my table. There was just the hint of an acknowledgment, the slightest incline of the head as he did so. I was sorry he was leaving so soon.

Later in the evening I sat around the family table in Doña Francesca's tiled kitchen with most of the family. Isa was there with her mother and father, and Norberto and his wife, Manuela. Missing were the two grandchildren, now in bed, and the younger brother of Isa and Norberto, Alejandro.

When I asked about Alejandro, I noticed once again the slight tension in the air as each paused just for an instant before answering the question. It was Isa who spoke. "We don't see much of him these days. He has a life and friends of his own," she said.

"He follows his own course," agreed Norberto. "He believes in his own causes."

Clearly this was all that was going to be said on the subject.

I suppose I was not really any more forthcoming myself on the subject of my divorce. But the evening passed pleasantly enough, and very late I went to bed.

That night, I had a most unpleasant dream, the first of what was to become a series of recurring nightmares. I was floating through space looking down at the earth, which metamorphosed into some kind of snakelike creature. The creature rose up as I flew over, and engulfed me. I began to fall through black space, and in the darkness I could hear angry voices. In my dream I knew what had happened. I had entered the maw of Xibalba, and the voices I heard were the Lords of the Underworld.

Prone to recurring dreams, I am nonetheless a little

15

slow figuring out what my subconscious is trying to tell me. A couple of years earlier I'd had a series of dreams in which I was standing in a doorway, my luggage in front of me, with no idea of where I was or where I was going. It took five or six repetitions of that one before I got the message and packed up and left Clive for good.

In retrospect, if I'd paid attention to that night's dream and those that were to follow, at a minimum I might have avoided some poor personal choices. At best, at least one death might have been averted.

IK

MÉRIDA MAY WELL MERIT ITS reputation as the White City, the cleanest and most beautiful in Mexico, but for me it is a city whose beginnings, like many Spanish colonial cities, are steeped in blood. Even now it remains one where the tensions between the colonial and the Indian, while giving the place a certain energy, are never entirely laid to rest.

Take, for instance, the square where Isa and I met for *almuerzo*, late breakfast, the day after my arrival. We were sitting at a café on what Meridanos call the Plaza Grande, tucking into *huevos rancheros* and getting caught up on each other's life.

We'd arrived just as a party of revelers left to sleep off the previous night's festivities. Mérida is one of the cities of Mexico that take Carnaval seriously, and while technically it is only celebrated the week leading up to Lent, some Meridanos get an early start on the festivities.

The plaza where we sat, officially the Plaza de la Independencia, is the heart of Mérida, just as this same great space was once the heart of a great Maya city called

T'ho. At one side is the cathedral, built in 1561 of stone taken from the razed buildings of T'ho. At the south side is Casa Montejo, now a bank, once the palace of Francisco de Montejo, the founder of Mérida—and the destroyer of T'ho. In case anyone misses the point, the facade of the palace depicts the Spanish conquerors standing on defeated Maya warriors.

The significance of the setting was apparently not lost on Isa, either.

"If I had to describe the character of this city, in some ways I would describe it as schizophrenic," she mused.

"To a certain extent Mérida, and indeed the whole Yucatán peninsula, is cut off from the rest of Mexico geographically. This has allowed it to develop a distinctive character. Mérida, for example, is a colonial city; just look at the buildings around this plaza.

"But the Maya roots are never very far below the surface and, quite frankly, are what give this place its very special feeling. It is quite a compelling mix. In a sense, Mexico's culture is the only one in the Americas where the old world and the new truly meet and mix.

"Sometimes there is an easy balance between the two, sometimes not.

"Sort of like my family." She smiled.

I told her of my sense the day before that all was not entirely well with the Ortiz family, and about the argument I thought I might have heard below my window.

"I am reasonably sure it was a Mayan language I heard, probably Yucatecan. But perhaps I just dreamed it."

She looked troubled for a moment. "I can't tell you about the argument—I didn't hear anything, and perhaps as you say, it really was a dream.

"As far as my family is concerned—perhaps my comparison between Mérida and us is very apt. Alejandro has discovered, or perhaps rediscovered, his Maya heritage.

"It is a cause for some friction in the family. He accuses Mother of selling out to the Spanish. Presumably that means by marrying my father." Again she smiled.

"Oh, I know we all go through stages as we are growing up when we are not exactly enamored of our parents, of course, but Alejandro seems to have gotten involved with a group of young people at the university we're not crazy about. He makes a lot of speeches, when he deigns to speak to us at all, that is, about fighting injustice, and there is a tone to it that worries parents a great deal.

"I'm sure his talk of rebellion is just youthful posturing, a phase all university students go through. But there is no question the Indígenas suffered greatly because of the conquest, and that disaffection is often very close to the surface. You may recall the riots in Chiapas not that long ago."

Indeed I did. I had been there, in fact, on a buying trip. The riots had occurred over the New Year, and had lasted several days.

"If I remember correctly," I said. "The riots were the work of a group called the Zapatista National Liberation Army, planned to coincide with the day the North

American Free Trade Agreement, NAFTA, came into effect."

"That's right. It is said that the Zapatistas trained for ten years in the jungle before coming out that New Year's," Isa said. "There were rumors, of course. We all heard them. You couldn't plan something like this for ten years in complete secrecy. But when it happened, it seemed to take the government completely by surprise. There had been nothing seen like this in Mexico since the Revolution.

"It was all over pretty quickly, but since then there have been flare-ups. Sometimes the Zapatistas and the government are talking, sometimes they aren't. But the possibility of violence always seems to be there.

"Anyway, I guess what I am saying is that our family problems mirror in some way the tensions that exist in our society. Alejandro talks a lot about injustice and hints at revolution.

"Mother is distraught of course," she continued. "Alejandro is her baby, the son born late in life. I was well into my teens when he was born, and I confess that while I thought he was an adorable baby, there was too much of a gap in our ages for me to find him very interesting. I guess I just find him irritating now, despite the fact I agree with him about many things.

"For example, Alejandro despises me because, like many of the children of the well-to-do in Mérida, I went to university in the United States. He has chosen to go to university here in Mérida, and I admire him for it, actually, although he is so tiresome on the subject that I have never told him."

"I'm sure he'll grow out of it," I said. "After all, when I was at university, I was the most conservative person on the campus, and that was only because my mother seemed embarrassingly flaky to me at the time. Now I realize she was just ahead of her time—she never let any of the rules about what women could, and could not, do influence her in any way."

"I'm sure you're right," Isa replied, and with that we parted company, she to visit her small factory where her designs were manufactured, I to prowl the museum—the Museo Emilio Garcia, named for its founder, a wealthy Mérida philanthropist. The *museo* was housed in a former monastery a few short blocks from the Plaza Grande.

I had hoped, I think, to run into Dr. Castillo Rivas, who had an office there. Santiago Ortiz had told me that Don Hernan had not returned to his room the previous night, but as that was not an unusual occurrence, no one gave it much thought. Don Hernan was often hot on the trail of some treasure or other, and when he was, he tended to get a little distracted, more so as the years went by. I had always regarded this as a sign of his genius, the absentminded-professor type. His wife, if I remember correctly, had found it less endearing.

I sneaked past the *"Prohibido Entrar"* sign on the staff door on the top floor of the *museo* and checked at his little office. It was dark and locked up tight.

I decided to try to solve the puzzle he had given me—the one about writing rabbits. I thought it a little coy of him, but Don Hernan and I had spent many a wonderful day together searching for goods for my shop, and I was determined to get into the spirit of the thing.

Because it had been Dr. Castillo who had first introduced me to the Tzolkin, the Maya count of days, I thought of that first. It was he who had explained to me that there are twenty name days, and thirteen numbers associated with them. Each day is linked to a number, 1 Imix, 2 Ik, 3 Akbal, and so on. Because there are more names than numbers, the fourteenth name is given the number one again. With thirteen numbers and twenty names, it is 260 days before the original day and number, 1 Imix in my example, comes round again.

Several visits earlier, sitting over a cup of very strong Mexican coffee in the darkened dining room at the Casa de las Buganvillas late one evening, Don Hernan had begun to explain all of this to me.

"To understand the Maya, you must understand their concept of time," he had told me.

"Like us, the Maya devised ways of recording the passage of time. Like us they gave names to days, but unlike us they attributed characteristics to those days.

"While most of us have forgotten these vestigial origins of our days—your Thursday was the Norse Thor's Day, Wednesday, Woden's Day, for example—many of the Maya have not.

"For the Maya, everything is influenced by the characteristics of the day, the number of the day, the character of the Haab or what we would call the month sign, and the character of the quadrant sign, four gods each characterized by a color, red for the east, black for the west, white for the north, and yellow for the south. Each of these gods, called Kawils, rules a quadrant of eight hundred and nineteen days."

"I suppose this is not dissimilar to our applying human characteristics to astrological signs and judging events by the cycles of the planets. Even American presidents have been known to do this," I said. "And the number/day-name correlation is not unlike our Friday the thirteenth."

"Yes, but as you will learn, theirs is a much more complex system, moving back and forward over enormous periods of time. While we measure time in years, decades, centuries, and so on, the Maya measure time in *katuns*, or twenty-year cycles, and *baktuns*, twenty times twenty, or four-hundred-year cycles.

"And while our largest unit of time is a millennium really, the Maya have much longer ones. They have, for example, a *calabtun*, a one-hundred-and-sixty-thousand-year unit. And they measure time from the beginning of what they consider to be the current cosmos, the fourth one to exist.

"There are dates and numbers carved on Maya temples that would predate the big bang many times over, and they predict dates millennia into the future. I think what I am trying to say is that for the Maya, the past is still with us, still alive."

Remembering that conversation as I walked through the *museo*, I tried to find a link with the riddle. The current day was Ik, the day of wind, breath, and life. Nothing to do with a rabbit. I mentally ran through the twenty day names. The day Lamat, six days hence, had some association with a rabbit and the moon or the planet

Venus, but if there were a connection, I didn't know what it might be.

Perhaps, I thought, it is a play on words, perhaps a translation to Spanish. But nothing came to mind.

Thinking that the answer might lie somewhere in the museum, I spent a good part of the afternoon wandering through the exhibits looking in vain for a Maya rabbit.

I was bent over an exhibit of artifacts taken from a sacred cenote when I heard the voice behind me.

"I say, didn't my eyes meet yours across a crowded room?" the very British voice asked.

I turned. It was the fellow from the dining room the evening before, looking every bit as good, I might add. Behind him lurked his dark friend.

"Ms. McClintoch, I believe," he said, extending his hand.

"You have me at a disadvantage," I replied.

"Sorry. Jonathan Hamelin and my associate, Lucas May. I managed to convince Norberto that I thought I knew you from school or something, and was able to pry your name out of him.

"Since we obviously frequent the same places, might we presume to invite you for a drink? A coffee, a tequila? If you don't mind a bit of a walk, I know a wonderful bar on the Paseo de Montejo."

He had such an air of assurance that I soon found myself being escorted from the building and propelled along several blocks toward the *paseo*, a tree-lined avenue, very European in character, that Meridanos somewhat optimistically refer to as their Champs-Élysées. There was a time, at the turn of the century when fortunes were being made by the Spanish in the henequen trade, when Mérida was one of the wealthiest cities in the world. The *paseo* was its centerpiece, the place where the wealthy lived in houses, palaces really, of blue, pink, buff, and peach, with wrought-iron gates and elaborately carved moldings modeled more on the style of Paris than the Americas, more Belle Époque than colonial.

The houses are still there, but by and large the families have moved on, the upkeep too much, perhaps, for diluted family fortunes. The houses stand, some lovingly restored and home to banks and other corporations that can afford them, others sinking, either gracefully or drearily, into decay.

We entered one of these old homes, painstakingly restored to its former glory, now the lobby and entrance-way of the Hotel Montserrat. Behind and adjoining it is a stucco-and-glass tower where guest rooms are located, designed to complement the original building. We headed for the bar, a large room at the front of the original house. Jonathan Hamelin was obviously well known there, and a table with a very nice view of the *paseo* materialized quickly.

Jonathan looked very comfortable in this setting. Even in more casual clothes, he was very nattily attired. His associate, however, was dressed very much the same as the night before, except that now he wore a black jacket. Once again, he looked rather out of place.

The bar was called Ek Balam, the Black Jaguar. Maya motifs featured prominently in the decor. At one end were two discreetly lit glass cases in which were displayed what appeared to be, at this distance at least, authentic pre-Columbian pieces.

But here any local references ended. Rather too large to be a conventionally cozy bar, the decor tended to cool peaches and aquas rather than the brilliant colors of the tropics. No mariachi or flamenco nouveau assaulted the delicate ears of the patrons. Instead, a string quartet at one end of the large room displayed what I think is called salon music: Ravel, Haydn, Copland, Strauss.

The air of the bar was filled with expensive perfume and cigar smoke. This was clearly where the beautiful people of Mérida came to see and be seen. The person many apparently wanted to be seen with sat, or more accurately held court, at a table in a dim corner.

He was a man of about sixty, short, I would say, somewhat paunchy, not particularly attractive, but with some kind of personal magnetism, perhaps the sensual appeal of money, that commanded the attention of at least half the women in the room, and the envy of most of the men. Two of the people at his table looked to me like bodyguards, not the least because their eyes constantly scanned the room and their conversational skills appeared to be just about nil.

"Señor Diego Maria Gomez Arias," Jonathan said, noting the direction of my gaze.

"The name is vaguely familiar."

"Very wealthy. Owns the hotel. Avid collector."

"Of what?"

"Beautiful things." Jonathan smiled.

"Including women?" I asked, watching the glances

several women in the room were casting in Señor Gomez Arias's direction.

"Including women," he agreed.

"Are the artifacts in the glass cases real?"

"Oh yes, I expect so."

"Shouldn't they be in a museum?"

"Quite possibly." He shrugged.

"I think I do recall his name. He is a client of Hernan Castillo Rivas?"

"Was, I believe. They had a falling-out of some sort from what I've heard. But how do you know Don Hernan?" Jonathan asked.

I told him about McClintoch and Swain.

"Well, we've met McClintoch. Who is Swain?"

"My ex-husband."

"Ah."

"'Ah' about sums it up."

I then told them about selling the business and the call that had brought me there the day before.

This seemed to attract the attention of both of them. Even Lucas, who had until this time barely uttered a word, leaned forward in expectation.

"Don't keep us in suspense, Lara," Jonathan said. "What's the project?"

"I don't know. Haven't seen him yet. He called to cancel dinner last night. He had to go out of town, hot on the trail of something or other."

I started to tell them about the rabbit, but something stopped me. In a way, I was beginning to wonder if Don Hernan had not gotten just a bit dotty, a little non compos mentis, since I had seen him last. He was pushing eighty, after all. I didn't want him—or me, for that matter—to look silly in the eyes of Jonathan Hamelin.

In any event, I stopped myself from saying more. Lucas was looking at me intently, as if he knew there must be more to this story, but the waiter arrived with our drinks—margaritas for Jonathan and me, a beer for Lucas—and the conversation veered off into the usual banalities you hear in bars.

Jonathan, I had learned as we walked over to the hotel, was an archaeologist from Cambridge University in England, Lucas the local archaeologist assigned by the Mexican authorities to work with him.

They, or at least Jonathan, since Lucas had settled back into his role of observer, told me about the work they were doing at a site a few miles from Chichén Itzá, the great postclassic Maya site near Mérida. I'd been to Chichén Itzá many times before, but thought it was always worth a visit, and said as much.

Jonathan was explaining to me in his upper-crust British accent about the interesting limestone caves and underground rivers in that part of the Yucatán and entertaining me with tales of the sacrifice of cross-eyed virgins in the sacred cenotes, when the most extraordinary thing happened.

Two people dressed entirely in black, kerchiefs over their faces, bandito-style, walked into the bar. One of them carried a rifle, the other a crowbar. Before anyone could react, they moved quickly to one of the glass cases at the end of the bar, smashed the glass, and grabbed one of the artifacts. They left the room as quickly as they had come in.

There was actually a moment of stunned silence, then an absolute din. Some patrons of the bar laughed, thinking, no doubt, that it was a preview of Carnaval celebrations. Gomez Arias was hustled from the room by his two bodyguards.

I looked at my two companions. Jonathan seemed quite startled. Lucas was as impassive as ever. But there was a look in his eyes that if I had to identify, I would call admiration.

All thoughts of Carnaval pranks were dispelled when the federal police arrived shortly thereafter.

The policeman in charge of the investigation was not, in my opinion, someone in whom anyone would wish to confide. Tall and thin, with an impressive mustache, he had a certain lean and hungry look, to borrow a phrase, a kind of hardness about the eyes, whether from a streak of cruelty or merely bitter disappointment, I couldn't tell.

I'm not sure what there was in his manner that made me dislike him so quickly. Perhaps it was his peremptory way of dealing with all of us, the patrons of the bar, or an undercurrent of brutality in the way he dealt with staff, the hotel's and his own. Or the arrogance with which he announced to us all that the guilty party—and here he looked at each of us in a way that implied that each of us in our own way was guilty—would be quickly apprehended.

Jonathan and Lucas, who seemed to be well known to the police, were called upon to identify which object had been taken, then all patrons were interviewed briefly and asked to leave an address and phone number where they could be reached, and permitted to leave.

Afterward Jonathan walked me to a taxi. He had been asked by the police to stay behind to assist with the investigation. The media had already arrived, and crowds of reporters and spectators milled outside the hotel.

"I'll repeat my question," I said. "Should those pieces not be in a museum?"

"Touché!" He smiled.

"I'm serious. How does Gomez Arias get away with keeping pieces like that in a glass case in a bar?"

"Maybe he wants to share his collection with the public."

"The public, by and large, does not get into his bar," I said acidly. "More likely he wants everyone who comes here to know he can afford them. It will be interesting to see if he can afford to lose them."

With that, we shook hands and I took the taxi back to the Casa de las Buganvillas. By the time I got back to the hotel, the news was already out, and the place was abuzz.

A rather sullen Alejandro was staffing the front desk with his father. He warmed slightly when he saw me. "Caught a glimpse of you on television," he said.

Suddenly I was exhausted. Even dinner seemed too much of an effort. I told Alejandro of my adventures, and he suggested that a bowl of his mother's *sopa de frijol*, black bean soup, be sent up. I gratefully accepted.

I showered, then answered the tap at the door. It was Isa bringing the *sopa*, fresh cheese, and crisp tortillas. After setting out the meal on a side table by the window, she pulled up a chair, saying, "Okay, tell me everything."

I laughed with relief. It was just like old times. I told her what had happened.

"We've been watching it on television," she said. "A group calling itself Children of the Talking Cross has claimed responsibility, saying it will be returning the statue to its rightful owners, the Maya."

"This Children of the Talking Cross—is this a, well . . . a mainstream terrorist group or something? I've never heard of them."

"No one has, as far as I know," Isa replied. "I certainly haven't."

"Did they identify the statue?" I asked, thinking of Jonathan and Lucas.

"Yes, there were two archaeologists—were they your friends?—right on the scene. They said it was a carving of the feathered serpent god, Itzamná."

After Isa had cleared away the dishes and gone downstairs to join her family, I climbed gratefully into bed.

Despite my fatigue, sleep did not come easily. I found myself on the horns of a dilemma. I was guilty of a rather major error of omission in my report to Isa. The big question was should I tell Isa that despite the mask I had recognized Alejandro in the Ek Balam? Should I tell him? Should I tell the federal police? I remembered my impression of the policeman. On that score at least, I rather thought not.

AKBAL

A LONG TIME AGO I had a boyfriend who described everyone he knew as a car. The worst thing he could think to say about someone was that they were an economy van.

I was, he told me, a '56 Thunderbird convertible. Not being much into cars, vintage or otherwise, I wasn't sure what that meant. One day, a couple of years after we parted company, I saw one, silver, on a revolving platform at a classic car show. Maybe he had liked me more than I realized.

Anyway, while I can barely remember what this guy looked like, he has left me with this particular way of categorizing people. Isa, for example, is the kind of car she drives. Elegant and snappy, a Mercedes 580SL convertible.

Jonathan? A British racing green Rover, leather upholstery. Refined, expensive in an understated way, and maybe just a little pretentious.

Lucas? I wasn't sure about him just yet. But whatever the model, the color would have to be black.

Waiting at the reception desk as I went downstairs the next morning to scrounge a cup of coffee was the person I had already come to think of as a Mack truck. The kind that roars up on your bumper so only the silver grille, like rows of sharks teeth, shows in your rearview mirror. Convinced that any moment you will be squashed like some insignificant bug on its front bumper, your relief is palpable when eventually it roars past, causing your car to jerk and lurch in its wake.

It was the investigating officer, one Major Ignacio Martinez, I had learned the previous night. Clearly this was a man who shot first and asked questions later, who made up his mind about the guilty party very early in an investigation, then went to great lengths to prove it, regardless of evidence to the contrary.

And the person he had decided was guilty of stealing the statue of Itzamná, I was soon to learn, was Dr. Hernan Castillo.

I had awakened late. The day was gloomy, fitting for Akbal, a day of evil and darkness. I had not arrived at any resolution of my dilemma of the night before, but when I saw Martinez standing at the reception desk, I thought my problem had been solved, though in the worst possible way.

But Martinez was not looking for Alejandro, he was looking for me. And it was Don Hernan he wanted to talk about.

We went into a small sitting room off the lobby.

"What brought you to Mexico, señora?" he began.

"I'm on a break from my studies, a holiday."

"What made you choose Mérida as your destination?"

34

"I'm studying Maya history and languages," I replied. There was a pause.

"I think you are not being entirely, shall we say, comprehensive, in your answers to my questions. Now, why would that be?"

"Perhaps you are not asking the right questions," I snapped. "What exactly is it you want to know?"

"I want to know the whereabouts of Dr. Hernan Castillo, and I believe you have the answer," he said.

Whereabouts? This man watches too many movies! I thought.

"What in heaven's name does Dr. Castillo have to do with this? Surely you cannot think he has anything to do with the robbery. He's a well-respected scholar."

"I believe I am the one authorized to ask the questions, señora, not you. Do I think he walked into the bar and took the statue personally? No, I do not. But yes, I do think he is involved. He and Señor Gomez Arias had an argument over the stolen sculpture, in fact only a few weeks ago."

"I don't know where he is," I replied. "I do know that he would not have anything to do with something as shabby as this."

He ignored the last comment. "But you did come to Mérida to meet him, did you not?" Obviously either Jonathan or Lucas had been more "comprehensive" in his testimony than I had been.

"Yes, but he canceled our first meeting, dinner the evening before last. I have not heard from him since."

"And the reason for his bad manners?"

"Bad manners?"

"Canceling dinner with a lovely foreign visitor whom you have invited to visit would not normally be considered good manners, would it, even in Canada?"

I ignored the gibe.

"What were you meeting him for? Perhaps to carry some stolen merchandise out of the country for him? I understand you have a fair knowledge of the import/export business."

"I really do not know what he wanted to talk to me about. It really was just an excuse to get away from my studies and the Canadian winter," I replied. My reply, though true, sounded questionable even to me. And no doubt I looked a little long in the tooth to be a student.

Another lengthy pause. Perhaps this is a technique I thought: wait long enough and the person will bleat something.

"May I see your passport, please?"

A new approach. I handed it to him, then watched in dismay as he slipped it into his jacket pocket and rose from his chair.

"You can't take that!" I sputtered.

"Ah yes, but I can. Do not, as they say in your American movies, leave town, señora."

Then he was gone, leaving me with the satisfaction, albeit minimal, of being right about the movies.

My first reaction was to try to reach my father to see what he and his diplomatic connections could do for me here. It's amazing how no matter how old we get, we still turn to our parents in a pinch. However, now that my father was retired, my parents, their wanderlust still unsated, were always traipsing off somewhere, usually somewhere obscure. Currently, if I remembered correctly, they were on the slow train for Ulan Bator.

Instead, I went looking for Don Santiago. After expressing his outrage in decidedly undiplomatic language, he propelled himself over to a telephone and began phoning some old acquaintances in the diplomatic corps.

As I left the sitting room I passed Alejandro at the front desk.

"You and I need to talk, Alejandro," I hissed on the way by.

He looked nonplussed for a brief moment, but then merely smiled and nodded. This was one composed young man.

"Meet me at the Café Escobar, in an hour," I said, naming a small restaurant just a couple of blocks from the hotel.

Reasonably calmed by my brief conversation with Santiago Ortiz, and his promise to try to fix the mess with the passport, I went into the kitchen to get some coffee. Isa and her mother were sitting at the big oak table having a companionable cup of coffee together. Don Santiago soon joined us. I told them about my day so far, then inquired about Don Hernan.

"Still not back, and we haven't heard from him either. We're getting worried," Francesca said.

"This would hardly be the first time he has disappeared on us," Santiago observed.

"Yes, but he usually calls," Francesca countered.

"I went to his office yesterday. It was locked up tight. I'd hoped he'd be there, or if not, I was hoping to get in to take a look around to see if there might be clues as to where he might be."

The Ortizes exchanged a glance, and Francesca rose from her seat.

Santiago said, "We have a key—Don Hernan was always misplacing his, so he left a spare with us. Francesca will get it for you. I'm sure Don Hernan would not mind."

As I was about to leave them a few minutes later, key in hand, a bell rang in the kitchen. The Casa de las Buganvillas still has the features of a gracious home of a bygone era, including a kind of upstairs/downstairs bell system where the aristocrat upstairs pulls a cord in the room and a bell rings down in the kitchen. This summons staff to receive commands, go back downstairs to act upon them, and then return upstairs with the task completed.

Most hotel guests, of course, simply telephoned the front desk when they wished something.

"I thought that system had been disconnected years ago," I said.

"It has"—Isa sighed—"except for the Empress."

Francesca rose from her chair to answer the bell in person.

"The Empress?" I asked.

"Señora Josefina Ramirez de Leon Tinoco," Isa replied. "She treats my family as if they were her personal servants!"

I don't pretend to understand the Mexican naming system, but I get the general idea that the longer your name, the higher your station in life. This name should put Doña Josefina pretty close to royalty, maybe just this side of God. Clearly she had never felt the need to learn to use the telephone.

"Does she wear a mantilla?" I asked.

"Always." Isa smiled.

And with that I left them.

Shortly thereafter I made my way to the Café Escobar. I had no idea whether Alejandro would show up or not.

The café was far from fancy, lots of Formica and what my neighbor Alex likes to call "little junks"—dangling Day of the Dead skulls and the like. But the food was good and plentiful and one wall had a Diego Rivera-like mural that appealed very much to students and aging dissidents. I thought it would be a place where Alejandro would feel comfortable.

As I waited for him I tried to calm myself. I had had nothing to eat yet and it was already well past noon, which didn't help any. I'd consumed several cups of very strong black coffee, and with this and the events of the day, I was almost dizzy with caffeine, adrenaline, and anxiety.

I ordered chicken *chilaquiles*, a casserole of tortillas, shredded chicken, *tomatillos,* chilis, cream, and cheese. To wash it down, a Dos XX beer. If he didn't show up, at least I'd have had lunch. I sat in a small banquette against the wall, watching the door, mentally plotting my approach to the subject.

Show up he did. Bold as brass.

He slid into the booth opposite me and quickly ordered a beer for himself. He was obviously well known here: he didn't have to tell them which brand.

"You wanted to talk to me about something?" He smiled.

This was a very self-possessed young man. I had to remind myself that he was only about half my age.

"Yes I do, Alejandro. About a robbery. In a bar. A robbery at which, as it turns out, I was present."

His expression did not change.

"Not only present," I continued, "but in which I am implicated."

"Implicated?" He looked surprised.

"Yes. In more ways than one. The police believe I have information that would lead them to the perpetrator."

Now I thought I was beginning to get through to him, judging by the way he kept nervously twirling the coaster on the table.

"I could, in fact, should I choose to, lead them to one of the perpetrators. Ironically, however, it is not the person they are looking for."

"I'm not sure I follow you," he said, but he looked a little uneasy now.

"Would it interest you to know that the police suspect Dr. Castillo of masterminding the whole event? And that he is now the object of search of that rather ruthless Major Martinez?"

A slight flicker of emotion, apprehension perhaps, crossed his face.

"I cannot imagine why they would do that," was all he said. But I had struck a nerve.

"Tell me, just who are these Children of the Talking Cross?" I asked.

"I have no idea," he said.

"Oh, I think you do, Alejandro. Why would these people, whoever they are, steal a statue of Itzamná and not the others?"

"Perhaps some political reasons you wouldn't understand," he said slowly.

"Or perhaps they are just a bunch of young hoodlums defying their parents, and making a nuisance of themselves, drawing innocent people in as they go!"

He gave me a look that I could not interpret, tossed a few coins on the table to pay for his beer, and hurried from the restaurant.

Well, that was brilliant! I told myself. He knows all you know, and you know nothing more than you did before. Furthermore he'll never tell you what he knows because now he is convinced you're a nasty old cow!

I paid for my meal and grabbed a taxi for the *museo*. I made the driver stop about a block away, and walked the rest of the way.

I paid my admission, made a pretense for a few minutes of looking at the exhibits, then, as I had the day before, ducked through the door on the top floor marked PROHIBIDO ENTRAR and very quietly let myself into Don Hernan's office, carefully locking the door behind me. I did not want to be surprised by anyone, least of all Major Martinez.

Despite the fact that he was well past retirement age, the museum board of governors had let Don Hernan keep his little office in recognition of his contribution to Maya studies in general, and his generosity to the museum in particular. Many of the exhibits on the floors below would not have been possible without his donations.

It wasn't much of an office really, just a dark little cubbyhole at the end of a long hallway on the top floor. The little room still reeked of the cigars he indulged in, and I very quietly unlocked the window and opened it a few inches to allow in some air.

There was not much light in the room, in part because of the gloominess of the day, but I was afraid to turn on the reading lamp. It would have been quite obvious, I thought, if anyone came into that dark hallway.

I could feel my face flush in mortification at the mere thought of being caught searching the office. Whatever would I say? I wondered. That Dr. Castillo had sent me to get something for him? And what would that something be? Indeed, when it came right down to it, what on earth was I doing here and what exactly had I hoped to accomplish? To find a road map pointing to his precise location? I felt a rush of annoyance at myself. Don Hernan had said he was going out of town and would call on his return. He did this all the time; at least he used to. He was probably just fine, and I was being silly.

But there I was, burdened by this niggling anxiety about the old man. I'd already committed a felony, minor though it might be, letting myself into this office without permission, so perhaps I'd just carry on, I reasoned.

I looked around. The room was much as I remembered it: stacks of books and papers everywhere, the odd pottery shard scattered on the desk. It was going to be difficult to find anything in this clutter, but I was able to locate his desk diary, a logical starting point, very quickly.

There was a comfortable ledge by the window, which

led, as is typical in many old buildings, to a fire-escape landing. After momentarily pondering the idiocy of having a fire escape off a locked room, I began to look at the entries in the diary made in Don Hernan's spidery scrawl.

I was just settling in nicely when I heard footsteps in the hall.

I stood motionless, hardly daring to breathe. The footsteps stopped right outside the door. I heard the rattle of keys as first one, then a second was tried in the door. I had no doubt that one would fit, and I looked frantically around the room for a place to hide.

At that moment there was a loud rumble as the rather antiquated freight elevator just down the hall groaned into use. Whoever was outside the door stopped fiddling with the lock and stood still. This person, or persons, apparently wished to be caught in this office as little as I did.

As the freight elevator clanged and rumbled I carefully slid the window open and crawled onto the fire escape, sliding the window down behind me. As I did so I heard the lock click and sensed rather than saw the door begin to open cautiously. I pressed my back to the wall to one side of the window.

It was a few minutes before I was able to regain a shred of composure and, standing as still as possible, to take stock of my surroundings. This was no easy task because I am not good with heights, and standing on an open fire escape, even on a building as low as four stories, makes me very uncomfortable at the best of times, which clearly these weren't.

Looking to the right and down, I could see that this

was the kind of fire escape where, presumably to discourage burglars, the stairs do not go right down to the ground, but lead instead to another window two floors below.

I did not relish the thought of climbing into someone's office. It was an academic point anyway, because to get to the stairs I would have to cross in front of the window. Since the window was open slightly, I knew that the unwanted visitor was still there, systematically searching the office. It did cross my mind that it could be Dr. Castillo, but I decided that he would not have had to try so many keys to get in, neither would he be searching his own office quite this methodically.

Looking straight down, I could see that I was on the back side of the museum, in an alleyway of sorts, which opened onto a larger street. Across the alley was another building, windowless on this side. My imagination, overactive at the best of times, began to see accomplices in the shadows of the alleyway.

The longer I stood there, the worse it got. The spurt of adrenaline that had got me out the window so quickly was now contributing to what I can only describe as a full-fledged panic attack. My heart was pounding so loudly I was sure it could be heard in the office, and I couldn't seem to get enough air no matter how often or how deeply I breathed. I tried concentrating on remaining motionless and breathing normally, but I felt overwhelmed by the need to get away from my precarious and exposed position on the fire escape, no matter what the risk.

A small rational part of my brain was still functional

and assessing my situation, I guess, because I became aware that I was leaning against something uncomfortable, which I eventually realized was an iron ladder. By craning my neck, I could see it led to what appeared to be a flat roof. As slowly and quietly as I could, I turned, put one foot on the first rung, then moved in slow motion to the second.

I was very close to the top of the ladder when I hit a loose step, which clanged, metal against metal, in what seemed to me to be the loudest noise in the world.

I heard someone start to raise the window, and with my last ounce of strength I hauled myself up and over the top to lie facedown on the gravel surface of the flat roof. I remained there, absolutely still, imagining someone coming out on the fire escape and up the ladder. But no one did, and after what seemed an eternity, I heard the window close, and a loud click as it was locked shut.

After several more minutes of motionless existence, I rolled onto my back and sat up. Over my shoulders I could see a large metal tank next to a brick wall, which I took to be the top of the elevator shaft.

I began to edge my way back toward the tank, thinking it might afford me some protection. I felt even more exposed on the roof than I had on the fire escape, and I wanted to huddle in a corner until the danger had passed. I thought if I could get to that tank, I could rest in its shadow, and figure out where to go next.

My hands were bleeding from pushing myself along on the stones, but eventually I felt my back touch the tank. I tried to wedge myself in tight against it. But as I reached out, my hand touched another, cold as death.

KAN

I CARRY A PICTURE IN my mind now, of Hernan Castillo Rivas, on this particular day. It is Kan, day of the lizard, symbol of the Maize Lord, bringer of abundance.

As I have reconstructed events, Don Hernan is sitting in a café in a dusty little village on a dirt road leading to nowhere.

The village consists of the tiny café in which he sits, a one-pump gas station, and a couple of stores. One of these is a souvenir shop, a triumph of hope over reason, since few tourists come this way.

There is also a small doctor's office—the doctor is in on Tuesdays only—and five or six little houses with whitewashed walls and thatched roofs, with chickens and small children scratching in the front yards.

Despite, or perhaps in defiance of the impoverished conditions, bright red flowers grow up trellises in the front yard of each house. Behind the little houses stretch the *milpas* of the occupants, gardens and fields of corn separated from their neighbors by fences of stone. Despite the dust, I can smell orange trees.

Because it is so hot, Don Hernan sits at the shadier of two tables on the veranda of the café. Because it is the day of the lizard, I picture one here, skittering from time to time across the tiles of the veranda and up the trellis at one end.

Guadelupe, the wife of the proprietor and mother of three-year-old Arturo, brings her visitor *panuchos*—tiny tortillas piled high with chicken, avocado, refried beans, and hardboiled eggs—and cold beer with lime.

Don Hernan is a big man. One is struck immediately by his size, but also by his expressive eyebrows, two circumflex accents over dark eyes. He has a mustache and goatee, still dashing, but a mop of gray and yellowing hair that would become unruly if not for constant attention.

Despite his girth and age, he has always been a dapper man. Since his wife's death, and now without benefit of her ministrations, he has become somewhat rumpled, but in a genteel sort of way, dressed always in the cream colors of the tropics, right down to his shoes and his cane.

Childless himself, he dotes on others' children. I can imagine little Arturo venturing to the veranda, curious about this stranger, being charmed by him and sent on his way with a peso or two.

Several days, or possibly weeks, earlier, poring through the myriad artifact drawers in the archives of the *museo*, peering at each piece through the magnifying glass he keeps on a chain around his neck, he finds and deciphers the message that brings him to this little café in this tiny village.

Knowing that he will need younger, stronger eyes, arms, and legs to help him, he tries to think of someone who will be impervious to the politics and avarice that will inevitably surround this discovery, and places the call that brings me to Mexico.

At some point, perhaps even as my flight crosses the Caribbean, he suspects that someone else has found it, too, and begins a hasty and ill-conceived journey.

Suspecting that he may be followed, he does not return to his room at the inn, but embarks on a circuitous route from his little office in the *museo*: by taxi through the back streets, then on foot for several blocks, puffing from exertion, by public bus to Valladolid, where he stays a day or two making his arrangements, and then on to this village by hired car.

At the general store he purchases a flashlight, compass, and a length of rope.

At some point during this process, mindful of his social obligations, he calls me at the Casa de las Buganvillas to cancel dinner, but tells me nothing of what he has found.

And so now he sits, folding and refolding the crumpled piece of paper that brought him here, waiting. For what? For help? For salvation? For his killer?

He does not call me again, or another friend or colleague. Perhaps he notices the battered blue pickup truck that passes his post rather too often on a road going nowhere. Perhaps he senses the gathering forces closing in on him, some good, some evil, and wants to protect us.

There is one person who might save him, who even now is desperately searching for clues to his location.

But how could Don Hernan know? How could he choose between those who can help him and those who wish him dead? The answer is far from obvious.

THE CORPSE BEHIND THE WATER tank, I learned the day after I found it, belonged to a young man by the name of Luis Vallespino.

To this day, my recollection of what happened right after I touched his dead hand is very hazy. What I do know is that I will never be able to forget his face. It was still smooth, with long, long eyelashes and just a hint of down above the mouth, the first attempt at a mustache perhaps, a youth on the threshold of adulthood. He could not have been more than fifteen or sixteen.

The mark of the blow on the side of the head that had killed him, and the rather Raggedy Andy appearance of the body stuffed so incongruously behind the water tank, added to the sense of youth and vulnerability.

Whatever attributes Luis Vallespino had possessed in life, in death there was a sort of sweetness about him. His face had, I thought, a sadness in its expression, as if in recognition of life's opportunities lost. But perhaps I am projecting my own sorrow to that still young face.

Time stood still for me for a few moments as I gazed at him. Then the horror of what I was looking at came over me. As in a nightmare, I remember trying to scream, but no sound would come out. I tried to get up, but I couldn't move.

Then I was up and clawing at a trapdoor. It was unlocked, and soon I was half falling down a wooden staircase that led to the floor below, then to a stairwell that exited at the back of the *museo*.

I have a vague recollection of flagging down a cab near the plaza in front of the building, and directing the driver to the Casa de las Buganvillas. I'm not sure how coherent I was, but Santiago understood enough to call the police. A doctor was also called. He gave me a shot, and I was out until morning.

When I got up I discovered there was a police officer stationed outside my room. This didn't do much for the ambience, in my opinion. It didn't do much for my mood either.

I guess that when I poked my head out the door, the police officer on duty had called in that I was awake, because by the time I'd showered and dressed, my favorite policeman, Ignacio Martinez, was waiting downstairs.

Now, this might prove to be a little tricky! No doubt his first question would be something along the lines of "What exactly were you doing on the roof of the *museo*, señora?"

In the shower, I'd rehearsed several answers. The trouble with lies, as we all know, is that once you get into them, it is difficult to extricate yourself. I had been guilty of a lie of omission in not telling Martinez what I knew about the robbery in the bar and anything about why I had come down to see Don Hernan, as unclear as that might be. I like to think that this would not be my normal way of dealing with situations—lying, that is—but Martinez was not the kind of man I was prepared to turn my friends over to—or myself, for that matter. I wasn't sure how he'd react to my trying to search the office, so now I was having to lie my way out of that one, too. The question was which answer would I use?

The "I'd gone up the stairs hoping to find Don Hernan, accidentally got lost in stairwell, found myself on roof" answer.

Or perhaps the one that was something a little closer to reality, the "I went to see Don Hernan, had key, climbed out on fire escape (why, God only knows!), window locked behind me, took ladder to roof to find way out" answer?

But Martinez, in his usual take-control manner, surprised me.

"I believe your life may be in danger, señora," was his opening gambit.

I was momentarily nonplussed.

"You really must tell me where Dr. Castillo Rivas is."

"Are you implying your first and second statements are related in some way?" I managed.

He looked at me as if I were mentally deficient or terminally naive.

"Let me lead you through this, señora," he said in his most patronizing tone. This man raised condescension to an art form. "Dr. Castillo and Señor Gomez Arias have a disagreement over, according to Señor Gomez Arias himself, a statue. This same statue is stolen shortly thereafter by a group calling itself Children"—he emphasized the word *children*—"of the Talking Cross.

"The very next day, a young man dies in, or in this particular case, on top of, the museum Dr. Castillo has been associated with for several years.

·

52

"Coincidence, señora? I rather think not."

I was inclined to agree with him there, although my conclusions were quite different.

"Very interesting, I'm sure. But"—as they say in the movies, I thought—"the evidence so far is circumstantial. What facts do you have to support this contention, and how exactly does this put my life in danger? I found a body. Unfortunate though that may be, I can't see any reason why someone would want to kill me for that reason."

"But not for that reason alone, señora. It is because you know too much."

Those movies again. What would the man say next? *Hasta la vista,* baby? Or perhaps we would soon be quoting dialogue directly from *High Noon.*

"I know nothing. I'm as baffled by all of this as apparently you are."

He, too, ignored the gibe.

"You knew where to find the body. Not everyone who visits our *museo* is so fascinated that they feel compelled to visit the roof!"

He had a point.

"I got lost. I was checking to see if Dr. Castillo was in his office—"

"And was he?"

"No. But I got lost in the stairwell, and saw blood on the roof. I thought someone might be hurt. . . ." I was launched into one of my well-rehearsed answers.

"Enough of this!" He rose from his seat. "Even if you insist on telling me this nonsense, I am responsible for your safety. You will remain in the hotel here under the protection of my officers until we have found Dr. Castillo."

So yesterday I was confined to the country, my passport confiscated. Today I was confined to the hotel. All for my personal safety, of course.

I walked with Martinez to the front door.

"You haven't even told me who the young man on the roof was," I said to him.

"I assumed you knew. Luis Vallespino."

The name meant nothing to me, but it certainly appeared to mean something to Alejandro, currently staffing the front desk.

His hands shook as he retrieved a key from one of the other hotel guests and handed her her mail.

Very interesting, I thought. Do I now know two of the robbers?

I wanted to talk to Alejandro, but it was not possible while he was at the desk. And as it turned out, this was the last I would see of him for a while. Soon after his father came to relieve him at the desk, he disappeared.

I spent the rest of the day, needless to say, at the hotel, under the watchful eyes of two policemen, one at the front door, one on patrol throughout the hotel.

For all the talk of this being for my personal protection, and despite the comfort of the surroundings, it felt like house arrest to me.

I paced the floor of my room for hours, going over everything in my mind. Was there really a connection between the robbery in the Hotel Montserrat and the murder of Luis Vallespino? Was Alejandro involved? Was he in danger? Where was Hernan Castillo, and what was his involvement, if any? Who were the Children of the Talking Cross?

It was clear to me that nothing was going to be solved in this hotel room, and the inactivity was beginning to drive me crazy. I decided I had to do something.

This hotel room, as I mentioned, is my favorite. Not just because of its beautiful view of the courtyard, however. When Isa and I were growing up together, those many years ago, we used this room, when it was unoccupied, as our center of operations. After all was quiet in the hotel, we would let ourselves in with the passkey. From there we had devised a way of getting out the bathroom window, onto a ledge that led around to the back of the inn where we were able to climb onto a large ceiba tree.

For hours we would sit in the branches of that big tree, gossip about the boys in our classes—we were both attending the international school at the time—and, of course, smoke. If our parents knew about this, they were polite enough not to mention it.

Partway through the school year, we discovered it was possible to move out along one of the large branches and lower ourselves onto the wall surrounding the hotel, and thence to the street. We only did it a couple of times: smoking was about as daring as we got, but it was a great secret that we shared.

And so it was off with the lights at about eleven P.M. as if I'd turned in for the night, into dark pants and turtleneck and running shoes, then into the bathroom. I put the vanity chair into the bathtub as Isa and I had always done, and then hauled myself out through the window.

It was more difficult than I remembered. The window, regrettably, seemed to have gotten smaller over the intervening years, as had the ledge. And I was already more than a little tired of hanging out on ledges and fire escapes. But the tree was still there, its branches would still hold me, and within a few minutes I was over the wall, and moving as quickly and as quietly as I could along the darkened street.

In a few minutes I found myself at the Café Escobar. I inquired if anyone had seen Alejandro and, when the answer was negative, asked to use the telephone. I was directed to a pay phone in a dark hallway behind the bar and placed a call to my neighbor Alex Stewart.

One of the best things about the little Victorian cottage in an old Toronto neighborhood that I bought when Clive and I parted is the neighbor I acquired with it.

Alex is a dapper little man who spent thirty-some years in the merchant marine before settling into the cottage next door to mine. He lives his retirement years growing native plants—the other neighbors call them weeds—and supporting various environmental and social causes. In the first few months after I met him, he dragged me to community meetings on several subjects, serving me herbal tea on our return and telling me stories of his life at sea.

He is also, quite unexpectedly, a whiz on the Internet and spends considerable time surfing in cyberspace. I'm not sure if he adopted me or I adopted him, but he reminds me of my favorite grandfather, long deceased, and I adore him. In many ways he has provided me with an emotional lifeline through the turbulent times of the past year.

Alex is a nighthawk, and even with the two-hour time difference, which would have made it about one-thirty in the morning, I was reasonably sure he would be up. I placed a collect call.

He picked up the phone immediately and accepted the charges with enthusiasm, quite charming when you considered the hour and the fact that he lives on a pension. I felt better just hearing his voice.

We talked briefly about my cat, whom, to my surprise, I actually missed, and my little house—both were, I gathered, just fine—and then I got to the point of my call. "Alex," I said. "You're up on all these various causes. Have you ever heard of a group called Children of the Talking Cross?"

"Children of the Talking Cross, no. Followers of the Talking Cross, yes indeed! The history will be a little too recent for you, I expect. Last century, actually. You're into much older stuff than this. But it's interesting nonetheless."

"Never mind the lecture on my lack of social conscience, Alex." I laughed. "Tell me about the Cross."

"I believe the miraculous Talking Cross first put in an appearance in about 1850 right in your part of the world, the Yucatán," he began.

"That would be shortly after the War of the Castes, wouldn't it?" I asked. "Just to prove to you that my knowledge of Mesoamerican history is not entirely restricted to the classical Maya period," I added.

"Perhaps I have underestimated you." He chuckled. "But, yes, you are right. As you and I have discussed from time to time, the Spanish conquest of the Maya was not in all respects successful.

"There are many reasons for this, not the least of which was the cruelty of the Spanish overlords, who subjected the Maya to forced labor and extracted the dreaded *encomienda* or tribute.

"Many Maya would not submit to the oppression. The War of the Castes—that was the European name for it of course—broke out in 1847. The Maya, driven no doubt by desperation, were stunningly successful. Soon the only part of the Yucatán peninsula that was still held by the Spanish was Mérida, more or less.

"The end of the war is the stuff of legend. When the time came to plant the corn, the Maya left for their villages, their army disintegrated, and the Spanish began to regain all that they had lost."

"Was that the end of it, then?"

"Oh no. In about 1850, in some village in the Yucatán, there was said to be a miraculous 'Talking Cross' that prophesied a holy war against the Spanish oppressors. Fighting continued from time to time, but the Spanish were ultimately victorious in 1901. But Talking Crosses proliferated throughout the region, and many say that they simply went underground after that. There have certainly been recorded accounts of Talking Crosses until fairly recent times."

"Do you consider them to be superstitious claptrap, as many would no doubt call it?" I asked.

"Well, of course I don't believe in talking inanimate objects of any kind. I'm not daft. But I do believe they were a very powerful symbol of resistance to oppression and may still be so, for all I know.

"It's kind of interesting that it's crosses, isn't it? From what I've read, the Maya have a profound belief in ritual, which the Spanish church capitalized on in subjugating them. Now the Maya have incorporated Christian symbolism and turned it against their oppressors."

"Sort of like being shot with your own gun, you mean?"

Alex laughed.

"Can you think of any reason why a rebel group would steal a statue of Itzamná?" I asked.

"Well, leaving aside something straightforward like monetary value—you know what a good price pre-Columbian art commands these days, what with all the controls of its export—isn't Itzamná one of the top gods in the Maya pantheon? Perhaps your statue of Itzamná is to be the newest symbol of rebellion—the 1990s' version of a Talking Cross. But I don't know, really. It's anybody's guess."

We chatted a little while longer. I told him I'd reimburse him later for the collect call and gave him a carefully edited version of my last few days, and I could hear the concern in his voice.

"Don't worry, Alex, I'll be fine," I said. But I hung up wondering if this was indeed so.

And then it was back through the café, carefully watched by all the late-night customers, and along the street to the wall. Isa and I had climbed back up by pulling a loose stone out slightly to give us a leg up. I checked the wall. Reassuringly, the stone was still there, all these years later. I reversed my earlier route and climbed into bed in the dark.

CHICCHAN

CHICCHAN IS THE DAY OF the celestial serpent, that double-headed creature that arches over the earth to create the sky. It is considered a good day in the Maya calendar, and by and large it was, an oasis of calm between the tragedy that had been and the horror that was to be.

It began well enough. It was still dark when I was awakened by a soft but persistent tapping at my door. It was Jonathan.

"You've been sprung," he whispered. In my semiconscious state, I wasn't sure what this meant.

"Santiago has got you released in Isa's and my custody until nine P.M. tonight. So hurry up, Lara. Bring your swimsuit and a sun hat."

I was downstairs, showered and dressed, in ten minutes. Lucas and Isa were there, both yawning, as I was. It seemed Jonathan and Lucas had come to check on me the previous evening, after I'd supposedly turned in for the night, had met Isa, and together they had hatched this plan to cheer me up. We tiptoed out the door so as not to wake the other guests, to a Jeep Cherokee outside.

Isa sat up front with Lucas, Jonathan and I in the back. As I began to doze off again I heard Isa valiantly trying to draw Lucas into some semblance of a conversation. It was not easy. I was trying not to fall asleep with my head slumped on Jonathan's shoulder. That wasn't easy, either.

We headed out on Highway 180, and with no traffic at this ungodly hour, Lucas covered his seventy-five miles to Chichén Itzá in record time, despite the fact that we forsook the new toll road and took the old highway through myriad little towns, all characterized by speed bumps and countless mangy dogs. My favorite town was called Libre Unión, free union, because, Isa told us, of the high percentage of couples living there without benefit of holy matrimony. With my less than satisfactory marital record, it sounded good to me.

By seven A.M. we were in the ruins, heading for El Castillo to catch the early-morning sun as it cleared the mist from the site. We had the place to ourselves, the site not yet open to the public. Lucas knew the gatekeeper.

Chichén Itzá was once a magnificent metropolis, built over several centuries by generations of people who ruled the northern Maya. El Castillo was, and is, its most impressive structure. Also known as the Temple of Kukulcán, the four-sided pyramid rises seventy-five feet from a grassy plaza. We scrambled up one of the restored stairways to the temple on its summit.

The sun began to cast its light on the Temple of the Warriors, below us and to the east of our position. This smaller temple, a three-tiered structure with rows of columns at its base that long ago formed a colonnade, has, at the top of the steps to its entrance, a Chac Mool, an ominous-looking reclining figure that guards the space, flanked by the heads of two carved serpents that must have formed the original doorway.

For an instant the early rays of the sun backlit the sculpture, adding its fiery glow to the chilling figure, then moved on.

I walked around the top of the temple, gazing out across miles of forest broken occasionally by a green mound that would one day reveal another lost structure. To the south the sun lit the top of El Caracol, the snail, visible above the trees, an unusual round building thought to have been the observatory from which the ancients tracked the planet Venus with great accuracy.

When I had circled around to where the others were sitting, Isa reached into the large tote bag she was never without and brought out a thermos of *café con leche,* four plastic cups, and some biscuits. We sat in companionable silence, our backs to the temple wall, and watched as more and more of the site was revealed from the mist.

In a few minutes the first busloads of tourists would arrive, but for now the place was ours. For a few minutes at least I was able to put the face of Luis Vallespino aside, distracted by the magic of this place.

None of us spoke for several minutes. Below and behind us, the vendors were arriving with their wares— soft drinks and handicrafts for the tourists—and their conversations carried across the great plaza to our vantage point.

Our personal reveries were broken by the sound of the

first tour group coming through the entranceway. Ahead of the pack were two young boys racing to be first up the pyramid, their mothers gasping behind them, telling them to be careful.

"Let's stay one jump ahead of them," Jonathan exclaimed, and we moved quickly to descend the steep staircase, I by gripping the heavy metal chain for support and sliding down on my rear end. Going up the pyramid in a hurry may be tiring; going down is positively terrifying.

We quickly crossed the plaza to the Temple of the Warriors. As I approached the top of the steps, I hesitated, savoring a short moment of anticipation.

This temple had been my favorite when I was first here as a young girl. When Isa and I told each other ghost stories up in that old tree, Chac Mool always featured prominently.

The carved stone figure reclines, knees drawn up and head twisted to face the west, the direction the Maya regarded as that of darkness and death. He—it could only be a "he"—holds to his chest a flat plate on which, legend has it, the hearts of sacrificial victims were placed, still beating, to appease the gods.

Worse yet, as you reach the top of the stairs, you find yourself looking right into his sightless eyes. He never blinks. He knows all. He waits. Isa and I, as sophisticated as we used to think we were, still clung to each other as we went up and over the top of the stairs, giggling in embarrassment and fear.

Lucas suddenly looked at me and smiled. "He is rather intimidating, isn't he?" I liked him for saying that, and thought there might be more to him than his conversation to date had indicated.

Then Isa came up behind me and, putting her arm through mine, said, "Here we go again, Lara, tempting the gods."

"It's just a statue," Jonathan scoffed. "A not particularly interesting example of Toltec carving in my opinion.

"It's only real interest is the inspiration it gave to Henry Moore, one of my more talented fellow countrymen." He smiled. "Spawned several rather famous Moore reclining figures."

"Tempting the gods yourself, aren't you, Jonathan?" Isa teased.

"Rubbish!"

"Oh, I don't know," I countered. "Didn't I hear someone got killed up here fairly recently?"

"Yes, indeed. Struck by lightning. An archaeologist, too, if I remember correctly," Isa said.

"It is true," Jonathan admitted. "These temples are not the safest places in a storm. A well-known archaeologist was unfortunate enough to be on the top of the Temple of the Warriors during one. He was struck dead."

"The Chac Mool, no doubt, was briefly appeased," I said. "Although he isn't saying, I suspect he regards Henry Moore as a mere blip in the passage of time." Lucas smiled for the second time since I had met him.

"Oh, no, here come those little monsters again," Isa groaned.

She was right. It was the two kids, leaders of the pack, their mothers still in hot and breathless pursuit.

Jonathan grabbed my hand and we descended the steps, turning north across the plaza, then past what is called the Venus platform, then onto a trail, now lined with numerous souvenir stands, heading east.

"This may look like an ordinary trail to you, or perhaps even an excuse for an outdoor market." Jonathan smiled, still holding my hand. "But it is, in fact, a remnant of an ancient Maya road or *sacbe*. There are traces of these *sacbaob* throughout the peninsula, many of them apparently linking the major cities."

His voice trailed on, noting various points of interest, but I was not really listening. Instead I was thinking how long it had been since I'd held someone's hand, and how nice it felt. Such simple gestures of closeness had so long been missing from my life—from most of my marriage, not to put too fine a point on it—that I felt I wanted to hold his hand forever.

Too soon we came to the end of the trail and stood by the edge of the Sacred Cenote or Well of Sacrifice.

The cenote, or *dzonot* in Mayan, is huge, 180 feet in diameter, almost exactly circular, and from the high edge, one looks at least eighty feet down to the water. The sides are striated limestone, with scrub bushes clinging to them.

Jonathan slipped amiably back into his role as professor and tour guide.

"As impressive as it is as a natural phenomenon—a cenote occurs when the walls of underground caves and rivers collapse and break through to the surface—it is its man-made context—"

"Cross-eyed virgins!" Isa interrupted, winking at me.

She was referring to the very popular notion that the Itzá sacrificed cross-eyed virgins in the cenote to appease the gods.

"As scarce as water is in this area," Jonathan continued, undeterred, "we don't believe this cenote was used as a water system. It may have been used for ritual or sacrificial purposes. The well has been dredged several times and a great trove of artifacts has been found—jade, gold, and about fifty skeletons."

"Aha, the cross-eyed virgins at last." Isa laughed.

"As it turns out," Jonathan said, "the skeletons are of adults and children, both male and female.

"And to borrow a phrase from one of my learned colleagues, if any or all of them were either cross-eyed, or virgins, let's just say their skeletal remains do not give us enough information to be definitive on the subject," Jonathan said dryly.

We all laughed at that.

"I think what is interesting about these places is that you always have a sense of something, some power, when you are in a place considered to be sacred," I said.

Lucas looked bemused, Jonathan slightly perplexed.

"Meaning?"

"You can understand why these walls were so special. They were supposed to be the entrances to the watery underworld, to Xibalba, the realm of the Lords of Death.

"Have you noticed how still and heavy the air is here. Almost oppressive. Back in the plaza there was quite a pleasant breeze. I'm sure there is a physical explanation for this—we're in a sort of a depression here, aren't we?—but to me there is an almost hypnotic quality to this place. Sacrificial victims might be drawn to their deaths by its power."

"Or maybe they just fell in," Jonathan suggested. "This place was occupied for centuries. Fifty skeletons is not a lot over that time period."

"If they fell in, why didn't they climb out?" Isa queried.

"Have you seen how far down the water is? And the sides are worn smooth down below by the water. It would be an extremely difficult climb," Jonathan explained.

"The Itzá were supposed to be water wizards or something, weren't they?" Isa asked.

"That's correct," Jonathan answered. "That's the literal translation of Itzá, and Chichén Itzá is the Mouth of the Well of the Itzá. This was, as Lara points out, a very sacred place.

"But all this talk of water is making me thirsty. How about lunch? If I remember correctly, there is a little café nearby. Not fancy but the food is good. You'll love it, Isa. It has a tacky mural of nubile cross-eyed virgins, all trussed up, being hurled into the cenote while lascivious gods look on."

We headed back along the *sacbe,* pausing to allow a gaggle of tourists following a guide carrying a sun umbrella to go by.

"Perfect timing," Isa murmured. "Let's get out of here!"

On our way, we took a detour through the famous ball court, where games of life and death were played. Jonathan told us that the Itzá did not record their history in hieroglyphics, as the classic Maya did, but instead chose to adorn the walls of the ball court with the most amazing pictorial carvings, some depicting their creation mythology, many others their ritual game.

"In this ball game, the ball is believed to have been a symbol of the movement of the sun through the sky, and the game itself therefore had the highest ritualistic importance," Jonathan said. "To lose was to die—by decapitation or by having your heart cut out. Such deaths ensured that the universe would continue to unfold as it should."

While Isa, Jonathan, and I lingered over the carvings, enjoying the sunshine, Lucas went off to talk to some of the guides and groundskeepers.

Later we crossed the great plaza, pausing only long enough to see hordes of tourists climbing up and down El Castillo like busy little ants at a picnic. Perfect timing, indeed.

We took the Jeep and headed west, Jonathan driving this time, doubling back along the old Highway 180 to the café he had spoken of.

He was right about its decor. There really was a mural depicting young women being hurled into the cenote. Whatever the artist lacked in skill he made up for in enthusiasm. We opted to eat in a little courtyard out back.

After a lunch of *sopa de lima* and grilled fish, we lingered over the last of our wine and beer, and inevitably the talk turned to the murder of Luis Vallespino and the disappearance of Don Hernan.

"Do either of you have any idea where Don Hernan might be?" Jonathan asked.

"None," we both agreed.

"I suppose we can take some comfort that the police are looking for him, even if it is for the wrong reason," I said, although I was not entirely convinced of this myself.

We all nodded at that.

"Does anyone really believe he had anything to do with the robbery?" Isa asked.

"Or the murder?" I added.

Isa looked surprised. I told her about my conversation with Major Martinez. "He really seems to feel Don Hernan is implicated in all of this."

"Speaking of Martinez," I said, "How did Don Santiago get me sprung, to use your expression, Jonathan?"

"He just called some of his former colleagues in the government. We should tell you a couple of things, though," Isa said, glancing at Jonathan, who nodded.

"My father does not much like what he is hearing about Major Martinez, and he suspects that your freedom today may not last, unfortunately. He thinks Martinez will have the ban on your leaving the hotel reinstated very soon."

"So enjoy your freedom while you can, Lara," Jonathan said.

I took that one in, then changed the subject.

"Does anyone know anything about Luis Vallespino?" I asked.

"Nothing at all," Jonathan replied.

"All I know about him is that his older brother is in one of Alejandro's classes at the university. No one has associated him with Don Hernan in any way," Isa said.

"Except that he was found dead right over Don Hernan's head, as it were," Jonathan interjected.

While we chatted Lucas left us again, and I could see him through the doorway, talking in an animated fashion to the waiter. Obviously he was not quite so taciturn in others' company.

"I have a suggestion," Jonathan said, changing to a more pleasant subject when Lucas returned to the table. "There's lots more of Chichén Itzá to see, and we could easily spend the rest of the afternoon here.

"But Lucas and I are working on a very interesting project not too far away. We're excavating in an underground cavern. Would you like to see it?"

"Definitely!" I said. Isa agreed.

Lucas drove this time, back to the highway, then east. Several miles from Chichén Itzá, he pulled onto a dusty dirt road marked NO EXIT. We followed it for another mile or two, until near its end, we sighted some activity. Lucas pulled the Jeep off the road and parked it beside a couple of old pickup trucks and three very ancient Volkswagens of the sort endearingly called Bugs.

"The fleet," Jonathan said, gesturing toward the vehicles with a smile.

We walked a few yards through the forest on a trail that had been cleared in a rudimentary fashion, soon coming upon what at a distance had appeared to be an outcropping of limestone. Up close, it was possible to see a narrow entrance to a cave. A small generator puffed and belched outside.

This part of the Yucatán is very, very flat and there are no surface rivers. There are only two physical features of note, one, the green mounds that often hide ancient ruins, the second, the unseen caves and rivers beneath the limestone surface.

"This is a little tricky here, at the start," Jonathan said as Lucas slid down a fairly steep slope and soon disappeared.

"Come on," he shouted, and Isa, casting a mock-terrified glance in my direction, followed him.

I went next. The entrance to the cave angled steeply downward, and it was rather muddy. I found myself sliding as the others had, and was very glad to have Lucas offering a steadying hand until I reached the point where the ground leveled out. Jonathan followed closely behind.

We were in a tunnel, lit by a few lightbulbs strung on a long wire from the generator at the entrance.

In this spot, it was possible for all of us, including Jonathan, who was tallest, to stand quite easily, but ahead there were some very low overhangs.

Lucas led the way, sticking to what appeared to be the main tunnel, which was barely wide enough for one person to pass. Workmen were coming and going, and when one of them approached with a wheelbarrow, we had to press ourselves flat against the wall of the tunnel.

Occasionally we needed to crawl on our hands and knees under low overhangs. From time to time I could see side tunnels branching off into darkness.

The tunnel always angled downward, and the air became increasingly warm and dank as we proceeded.

After several minutes of this, when we must have been many feet below the surface, the tunnel came to an abrupt end, and we found ourselves in a large round cavern, several yards in diameter.

Here a very bright spotlight had been set up, and in its beam, three or four workmen were patiently brushing away at the rock face on one side of the cavern.

Two huge carved masks dominated the cavern, one on each side. Still partially covered in dirt, they were nonetheless impressive, at least seven or eight feet high, with large eyes complete with staring pupils, long noses, and earlobes adorned with large round ornaments. Mouths agape, lips drawn back, tongues protruding, they were Chacs, Maya rain gods, much revered by the Yucatecan Maya at the time of the conquest.

After several minutes of gazing almost hypnotically at the masks, I became aware of the sound of water. At the far side of the cavern was another tunnel. This one, however, dropped off precipitously into darkness.

At the bottom, Jonathan told us, was a cenote, a smaller version of the Well of Sacrifice we had seen earlier at Chichén Itzá. A rather rudimentary rope fence strung from wooden stakes protected the edge. Leaning over, it was not possible to see the water below. Jonathan dropped a pebble. It bounced down the sides, and then splashed. The water was a long way down.

"Are there artifacts down there?" I asked.

"Don't know yet," Jonathan replied. "We aren't planning to dredge the cenote until we finish the work up here, several weeks from now. As you can appreciate, it will be quite a task, with no daylight to help us."

Over to one side was a mound of pieces of rock, bits of bone, pottery, and other things.

"What are these?" I asked.

"That"—Jonathan smiled—"is what we archaeologists lovingly refer to as the GOK pile—God Only Knows. We'll work on identifying it all later.

"But come and see what we can identify," Jonathan urged, taking us over to some large wooden crates, about three feet by four feet, in which were laid out trays of pottery shards, all carefully numbered and cataloged and set in unbleached cotton, beads that might be jade, and in one tray, beautifully carved flint blades, each different, and each a magnificent work of art.

"So far we have found eight of these blades," Jonathan explained.

"There will be nine," Lucas said. "Nine blades for the nine Lords of Darkness." His infrequent contributions to the conversations never failed to surprise me.

"Lucas may be right. There is no question these caves were considered to be entrances to the underworld, to Xibalba. We believe this must have been a very sacred spot. We don't really know why these blades were hidden here, or what ceremonies may have taken place beneath the surface of the earth, but we feel it must have been important," Jonathan said.

"Perhaps this was a place their king, the ahau, would come alone to fast and commune with the ancestors and gods. After days of fasting and praying, in a trancelike state, the king would pierce his tongue or his genitals with a stingray spine. The blood thus shed dripped onto paper which was burned to appease the gods. The king would then appear before his people, his white robe stained with his own blood. As gruesome as it might seem to us, blood was believed to carry the soul, and this was a powerful ritual for the Maya, one that, like the ball game, ensured the continuing cycle of life."

"Think of the people working underground, without benefit of electric lights, carving these magnificent masks," Isa breathed.

She was right. While their friends and families toiled and played above them, Maya artists must have conquered the most primitive of fears, that of the dark, and with the aid only of torches, made their way to this spot to carve these awesome faces.

As we turned to leave I noticed on the wall around the tunnel opening the faint outline of a carving that the workmen had not yet uncovered. It was of a rather intricate design with what appeared to be two tendrils extending up from a base, rather like two raised arms.

I would have liked to ask more about it and to take a closer look, but it was clearly time to go. We were each immersed in our own thoughts as we left the cavern and made our way slowly to the surface.

We returned to the Jeep and headed back toward Mérida. About halfway, we once again pulled off the road and stopped at a charming little house.

"Humble, but mine own," Jonathan announced. "Or at least it's mine while I'm supervising the dig. Let's go for a swim!"

The house may have been small, but it had everything one could want. A large open kitchen, a fireplace in the living/dining area, and a very nice bedroom overlooking a patio and swimming pool. We all had a dip and a cold drink beside the pool.

After about an hour, as the sun set, we began the long journey to Mérida.

Even seeing Major Martinez at the front desk could not spoil the day for me, although it was obvious that my escape had made him even more irritable than usual. He merely harrumphed when he saw me and made a big show of looking at his watch.

But we were not late, and there was nothing much he could do about it.

I invited the others to join me for dinner but all had other plans: Isa to help her mother in the kitchen, Lucas and Jonathan some other engagement.

As they left, Jonathan's hand brushed mine. "I hope you will come back to visit my little house very soon, just you and me. Would you do that?"

"Love to," I said. And I meant it.

When I went upstairs to my room, I had a very strong feeling that someone had been there. Not the young woman who made up the room, but someone else. It's strange how you always know, even when nothing appears to be out of place.

I tried to cast the idea out of my mind. The thought of an evening with Jonathan in his delightful little house helped a lot.

CIMI

CIMI. ANOTHER DEATH DAY.

The Popol Vuh, the great epic of the Quiché Maya, portrays a mythic battle between the Lords of Death, denizens of an underworld called Xibalba, and the Hero Twins. The Twins, Hunahpu and Xbalanque, offspring of the Maize Lord and a banished underworld princess, play a ball game with the Xibalbans by day and submit to a series of tests by night.

They survive tests of fire, rain and hail, bats, razorsharp stones that come to life and try to slash them. One is beheaded; they are drowned, their bones ground up and thrown into the sea. In the end, of course, they outwit the Lords of Death and rise through the earth into the sky to become the sun and the moon. In so doing, the heroes are said to have brought hope to the world: a soul called to Xibalba can defeat the Lords of the Underworld as they did, and triumph over death.

Today, although I do not know it yet, is Don Hernan's last, the day that his soul enters the maw of Xibalba and begins his personal battle with the Lords of Death. He dies without finding what he sought.

That he does so on Cimi, the day of the human skull hieroglyph, would have seemed only natural to the ancient Maya.

But his death is anything but natural. Whichever human emissary of the Lords of Xibalba has been the cause of his death has a sense of history—and theater.

TODAY I WAS ONCE AGAIN confined to barracks, as it were. Isa and I had a late breakfast with Francesca and Santiago in the kitchen while Santiago told me of the efforts to have me sprung from captivity again.

I myself made a call to the Canadian embassy in Mexico City, and after several infuriating attempts to get through the bureaucratic morass, I found someone, a Margaret Semple, who had worked with my father several years earlier and said she would get right on this.

Knowing that "get right on this" in Mexico meant something different and more protracted than the same statement back home, I decided to relax and enjoy the day with the Ortiz family.

Alejandro was in the hotel, and he looked pale and withdrawn, not the least the cocky kid I'd had a short beer with a couple of days earlier. That morning he had attended the funeral of Luis Vallespino with a group of his friends, and the experience had obviously subdued him.

"I'm sorry I was so rude to you the other day, Alejandro," I said to him when we had a minute alone. His eyes teared up a little. "I am terribly worried about

Don Hernan. I don't know what any of this is about, Alejandro. But I will remain silent, I promise you. I just wish you'd talk to me about it."

His mouth moved as if he were about to speak, but then he turned and walked away.

Later Isa and I swam in the pool in the courtyard, sunned ourselves, and gossiped, supervised, in a manner of speaking, by Doña Josefina, who, in keeping with her epithet, *The Empress*, regally surveyed the comings and goings of everyone from the shade of the veranda.

"Okay, Isa, tell me about the boyfriend."

"He's lovely. He's a banker, but not too stuffy. From France. Fortunately for me he got posted to Mexico two years ago. We met shortly after he got here. With the Mexican peso as volatile as it is, I don't think he regarded this as a plum assignment. Now the question is what we will do if he gets called back to Paris?"

"What kind of banking does he do?"

"Currency, international transfers of money for large accounts. That kind of thing. He's been very helpful with my business actually. He's always giving me advice as to when to buy and sell US or Eurodollars. He's very talented."

"Talented and . . . ?"

"Cute. Maybe even adorable, what can I say? Very French, very charming, very funny, nice dresser. And he gets along with my family; even Alejandro. But your turn. Where are we, exactly, on the subject of our two archaeologists?"

"Actually I was thinking about Alejandro. He's rather quiet these days, isn't he?"

"Yes, we're concerned about him. I think this is the first funeral he's ever attended. Luis, as I told you, was the younger brother of a friend of Alejandro's, Ricardo Vallespino. I didn't know they were such good friends, just part of the same circle, but I suppose at that age, death, particularly such a violent one, always seems remote.

"But don't try and change the subject. Back to the archaeologists!"

"I'm not sure, I guess. You know my history with men as well as anyone, Isa. I always go for the cads. So what should we think would you say?

"Well, there's no question which one is the better conversationalist. Or the better dresser. Gucci loafers, no less!"

"That's good, is it?" I asked, grinning. Isa thought I knew absolutely nothing about fashion, and I loved to tease her, and she me, about it.

Isa sighed. "Lara, your knowledge of fashion is appalling. I really will have to take you in hand. G-U-C-C-I. Italian, trendy, expensive. Jonathan is unquestionably the best-dressed archaeologist I've ever seen. Even his casual clothes are Savile Row. He's also the better conversationalist. Lucas isn't exactly wordy, is he?"

"No, but he dresses like an archaeologist. I don't suppose there is any point in asking who, where, or what is a Savile Row?"

Isa treated my question with the contempt it deserved. "I think we can safely assume Jonathan is not living off an archaeologist's salary. He must be independently wealthy, upper-crust, Oxford-educated, old school tie, tea parties at Buckingham Palace, that sort of thing. I think we should make inquiries."

Just then Norberto came over with a tray with two margaritas for us. "On the house." He smiled. "Mother says to just get whatever you want to eat from the kitchen. She's gone to pay her respects to Luis and Ricardo's mother."

"Have you heard anything more about the police investigation, Isa?" I asked after Norberto had gone back inside.

"The police are saying it was some kind of gang war," Isa replied.

"That may be what they are saying officially, Isa, but as I told you, Major Martinez has hinted—more than hinted—that Don Hernan is involved."

"That's ridiculous!"

"Try telling that to Martinez. And Luis was found on the roof of the *museo*. How on earth would a gang war put him there?"

We both pondered that for a while.

"Isa, I have a favor to ask."

"Sure."

"I need an address and directions to the home of Diego Maria Gomez Arias."

She raised an eyebrow.

"His name or rather the initials D.M.G.A. appear rather often in Don Hernan's diary, if I remember correctly."

"How are you going to—*the tree!*"

I nodded.

Later that afternoon she went out, and returned in an hour or two.

She handed me a slip of paper with an address and a hand-drawn route map. She also slipped me a set of car keys.

"You'll need transportation," she whispered conspiratorially. "My car will be on the side street by eleven P.M. I'll go stay with friends for a couple of hours, then pick it up on the way home and drive it to the garage."

The day dragged on after that, except for the time when Jonathan dropped in for a drink, "to visit the prisoner," as he put it. We had a pleasant visit, but he couldn't stay for dinner. He had work to do, he said. I looked at his shoes with new respect. Italian, trendy, expensive . . .

We watched the television news in the kitchen. The death of Luis Vallespino had caused an outpouring of rage and grief in the city. His funeral had made the news, and was obviously well attended. I scanned the crowd for signs of Alejandro, but did not see him.

Right after eleven, I turned out the light, put the dark pants and sweater on again, and crawled out through the bathroom window as I had previously.

I had to wait up in the tree until a couple out for a stroll passed by, then I was down and around the corner.

The Mercedes was there, as promised, and I pulled away as quickly as I could.

Isa's directions took me north on the extension of the Paseo de Montejo to a part of town known to be the haunt of the nouveau riche and famous. When the henequen trade had dried up, victim of the arrival of man-made fibers, and the upkeep and modernization of the houses on the *paseo* became too expensive for succeeding generations, the rich moved north along the road to Progreso.

Indeed, if you take the Plaza Major as the heart of Mérida, the farther north you go, the wealthier the residents. The Gomez Arias family lived well to the north, out beyond even the country-club set. The houses out here were enormous, and even though it was now about eleven-thirty, almost all were still ablaze, a testimony to the Mexican penchant for staying up half the night.

I was glad to have the Mercedes. There were several private security personnel on patrol, some in cars, some on foot with dogs. The Mercedes, in this neighborhood, raised no suspicions.

I had a little trouble finding my way through the winding streets, but eventually I pulled up at the gate of the palatial estate Diego Maria Gomez Arias called home. I pushed a button at the entrance and spoke my name into a little box, asking in what I hoped was impeccable Spanish for a brief meeting with Señor Gomez Arias. There was a lengthy pause, during which I got to consider how silly this all was. Of course they would not open the gates to a stranger at eleven-thirty at night.

I was about to give up and go back to the hotel, fearful the dogs had been called, when the huge wrought-iron gates began to swing open.

I piloted the Mercedes along a sweeping drive, the

headlights illuminating bushes of hibiscus that must have been absolutely gorgeous in the light of day.

The house itself struck me as rather odd for Mérida, its architecture more English or French manor house than traditional Spanish: portico entrance, leaded glass windows, none of the tilework or heavy wood carving I would have expected.

This impression was borne out when the door was opened at my ring, and I was ushered into a spectacular mirrored black-and-white marble-tiled foyer. The maid who opened the door was also dressed in black and white, and looked rather disdainfully at my attire. At least all in black, I, too, matched the decor. I was left to cool my heels for a while.

This gave me plenty of opportunity to gawk. A huge crystal chandelier graced the entranceway, a circular staircase curved up one side of the foyer, and to my right, a door led into what I was soon to learn was a sitting room.

The walls were all mirrored, and in a decorating affectation I have never liked, pictures were hung against the mirrors, held there by thin wires from the ceiling. The paintings were nonetheless impressive. One was, I was almost certain, a real Picasso, another a Matisse. Señor Gomez Arias was obviously doing quite nicely, thank you. And he had good taste in art.

Another door to the left opened to a dining room, complete with another crystal chandelier. Both fixtures were so large I wondered if Don Diego Maria had borrowed a couple of spares from the ballroom of his hotel.

After a few minutes I heard someone descending the stairs. It was not Don Diego, but instead a smart-looking woman of about forty who clutched the banister in one hand and a martini glass in the other.

She made her way down the stairs with some care.

She was attractive in a kind of beige way: beigy-blond hair that she wore long and pulled back, a creamy beige sweater that I could only assume was cashmere, and a beige suede skirt.

"Sheila Stratton Gomez," she said, addressing me in Spanish. "Diego's wife. His third wife, to be precise. And you are . . . ?"

"Lara McClintoch."

"With a name like that, you must speak English, thank God. Come in," she said, beckoning in the general direction of the door to the right in a way that, in those very high heels, the kind men love but give me vertigo. I couldn't imagine how she could walk in them, even at the best of times. And judging by the martini glass and her general unsteadiness, these were not the best of times.

"You'll have a drink, of course," she said when we were seated in large crushed-velvet armchairs in front of a large marble fireplace of baronial proportions. I gathered she wanted another one.

The maid reappeared, and Sheila Gomez ordered a white wine for me, another martini for herself.

While she addressed me in English and was clearly an American, she ordered the drinks in formal Castilian Spanish, a language I find exotic when spoken by a native, but from someone like Sheila, who obviously learned it later in life, it always sounds affected. Her current tipsy state only exaggerated the rather lisping quality of her speech.

"My husband is not at home. How may I help you?" she said when the drinks arrived.

"I'm looking for someone," I said, "and I had hoped Señor Gomez Arias might be able to help me."

"How deliciously mysterious," she said. She had a little trouble with *deliciously.* "Tell me more."

"I'm trying to find Señor Hernan Castillo. I came to Mexico at his request a few days ago, but he phoned the first evening to say he had been called away, and has not been heard of since."

"Don Hernan. A lovely man. Cultured, kind. I was so sorry when he stopped coming here. He used to come for dinner quite often. We talked about New York, Boston, my hometown of Philadelphia. Don Hernan was very interested in things American, you know. A lovely man," she repeated.

"When and why did he stop coming here?" I asked, trying to focus the conversation a little before the next martini took effect.

"About a month or so ago, I think. He and Diego had an argument of some sort—they were in Diego's study with the door closed, so I don't know what it was about, but it sounded unpleasant," she said.

"Did your husband and Don Hernan have business dealings?" I asked.

"I think so. Diego is on the board of directors of the museum. Beyond that, Diego does not talk to me much about his business. I'm the trophy wife, you know. Good

American family, by which I mean wealthy. I'm brought out on ceremonial occasions only," she said bitterly.

I made sympathetic noises of some kind.

"He's not a bad man, really. I know he has a reputation for ruthless business dealings but . . ." She trailed off.

We both heard someone out in the hall. A young, very attractive woman in her mid-twenties, I would say, dark hair and eyes, looked in. She seemed vaguely familiar. She glanced at the martini glass in Sheila's hand, then briefly at me, and left without a word.

Sheila looked alarmed.

"Who's that?"

"That's Montserrat, Diego's daughter by his much-loved first wife. They fight all the time, but he adores her."

"He named the hotel after her, I take it," I said.

"Yes." She paused and then giggled into her martini glass. "At least I hope that's the way it worked. It wouldn't be very nice for a girl to be named after a hotel, now, would it?

"Actually, she is the manager of the hotel and vice-president of some other businesses Diego owns. He is very proud of her."

"She doesn't look like her father, does she?" I said, thinking of the rather unattractive man in the Ek Balam.

"No, she takes after her mother, Innocentia, who died when Montserrat was very young. Her mother's picture is all over the house." Sheila looked as if she were going to start sobbing in an alcoholic haze.

"Tell me about your husband's businesses," I said,

trying to drag her back from the brink of self-pity. "He owns a hotel, obviously."

"Yes. His original business, the one that made him rich, though, is water."

"Water, as in—"

"As in the stuff they make ice for martinis out of." She giggled again. "Well, have you seen much in the way of fresh water around here? The water for this city comes from the aquifer beneath the city."

"The windmills!" I said, remembering this significant feature of the city when I had first come here as a young girl.

"Right. All of Mérida's water used to be brought to the surface by the windmills you saw everywhere. That's why it was sometimes called the City of Windmills. Diego's father died when Diego was quite young, and I guess his mother didn't feel an education was important for the youngest in the family. Diego is essentially self-taught. He recognized that the water supply here is always a problem, so he learned all about soil mechanics, the underground rivers and everything, and invented a more efficient windmill—sort of like building a better mousetrap—and the rest, as they say, is history. When Mérida switched to a city water system, Diego bought up the old windmills for a song, converted them, and sold them for a premium in the countryside."

"How does he feel about the theft of the statue from the bar?" I asked.

"He is devastated. It was one of his favorite pieces. Actually, Diego and Don Hernan had an argument over that very statue one night at dinner."

I waited while she took another sip of her martini.

"There is one thing you need to know about Diego to understand him. It is not enough for him to admire rare or beautiful things. He must possess them. And the rarer they are, or the harder to obtain, the more he wants them.

"You must have noticed this house. Rather different from the neighbors', wouldn't you say? He saw this little manor house on a country estate in England. The owner, some English earl or something, said it had been in the family for centuries and there was no way he would sell.

"But Diego managed it—found out something about the earl—one would rather not know what—that convinced him to sell.

"Then Diego moved the building, stone by stone, to his property here, and had it reassembled. Fortunately he also owns a small shipping company!" She laughed.

"And then there's me. We met at an official dinner at the governor's residence back home. Diego was a guest of the governor. I was married at the time, but that didn't stop Diego. He pursued me with an enthusiasm that was very flattering. Now I am one of his possessions."

"And Itzamná, the statue?"

"Apparently it was really very old, and a very sacred relic for the Maya. Don Hernan had always felt objects of such antiquity belong in museums, not private collections. After several visits to U.S. museums, he was also coming around to the view that something he called comanagement—sharing ownership of and responsibility for an artifact between an institution like the *museo* and the people to whom it had originally belonged—was the way of the future.

"Anyway, Don Hernan had heard about the Itzamná and had mentioned it to Diego. Both men went after it, for the reasons I've told you, and Diego got to it first.

"It was the beginning of the end of the friendship, and a very sad day for me."

Sheila looked at her empty martini glass and rang the bell for the maid. But instead of the maid, Montserrat appeared. "I believe you've had enough, Sheila," she said.

Sheila looked cowed. Montserrat nodded in my general direction and left the room again.

"Perhaps it's time I left," I said, stating the obvious. "Thank you for your hospitality."

"I don't suppose you'd come again," she said rather wistfully.

"I'd like to," I said, momentarily forgetting I was under house arrest.

"Where would I find you?"

"Casa de las Buganvillas."

"Where Don Hernan lived. I've heard it's lovely."

We shook hands and I headed back down the drive and then toward the hotel. I did not have to ask why Sheila had let a total stranger into the house late at night. This was one very sad and lonely woman.

But there was something about our conversation that was nagging at me as I drove back to the hotel. I was about halfway back when I realized that she had spoken about Don Hernan in the past tense the whole time.

And I remembered where I had seen Montserrat. On television, in the crowd at Luis Vallespino's funeral.

I parked the Mercedes on a side street, crept stealthily

along the sidewalk, climbed the wall into the tree, and then slipped through the window onto the chair in the bathtub.

It was then I noticed the light shining in under the bathroom door from my room. I opened the door with real apprehension.

Isa was sitting on my bed, her eyes red from crying.

"Don Hernan is dead," she said.

MANIK

DON HERNAN HAD BEEN FOUND by the cleaning staff, seated on the floor of his little office at the *museo*. Knees drawn up, his torso and head twisted to face the doorway, and held there by the rigor of death, his body was a human caricature of the Chac Mool that guards the Temple of the Warriors at Chichén Itzá.

He had been stabbed through the heart. There was very little blood in his office, and the murder weapon was not to be found.

Santiago Ortiz Menendez, as one of Don Hernan's oldest friends, was given the unenviable task of identifying the body the next morning. Isa and I accompanied him, my presence permitted, and shall we say even encouraged, by Major Martinez himself. Francesca remained at the inn to break the sad news to the other permanent guests.

It was Manik, day of the deer, day of the hunt, and the day, to force an analogy, that it became very clear to me that Don Hernan's search, the hunt for whatever the elusive rabbit might write, was no whimsical diversion of an elderly man, but like the game in the ball court at Chichén Itzá, a deadly serious contest in which the loser paid with his life.

We took the Ortiz family van, outfitted to accommodate Don Santiago's wheelchair, to the morgue.

Major Martinez was waiting for us when we arrived. In anticipation of just this eventuality, Don Santiago had suggested in the van that I give him—Don Santiago—ten pesos and ask to hire his services. He had trained as a lawyer before joining the diplomatic corps, and although his chosen field was international law, we all agreed that should Martinez regularly feel the need to interview me, it might be well to have Don Santiago along.

Martinez led us down sterile corridors and stairs to the basement, and then to a window marked RECEPCION, behind which sat a young man energetically eating tacos filled with pork, if my sense of smell was functioning properly in this place, which I couldn't swear to. A reddish-brown liquid dribbled down his chin and spattered onto a sheet of wax paper on the desk. Apparently working in a morgue does not put everyone off their food.

Martinez flashed his badge, we all signed in, and the young man used a greasy finger to push a button that unlatched the door beside him. We passed into the heart of the morgue.

With Martinez leading, we came into a room with a row of body lockers against one wall. The place felt cold and clammy to me, and I could see Isa shiver. Whether or not it actually was cold, I couldn't tell.

The drawer containing the remains of Don Hernan was pulled out by a young woman in a lab coat, and his face exposed for Don Santiago's perusal.

I suppose all those of us confronted by this moment hope against hope that a mistake has been made, that a total stranger will be uncovered when the drawer slides out.

But it was not to be. Santiago nodded mutely, and we were led quickly away. Santiago's hands shook as he rearranged the light blanket that covered his emaciated legs. Isa kept one hand on his shoulder as we made our way back to the young man with the tacos. He in turn looked mildly annoyed at having his meal interrupted a second time, but condescended to hand a box over to Martinez. We were then escorted to a small room with a table and a couple of chairs and asked to inspect the contents of the box.

It contained everything that had been found on Don Hernan's body. His watch, an elegant late-nineteenth-century timepiece and chain that had belonged to his mother and contained a picture of his late wife, his clothes, an absolutely empty billfold, a few loose pesos. Only one object looked out of place, and this was a small green jade bead. The young woman in the lab coat, who had accompanied us, saw me looking at it.

"Found it in his mouth," she said. "It was put there with some difficulty several hours after he died."

"When did he die?" I asked.

"Very early yesterday, I would estimate," she said, ignoring the warning stare coming her way from Martinez. Clearly the major was not king of the morgue.

While Martinez asked Santiago whether or not he could recall these belongings as Don Hernan's, I touched the cream-colored shoes. While it was difficult to tell just looking at them, they were covered in the light dust so pervasive outside the city. The trouser cuffs were also dusty.

Perhaps the question I should have asked was where did he die, not when.

"Who has done such a thing?" Santiago asked, almost in a whisper.

"Robbery, apparently," Martinez replied. "Empty wallet," he added as Santiago looked up at him. "Every effort will, of course, be made to apprehend the perpetrator or perpetrators."

"Of course," we all agreed.

"However, there are many robberies here every day. It will take some time to conduct this investigation."

"Where was he killed?" I asked Martinez.

"We are still conducting tests, but in the meantime we assume it was in his office in which he was found," he replied. The young woman in the lab coat looked dubious, but said nothing.

I didn't believe this, but also said nothing. Isa and I asked Martinez when the police would finish their work on the body, and were told it would probably be later that day or early the next.

"I think we can safely assume that what we have here is a case of death at the hands of person or persons unknown," he concluded.

As we left the building, Don Santiago pulled himself

together and addressed Martinez in his new capacity as my lawyer.

"I have been retained by Señora McClintoch in this matter," he began.

"Have you indeed?" Martinez interrupted. "Now, why might the señora feel she has need of a lawyer?"

"Because of your unconscionable move of confiscating her passport, and confining her to the hotel, I am sure you will agree that since it was information on Dr. Castillo's whereabouts that you were looking for, and since his present location is well known, there is no longer any need to restrict her activities.

"And since she could not be implicated in Dr. Castillo's death—she has been, if you recall, under house arrest for the last few days, and several of us can attest to that—no doubt you will also be returning her passport shortly."

"If Señora McClintoch does not feel the need for our protection, then that is up to her," the policeman said smoothly. "As far as the passport is concerned, you will understand that we are now investigating two murders, and we will have to have extensive discussions with our superiors to determine whether we can allow her to leave the country before our investigations are complete."

So it was a standoff, one for him, one for me. It would be a relief to be able to leave the hotel at will, and by the door rather than the window. I'd work on the passport later.

We were a silent group as we made our way back to the van and returned to the hotel. It was Isa who broke the silence partway home.

"Seeing his belongings in a box was so sad," she said. "It seemed like such a small amount of stuff for such a big man—and I mean that not just in terms of his physique, but his personality. He always seemed larger than life to me. It just seemed too little."

"It really was too little," I said slowly.

Both Isa and Don Santiago looked at me.

"No glasses. No cane."

A pause.

"So you're saying he wasn't murdered in his office, or both those things would be there. He couldn't go anywhere without his glasses, and hardly anywhere without his cane. Maybe they are still in his office," Isa said.

Maybe not, I thought. But I knew I would find out.

Back at the Casa de las Buganvillas, Francesca and her daughter-in-law, Manuela, were ministering to the permanent residents of the hotel.

Most of them elderly like Don Hernan, their shock and disbelief were almost palpable. Theories were exchanged, tears flowed, each in their own way trying to come to terms with this most awful of crimes.

Doña Josefina, she of the mantilla, sat like a broken doll, all lace and wobbly gestures, in a chair suddenly way too big for her. Manuela sat beside her, trying to get her to drink hot lemon tea.

I felt very sorry for her. She was what I used to refer to in the shop as a high-maintenance customer, and she did expect to be attended to rather more than most.

But Don Hernan, I'd heard, had a way of dealing with her. Courtly, patient, he had been able to make her smile.

It was even rumored in that little community that she had set her sights on him—the younger man as her second husband.

Into this room awash with fear and loneliness strode Jonathan, with Lucas May shadowing him once more. Catching the mood in the room at once and seeing the two bright pink spots on Doña Josefina's cheeks, he called for a restorative, Xtabentun, the Mexican anise liqueur, and Manuela was quick to comply.

Soon everyone was sipping the fiery liquid as Jonathan moved about the room talking quietly to each in turn. Within a few minutes they were exchanging their favorite stories about Don Hernan. Lucas placed himself beside Doña Josefina and sat quietly holding her hand.

Suddenly Josefina roused herself.

"He was onto something very important," she said, her voice carrying across the room.

"Very important," she repeated. "And I know what it was."

All eyes in the room turned to her. But that was all she said. A look of fear crossed her face, as if for the first time she had realized that this very important thing, whatever it might be, might be sufficient motive for murder.

Lucas whispered something to her, and then Jonathan crossed the room and asked her what she meant.

But she shook her head, her lips compressed into a thin line.

I should have spoken to her right then, of course, tried to cajole the information out of her, but at this particular point in time, it looked as if the Ortiz family had everything under control. I knew I needed to talk to Doña Josefina, but not in this public place, and there was something I wanted to do first.

Jonathan and Lucas left the sitting room with me, and Jonathan asked me where I was heading.

"Back to the morgue," I said. He looked startled, but gamely offered to accompany me.

We took the Jeep, and parked just down the street from the dreaded building. Much to my surprise, it was not difficult to get inside. I retraced our steps of earlier that day and soon found myself at the reception window.

The young man with the greasy tacos had been replaced by a thin young woman doing her nails.

"Excuse me," I said. "I was here earlier today to assist in the identification of a body."

She nodded as if this was a perfectly normal occurrence.

"There was a very nice woman, she was wearing a lab coat, and she was very helpful. I left without thanking her for her kindness, and would like to do so if she is here now."

Jonathan looked slightly skeptical, but kept his opinion to himself.

"She's left for the day."

"Would she be in again tomorrow?" I asked. The young woman sighed, got out of her chair, holding her hands carefully so as not to damage her manicure, and too vain to wear her glasses, peered at a large scheduling chart.

"Not back for four days," she said. "Flextime," she

added. I thought all time in Mexico was flextime, but I kept that opinion to myself.

But I had a name. Eulalia Gonzales. There was only one woman on the chart who had been in today, and wouldn't be back for four days.

"Gracias," I said, and Jonathan and I headed back up to the entrance.

"What was that all about, may I ask?" he said as we left that horrible building to breathe real air again.

"I wanted to ask her for more information about what happened to Don Hernan," I said.

"Shouldn't this be left to the police?"

"I have a bad feeling about Martinez's investigation of this case. I think in his haste to wrap up a high-profile case like this one—Don Hernan has, after all, an international reputation in his field—he's prepared to overlook some discrepancies."

"Such as?"

"Such as the scene of the crime. About as basic a detail as you can get, wouldn't you say? When we went to identify the body, Martinez said that Don Hernan was probably killed in his office, but I don't think that's right. There was dust all over his shoes and the cuffs of his trousers. You don't get that kind of dust on you working at your desk. I got the impression Eulalia Gonzales didn't think he was murdered in his office, either. Don't you have to wonder why Martinez would insist that he was?"

"You may be being unfair to the police, Lara. Maybe Martinez just isn't saying anything publicly. I'm going to take you back to the hotel. You should get some rest after this ordeal."

Part of me agreed with him. In any event, I had another plan. So I let him drive me back to the hotel. On the way back, he reached over and squeezed my hand.

"When this all settles down, let's keep that date we had for a day out in the country again, just the two of us."

"Great idea," I said, hoping he meant it.

I spent the rest of the day helping the Ortiz family make the funeral arrangements. The police had promised to release the body that evening, and the funeral was to be two days hence.

We all turned in early, exhausted beyond words. Doña Josefina had retired to her room before I had returned to the hotel. I did not see her that evening.

I set the alarm for three A.M., and it took me a minute or two to get my bearings when it went off. Then I was back in the black clothes. This was a task that required going out the window again. I did not wish to be seen leaving the hotel at this hour.

I figured the *museo* was less than a mile from the inn. Not wishing to flag down a cab, I jogged, keeping to the residential streets as much as possible and clinging to the shadows. When I reached the *museo*, I hid in the little garden at the back while I caught my breath. I could see no sign of police—no cars, no guards.

I still had the key to Don Hernan's office, and since there was only one key at the hotel, I was reasonably sure it was a master. It was marked *MUSEO*, not *OFFICE*, and Don Hernan had been executive director of the *museo*. I carefully made my way to the back door.

In a couple of seconds I was inside and moving up the stairs as quietly as I could. When I got to the top floor, I waited for my eyes to adjust to the darkness. I could see police tape across the office doorway, but no guard was posted. The police work there had by and large been done.

I crept down the hallway. It was very easy to slide under the yellow tape and let myself into the office. I had brought a flashlight from the kitchen at the inn, and I did a quick sweep of the room. No eyeglasses. No cane. Only the sad chalk outline where the body had been found.

The diary, which I had dropped in my haste to escape on my last visit, was wedged between the window ledge and a filing cabinet, and had obviously been missed in a cursory police search. I grabbed it, and then retraced my steps, pausing at the *museo* door to make sure no one was outside before stepping into the plaza.

By four-thirty I was back in bed. But I did not sleep. I had a lot of thinking to do.

Up to this point, I'd been tinkering around the edges. But it was like trying to stick your toe into the water just above Niagara Falls. You could not help but be swept away. In this case, I found myself being pulled inexorably into a world of masks, a world of evil. Perhaps, I thought, I was about to live my dream of my first night in Mérida, falling into the black world of Xibalba where the Lords of Death await.

Why did I go willingly?

Maybe some recessive impulsive gene surfaced in me at this late stage. Maybe all the hurt and resentment of the past year or so got focused on these events. Or maybe I just got mad.

I think, though, it was something more fundamental:

Don Hernan had called me *amiga*. He'd thought he needed a partner in this undertaking, and he'd called on me.

I guess I just had to do something.

The next day, Lamat, a day associated with the rabbit, was as good a day as any to start. I'd have to solve the riddle, find the rabbit, and follow it wherever it took me.

I'd already committed at least one illegal act—theft—and from a murder scene at that. Better make that two. I'd withheld information about a crime, the robbery in the bar, from the police. Before this was played out, there might be more.

This would not make the federal police, particularly Major Ignacio Martinez, happy.

I decided that when it came right down to it, I didn't much care what Major Martinez thought.

LAMAT

It is the bottom of the eighth inning of the final ball game between the mythic Hero Twins and the Lords of Xibalba. It does not look good for our heroes. The evil lords have cut off Hunahpu's head and have substituted it for the ball!

The other twin, Xbalanque, however, has a plan of his own. Taking a leaf from the Xibalbans' book, he asks a rabbit to wait in the bushes near the edge of the ball court and then lobs his brother's head in that direction.

The rabbit, in a star turn if ever there was one, bounds away right on cue. The Xibalbans think the rabbit is the head, of course, and run shrieking after it. With the Xibalbans thus distracted, Xbalanque has time to replace Hanahpu's head. Victory over the Xibalbans is near.

Rabbits pop up everywhere in Maya mythology and history, I found as I worked my way through the reference library at the *museo*. It was a tedious process. The *museo*, a private institution, always suffered from inadequate funding, and while the office was the proud owner of a new computer, and the collection itself was gradually being cataloged electronically, the reference-library contents were still cataloged on little cards in little drawers.

Other rabbits I found that day: there is a ruin of a classic Maya structure called Muyil on the eastern coast of the Yucatán peninsula, south of Tulum Pueblo. Muyil means the "Place of Rabbits."

The Moon Goddess, a young woman sitting in the crescent of the moon, is often shown holding a rabbit, according to the texts. This is probably because the Maya discerned the outline of a rabbit in the dark areas of the full moon, just as we think we see a man.

Rabbits are also listed in Friar Diego de Landa's *Relación de las cosas de Yucatán,* a document the infamous Spanish priest wrote in 1566 to defend himself against accusations that he had been too harsh in his treatment of the Maya—even for the times of the Inquisition! He describes the local hare as large and good to eat.

I even found a traditional recipe for rabbit cooked in sherry, tomatoes, and jalapeño peppers.

As far as I knew, none of these rabbits was known to have written anything.

The library at the *museo* was a dusty, airless old place with only one window, presided over by one Señor Dr. Antonio Valesquez.

Valesquez struck me as the quintessential librarian, a man with an obsession about order, procedure, and silence. I don't expect anyone ever called him Antonio in that place.

I got an early start, and learning that Doña Josefina

was still indisposed, due to the shock of Don Hernan's death, made my way directly to the library when the *museo* opened at nine. Exactly at the appointed opening time of nine-fifteen, Valesquez opened the library doors, a most unusual occurrence in Mexico.

Considering the events of the last few days, this punctuality was particularly surprising, but Valesquez was not the type of person to let a murder or two disrupt the order of his day. Fiftyish, with a shock of gray hair and a habit of absentmindedly picking imaginary lint off everything, he looked at me over the tops of his reading glasses and stated quite firmly that this library was for serious research only, and not open to the general public.

Fortunately I had brought my University of Toronto student card, which identified me as a graduate student in Mesoamerican studies. That was enough to get me through the door, but not as a welcome guest.

"Señor doctor," I began. I found myself whispering as he was, even though only two of us were in the room. "I am doing a research paper on natural symbolism in the Maya pantheon, and was directed to you as a possible source of material."

"And who might have directed you here?" He sniffed.

"Dr. Hernan Castillo," I lied. I'd rehearsed this lie, as usual, and it slid off my tongue with amazing facility. "Dr. Castillo has been most helpful with my research, which he felt was an unusual subject that held much promise. I've had several conversations with him from Toronto, and I hoped to be able to speak with him on this visit, but have been unable to reach him," I continued.

It looked for a moment as if Valesquez's composure would crack, but his library training took over.

"Dr. Castillo has met with an unfortunate accident," he said, ignoring as I had the lurid headlines on the front pages of all the local papers. I made suitable noises of surprise and regret.

"While his expertise clearly exceeds mine manyfold," he went on, "I will assist you in any way I can. What particular natural symbolism are you interested in?" he whispered.

"Rabbits," I said.

He nodded gravely. If he was surprised, he didn't show it. I expect one gets all kinds of weird requests in a library such as this. He showed me to the card catalog and led me through it. As he spoke he patted any index card foolhardy enough to be even a millimeter out of line back into place.

"Everything here is cataloged by subject and author using the Dewey Decimal System. I am personally familiar with most of the books here, and can direct you to some to begin your work. Rare books and first editions are available only on special request, in writing, to my office. No book may be removed from the premises. And of course, no food or drink is allowed here," he concluded.

He didn't need to tell me this. There were signs everywhere.

I made my way to a table at the back of the room protected by the book stacks and pulled out a chair. It made a scraping sound as it slid against the marble floor, and brought the inevitable "look" from the librarian. I would obviously have to mind my library manners here.

After a couple of hours I had found the rabbits I've already mentioned, and had several more books to work through. It was laborious work hand-copying anything I wanted to remember. There was no photocopier in sight and I was afraid to ask if one might be available. Clearly I was here on sufferance, and I didn't wish to wear out my welcome.

I still had not told anyone about the writing rabbit, and I would have dearly liked to ask advice from someone more knowledgeable in this field. My study had been restricted to the Mayan language, to hieroglyphics, and while one inevitably learns a great deal about a civilization this way, my studies were still at a very rudimentary level.

The only two people I knew who would know more about this than I, now that Don Hernan was gone, were Jonathan and Lucas.

And what did I know of them, other than that both were archaeologists? Jonathan Hamelin was British—Cambridge University, he had said—pale and aristocratic in bearing, wore nice shoes, and rented a nice little house. I also liked holding his hand.

Lucas May? The dark, brooding one. I knew even less about him. According to Isa, he didn't have nice shoes, and I was inclined to agree with her low opinion of his conversational skills. I had no idea where he lived or where he'd studied archaeology. I had a sense of something hidden, something deep, but it was a feeling only. He also had a nicely ironic smile, infrequently though it appeared.

For a few minutes I was lost in reverie, watching dust motes floating in a beam of light from the lamp on the table. Dr. Valesquez appeared soundlessly at my table and whispered that he was regrettably closing the library, but would reopen between four and six P.M.

I was amazed that almost three hours had passed and dismayed that I was no closer to the writing rabbit. I thanked him for his assistance, for which I received a courtly bow, and told him I would return at four.

I made my way down the back staircase, and moments later was blinking in the now unfamiliar sunlight like some lizard whose dark hiding place has suddenly been uncovered.

I did notice, however, that while one might need a key to get in, one merely pushed a bar on the door to get out. So if you were up to any skulduggery after hours, you had only to hide in the *museo* until closing, then let yourself out at your leisure.

I wandered rather aimlessly to pass the time until the library reopened, and soon I found myself in the market area, absorbing the sights, sounds, and smells, as always almost overwhelmed by the colors, so intense to my northern eye.

It was the time of Carnaval, Ash Wednesday fast approaching, and brightly colored masks and capes were prominently displayed. Here once again the old and new worlds coexisted. While Carnaval may have Christian beginnings, the costumes were decidedly Maya—monkey beings, creatures of a previous Maya creation, and various representations of Xibalbans with grotesque horned masks. One enterprising shopkeeper was offering for sale a Children of the Talking Cross costume, complete with black bandanna and wooden rifle.

There were stalls piled high with fruits and vegetables, some familiar, others not; the heaps of dried peppers, large and dark, intense in flavor I knew; the Mexican tomatoes, *tomatillos,* small green fruits with a natural brown tissuelike wrapping; the prickly *nopales,* cactus-type vegetables whose needles must be removed before they can be used in salads and *moles;* the pungent spices—*epazote, achiote,* or *annatto* seeds, cumin, chili, and saffron.

Tired of wandering, I eventually stopped at a little café for a Mexican sandwich, a *torta,* stuffed with *frijoles*—refried black beans—avocado, and *anejo* cheese, and an order of jalapeño peppers, stuffed with cheese and shrimp and lightly fried.

The air was pleasantly hot, and as I sat there I tried to sift through the patterns within patterns in this situation in which I found myself.

A very public robbery and two murders, and there seemed to be threads, however tenuous, linking all three events.

First the robbery. Alejandro was surely involved. It took place in the bar of a hotel owned by Diego Maria Gomcz Arias. The object stolen is a statue that Hernan Castillo and Gomez Arias had argued about in the recent past. It is stolen by a self-defined terrorist group called the Children of the Talking Cross. But whoever heard of a terrorist group that steals statues from bars? Bank heists, skyjackings, car bombs, maybe. But theft of pre-Columbian carvings?

The murder of Luis Vallespino. Luis's brother is a friend of Alejandro, and Montserrat, Gomez Arias's daughter, attends the funeral. And of course, Luis is found murdered on the roof of the *museo,* of which Gomez Arias is on the board of directors, as is Don Hernan, who was also a staff member and important benefactor.

Don Hernan's murder. Occurring somewhere else, perhaps, but he ends up in his office at the *museo* with a jade bead in his mouth, the significance of which I did not understand. He's looking for something, which is obviously Maya, since he made it clear that whatever it was fit in with my university studies, and it was important enough for him to ask me to come to Mérida.

Don Hernan used to work with Gomez Arias, but they had an argument. Gomez Arias is a compulsive collector. Could the two men have been looking for the same thing? And if so, exactly how far was Gomez Arias prepared to go to get it?

There had to be something or someone linking all of these things. Right now that appeared to be me. I'd come here at Don Hernan's request, I'd witnessed the robbery, I'd found Luis Vallespino's body. I was actually becoming sympathetic to Major Martinez's interest in me.

I wandered back to the *museo,* pausing once again for a few moments in the small rear garden, thinking about the times I had spent with Don Hernan. I was trying very hard to remember the good times, and put the sights and smells of our farewell, in the basement of the morgue, behind me.

As I stood there I saw Antonio Valesquez let himself in

at the back door, the one I'd made use of a couple of times myself. I wondered how many people had a key to that door.

I once again wandered into the building and arrived just as Valesquez, punctual as ever, opened the library doors. A new stack of books was on the table at the back.

"More rabbits," was all he said. This dark little corner was beginning to feel like home, and soon I was attacking the books with renewed enthusiasm. While I worked, Valesquez continued his librarian tasks of bringing order to the room and discouraging visitors.

In 695 A.D., I learned, 18-Rabbit succeeded Smoke-Imix-God K as king of the city state Copán in the southern Yucatán peninsula in what is now Honduras. An avid patron of the arts, 18-Rabbit spent the forty-two years of his reign, until his defeat and sacrifice at the hands of Cauac-Sky of nearby Quirigua, building some of the most glorious monuments of Maya civilization, with temple carvings and stelae unequaled elsewhere in the Maya world. His likeness can still be seen in the magnificent stone stelae around Copán, in which he had himself depicted as the reincarnation of the Hero Twins and as various other Maya gods.

Nonetheless, to be defeated by a rival king, particularly one installed on the neighboring throne some years earlier by 18-Rabbit himself, and then sacrificed, is about as ignominious an end as one could imagine. It took his great grandson Yax-Pac to rehabilitate his memory some three decades later.

After about an hour of frustrating research, I was about to call it a day when, on impulse, I asked Valesquez if he had anything on the War of the Castes and the villages of the Talking Cross.

As it turned out, Alex had been right about the miraculous Talking Crosses. In 1850, in a cave with a cenote in the town of Chan Santa Cruz, a cross carved in a tree spoke to the Maya, urging them to rise up against their oppressors, the Spanish, and defeat them once and for all. It was the first of many Talking Crosses, all carrying much the same message.

From this account I learned two interesting things. One was that the Maya had always known that the Talking Crosses were not really voices sent from the gods, but simply those of their neighbors. Some argued it was the gods, talking through their neighbors. Others were more machiavellian: they had known how to use these voices as a powerful symbol of resistance. In any event, the Maya began to build a capital of sorts in Chan Santa Cruz where the cross first presented itself.

The second item of interest was more complicated, and I wasn't sure how relevant. I was skimming through an account of the various victories on both the Spanish and Maya sides, most particularly the advance of the Mexican army against the Maya in Chan Santa Cruz, when a name caught my eye: General Francisco May.

It seems that while the Mexicans were successful by the turn of the century in regaining ground lost during the War of the Castes, guerrilla raids continued, and eventually the Mexican army had to withdraw from the conflict in 1915 because of the Mexican Revolution.

After the Mexicans withdrew, a Maya general by the name of Francisco May rose to power and set up his headquarters in a town called Chan Coh Veracruz, Little Town of the True Cross.

In an act for which he is infamous in the annals of the Maya resistance, General May, who had become very rich from the chicle trade, made peace with the Mexican government.

The Mexicans returned and stripped May of his power, and the resistance moved on to other people and places.

May died in 1969 and a plaque commemorating his death, I learned, can be found in a town now called Felipe Carrillo Puerto. Once it was called Chan Santa Cruz, the original town of the Talking Cross.

Interesting name, Francisco May, and interesting association with the Villages of the Talking Cross. Remembering the look on his face as the Itzamná statue was stolen from the Ek Balam bar, I thought that perhaps I needed to draw Lucas May into the patterns within patterns of the last few days.

It was now very close to closing time and I packed up to leave. At the front desk I expressed my thanks to Valesquez, who asked me if I was planning to return.

"I regret that we will not be open tomorrow," he said. He hesitated, then said, "I have not been entirely honest with you. Dr. Castillo has not just met with an unfortunate accident as I told you this morning. He has been brutally murdered. The *museo* will be closed tomorrow to permit staff to attend his funeral."

I looked at this man with the mop of gray hair and the nervous gestures and thought I saw the beginnings of tears in his eyes.

"I've not been entirely honest with you, either," I said.

"I, too, will be at the funeral tomorrow. Don Hernan was a friend of mine."

He digested that information. "And are you really looking for rabbits?" he asked nervously.

"Yes," I said. "But a particular kind of rabbit. And I'm doing it for Don Hernan."

I paused, took a deep breath, and plunged on. "I'm looking for a rabbit that writes. I'd prefer no one else know about it, because I have a horrible feeling that it may be dangerous to look for it!"

This brought an orgy of imaginary lint picking from Valesquez, but he managed to nod his understanding of what I had said.

Night comes quickly this close to the equator, and it was dark when I exited by the back stairway once more. I looked toward the lights of the Paseo de Montejo a block or so away, but chose, as I had the night before, the back streets.

I had a sense of being, if not followed, then watched, as I made my way back to the Casa de las Buganvillas. A couple of times I turned, but saw nothing, except perhaps, a slight movement in the shadows, perhaps only a distortion in the darkness caused by distant headlights, or a lamp turned on in one of the houses along the route.

When I reached the hotel, I was greeted by more bad news. At some point during the day Francesca had become aware that the Empress's bell had been still for several hours, and checking the room had found Doña Josefina unconscious, the victim of a stroke. She had been whisked to hospital, where her condition was said to be "guarded," whatever that meant.

She was not able to speak, and could only see through one eye. Whatever she knew, she would not be telling anyone for some time—if ever.

MULUC

THAT HERNAN CASTILLO WAS HELD in great esteem was evident from the crowds and tributes at his funeral.

The cathedral was packed. Representatives from universities and museums as far away as Europe were there, as were many public personages. It was even rumored that the president of Mexico might attend. If he was there, I didn't see him.

Perhaps he had other things on his mind. The peso was in a free fall and allegations of wrongdoing in his government had extended to members of his immediate family. It was politics as usual in Mexico City.

Jonathan was there, though. He'd have come to keep me company in any event, he told me, but Cambridge University had asked him to be its official representative and he was sitting with the official delegation. I saw no sign of Lucas.

The funeral was held in the main cathedral on the Plaza Grande. I suppose there was a certain resonance in this, considering Don Hernan's interest in the Maya. It had taken hundreds of Maya laborers some thirty-six years to build the place, with stone torn from their own ravaged city.

It is a rather stolid, gloomy place. Cathedrals of those times also often had to serve as fortresses, the Maya not yet entirely subdued, and this was clearly the case here. Instead of the huge stained-glass windows we North Americans have come to associate with cathedrals, this one has gunnery slits instead. The facade is very plain, as is the interior, which has, as its one spot of light, brightly embroidered altar cloths, done in the Maya style.

For those for whom such things matter, it is the oldest cathedral on the North American mainland, and the cross above the main altar is supposed to be the second largest in the world. Probably at some time it would have been decorated in gold, but most gold disappeared from churches during the Revolution.

As the crowds began to file in I found myself thinking about the conversation I had had earlier in the morning with Doña Francesca. I'd been helping as best I could in the kitchen, carrying trays of coffee and pastries to the guests, many of whom were bordering on hysteria because of the last few days' events.

Francesca suggested that I take a coffee break after several of these trips, and I was grateful. As we both sat sipping *café con leche* I talked to her about the Empress.

"I thought you were remarkably patient with her," I began. "She cannot have been an easy person to please."

"On the contrary, I thought she was the remarkable one," Doña Francesca said.

She paused for a moment. "She had a difficult life. She was actually born in England, you know. I imagine her name was Josephine, originally. I have no idea what her surname was. I gather from certain references that her family was very poor, and she saved her money for years before she was able to book passage on a ship bound for North America.

"She had wanted to go to New York, of course. Doesn't everyone? But the fare for Mérida was cheaper—I think she said she had come on a freighter."

"When would this have been?"

"A long time ago. She said she was very young. In the late twenties, I would think."

"That must have been considered very daring in those days, for a young woman," I said.

"Oh yes, I think it was. But in her case, I think it was more desperation than daring.

"In any event, she told me she worked as a nanny for a wealthy Mexican family. She was occasionally allowed to join their guests at dinner parties, and it was there she met the love of her life.

"He was a married man, and a legal union was never in the picture. She became pregnant shortly after they met, and for four years he supported her and the child. Both she and her lover doted on the boy. For her he was everything. And I guess for her lover too, judging by what happened.

"One day she returned from a shopping trip to find her son gone. The woman who looked after him had been pushed into a closet, and trapped there. She did not recognize the men who had taken the child.

"Josefina has a very good idea who had been responsible, however. She ran to the home of her lover, but found it empty. The family had gone abroad, she was told. She searched the docks for a ship leaving for Europe; she waited day and night at the house. But she never saw her son again. She stayed in Mérida, waiting for the family to return, hoping in the end to hear some word, or even to catch a glimpse of her child.

"To support herself, she did the only thing she could think of. Having lived in a fine family's home for a few years in her early days in Mérida, her manners were impeccable. She was not well educated, perhaps, but she had borrowed books from the family's library, and she was a quick study.

"She became what I guess you would politely call a courtesan. She always referred to herself as a widow, and I guess in some ways she was.

"I know some people saw her as difficult. I always felt that it was real strength of character that saw her through."

I could feel my throat constricting as Francesca told me the story of this woman I had found somewhat laughable, and now I could feel the tears burning in my eyes as I sat in the cathedral. She of the aristocratic name, who had held constant for fifty years waiting to see her son, engaging men's attentions, if not their hearts, while she waited. A prayer for Doña Josefina would be in order that day, too.

As the lights over the main altar came on, and the service began, I began to have a strange sensation: a mental disorientation more than dizziness. I tried to concentrate on the words of the sermon, and to take comfort from them, but I could not.

The pastor was talking about Christ as a fisherman, a fisher of men, and I remembered that today was Muluc, the day in the Maya calendar associated with water and fish. Suddenly the dark contradictions in this city, the melding of the Western world with that of the Maya this cathedral embodied, seemed ominous and threatening.

I found myself longing for coolness and darkness. Somewhere in my mind, a rational being was telling me that this was a result of the shock and pain of the last few days, but the rational voice was losing. I felt an overwhelming need to find a dark corner, away from the light. Rising from my seat, I disturbed my neighbors as I made my way to the side of the church.

To the left of the main altar is a small chapel with what is called the *Cristo de las Ampollas*, the Christ of the Blisters, supposedly carved in the 1500s from the wood of a tree that was engulfed in flames all night, but was not charred. When the church in which it was originally housed was also burned, it is said both the church and the statue were covered in blisters.

Hugging the walls of the darkened side aisles of the cathedral, I was transfixed as I saw kneeling before the Cristo, lighting a votive candle in prayer, a fair-haired woman in a black dress, black gloves, and a black mantilla.

For a moment I was convinced it was Doña Josefina, fully recovered. Then the woman rose and turned in my direction. It was Sheila Stratton Gomez.

As she saw me, she gave me a wan smile. Her eyes were red from crying. I thought how many similarities there might be between her and Josefina, both pale foreigners, lonely, if for very different reasons, both victims in a way, of ruthless men.

She must have recognized the shock on my face, because she quickly took my arm and pulled me to a seat on the side. While we sat there she quietly opened her purse and gestured at the contents. I saw only two things. A platinum credit card and a small silver flask.

Using a handkerchief for cover, she quickly took a swig, then passed the flask to me. I took a sip. It was a very chilled martini. Horrified though I was, I have to admit it helped.

We sat there side by side, her arm through mine, while the service continued, and then we followed the coffin procession, led by Santiago and his wheelchair, Norberto and Alejandro among the pallbearers.

Both Sheila and I put on sunglasses as we emerged from the church and followed the procession to the cemetery. The cemetery in Mérida, like others in Mexico, seems so much brighter and more extravagant than those I am accustomed to, the monuments in cobalt blue, coral, green, and white, many of them with pictures of the deceased surrounded by garlands of flowers. The colors of the flowers are extraordinary: lilies, carnations, roses, and marguerites, sold by Maya women from little stalls set up under awnings on the main road of the cemetery. The monuments themselves, everything from simple crosses to little chapels decorated like wedding cakes in white marble, testify to the obsession Mexicans have with death.

It was almost like a festival as we made our way to Don Hernan's family crypt, where he was to be buried next to his wife and near his ancestors. There was one jarring note, however: large numbers of federal police near the perimeter of the crowd. Partially hidden by a large chapel, a policeman was busy videotaping the crowd at the cemetery.

Major Martinez was there, and I was convinced he had his eyes on me virtually all the time. But perhaps it was my hyperactive imagination. It was an impressive display of police might all right, perfect for the media covering the event. But what it meant, and how close Martinez was to an arrest, I couldn't imagine.

At the end of the interment ceremony, a sleek black limousine with very dark windows pulled up at the entrance to the cemetery. "Do you feel all right now?" Sheila asked, glancing toward the limo. "I could give you a lift back to the inn."

I told her that I would stay with the Ortiz family, but thanked her for her kindness.

She gave me that sad smile again. "I really meant it when I said I hoped you would come to the house again. I'd like you to meet my husband. Perhaps dinner later this week?"

I wondered how often Gomez Arias was actually home for dinner, but I told her I would love to come. After all, he was on my personal suspect list, and I did want to meet him.

She disappeared quickly into the limo and it pulled away.

Close friends of Don Hernan had been invited back to the Casa de las Buganvillas for tea. Much to my surprise, Antonio Valesquez was there. He looked totally out of his element, except when browsing through the books in Santiago's collection in the sitting room.

"So it is indeed true that you and I are—were—both friends of Don Hernan," he said as I brought him a cup of tea. I nodded.

"Perhaps you could tell me how you know him," he said.

In the volubility that sometimes accompanies shock, I told this strange little man about my long friendship with the Ortiz family, and how I had met Don Hernan through them. I told him about my beloved business, its loss, the failure of my marriage, the call that had brought me to the Yucatán, and the clue about the rabbit. Not once during the conversation did the rational interior voice ask me if this was a good idea or whether someone else might be listening.

"Now it's your turn," I said conversationally, having exhausted my story, and my voice.

"I live with my mother," he said in an apparent non sequitur. "About what you would expect from a man who finds reality only in books, wouldn't you say?" he asked with an ironic smile.

"My mother became very ill about three years ago. She required very expensive medical treatment that I could not afford. When I was about to take her out of the hospital because I could no longer afford it, I found that the bills had all been paid."

"Don Hernan," I said, finally grasping the point.

"For a long time I did not know it was he. At the hospital they would not tell me. For a while I thought it might be Diego Maria Gomez Arias. He could surely

126

afford it. One day I saw Don Hernan in the business office of the hospital. I confronted him, and with some reluctance he admitted it. He told me not to worry about my mother. He would see to it that she was taken care of.

"Until that time I had always regarded him with some awe, as some distant personage. After all, he was the executive director of the *museo* for much of my tenure as librarian. I certainly had always found him pleasant, and he had defended my little acquisitions budget every year when the time came to submit estimates for the next year, but to do such a thing! I will be forever grateful."

I would have liked to talk to Valesquez longer, but I noticed that many of the guests had begun to drift away, so I excused myself and began helping with wraps and canes. Francesca and Santiago both looked exhausted, and Isa soon bundled them off to their quarters at the back of the hotel.

She and I cleaned up, and Manuela, her two little children racing around the kitchen, began the preparations for *cena* that evening while Norberto set up the dining room. In the hotel business, the work never stops, even for murders and funerals.

"About time you got down to some honest work," the English voice said. It was Jonathan, of course.

"Maybe you could stop digging around in the dirt and do some honest work yourself," I said, handing him a vegetable peeler and pointing at a pile of potatoes.

Good-humoredly, he pitched in, although when the young woman who assisted Francesca and Manuela in the kitchen in the evenings arrived, he was quick to hand her the peeler.

"I've come to make a firm date," he said. "Dinner, a late-night swim, perhaps?"

We made a date for three days hence, and I walked him to the front steps of the inn. As I leaned over to take in the fragrance of some flowers near the steps, I felt his lips brush the back of my neck. Neither of us said anything. I simply watched as he got into the Jeep and pulled away with a brief wave of his hand.

I helped Isa and Manuela as best I could for the remainder of the evening and then shared a light supper with them in the kitchen. Isa told me that Don Hernan's solicitor had called to say that the family was expected at the reading of the will at his offices the next afternoon, and that I, too, was invited.

Late in the evening, as I began to ascend the stairs to my room, Alejandro, who was staffing the front desk, signaled that I had a phone call.

I took the call in the little sitting room behind the front desk. It was Antonio Valesquez.

"I've found it! The rabbit that writes. Can you meet me at the *museo* tomorrow at nine A.M.? As you know, it's closed. I'll meet you at the back door to let you in."

"I'll be there," I said, neglecting to mention that getting into the *museo* was no problem for me, unless someone had got smart after two murders and changed the locks.

Good old Antonio Valesquez. The nervous little man with a large debt to Don Hernan. He must have gone straight to the *museo* after leaving the inn, and applied his considerable research skills to the problem.

When I got into bed, I was exhausted to the bone. This

time I dreamed I was chasing a rabbit, a kind of Alice-Through-the-Looking-Glass rabbit that walked on its hind legs.

I followed it through the *museo*. Just as I was about to catch it, a hole opened up beneath me, and once again I was falling through black space, a babble of voices around me.

I sat up, awakened by my own cry, I think. It was a while before I could get back to sleep.

As I drifted off again I found myself praying that Valesquez would stay alive long enough to show me the rabbit. Knowing about writing rabbits would appear to shorten one's life span. Once I knew about it, I'd have to remember that myself.

O C

ONE DEATH, HEAD LORD OF of Xibalba, sits compla-
cently on his throne, a smile of sorts on his face.

And why should he not smile? He is surrounded by
bald-headed goddesses, there to attend to his every
whim. One of them kneels at his feet. Others hover
around him.

For his entertainment, two jester priests are about to
sacrifice a human victim, bound hand and foot below the
throne.

And his arch enemies, the Hero Twins? Gone, cooked
in an oven, their bones ground to dust and thrown into
the underworld river.

Life, or in this case death, is unfolding as it should.

But let us look more closely at the two jester priests.
Beneath their masks, do they not look familiar? Could it
be that our heroes are not vanquished? The fate of our
souls hangs in the balance. Is there still hope?

And who, or what, is there to record this pivotal
moment in the history of the gods? Below the temple
platform on which One Death presides, a scribe indus-

triously records the story of our Hero Twins and their travels in the underworld.

Antonio Valesquez met me at the back door of the *museo*, as promised. His hands were shaking, whether with fear or excitement I could not tell, as he checked the door behind us and led the way to the old elevator and thence to the basement of the *museo*. It occurred to me that meeting me this way might be the most daring act he had ever committed.

The *museo* was closed, the building deserted except, I presumed, for a security guard who made casual rounds from time to time.

Like Oc, the dog that nightly leads the sun through the underworld, Valesquez led the way through the labyrinthine passageways.

He did not turn on any lights, relying instead on the faint daylight that filtered through a few small windows at ground level and on the emergency lighting in the dark hallways.

Several sections of hallway were lined with metal shelving filled with artifacts. In one hallway I paused to look at a large wooden crate, similar to the ones I had seen at Jonathan's cave dig site.

Eventually Antonio unlocked an unmarked door, and we entered what appeared to be a conservation lab. There were a couple of ventilation chambers and hoods for use with chemicals, and rows of implements that reminded me of a dentist's office. I noticed as well bottles of liquids marked with the universal symbol of poison, the skull and crossbones.

There were two large worktables. On one, an ancient

skeleton was being pieced together, bone by bone, each one sorted from a box of dirt and bones on the floor under the table, like some life-size jigsaw puzzle.

Valesquez stopped triumphantly at the second. Here someone had been laboriously fitting together tiny pieces of a terra-cotta pot with a cream-colored background and a red rim. On it there was a scene done in very fine brushwork, and without touching it, and scarcely daring to breathe it looked so fragile, I leaned over to scan it.

The scene contained some text, which I strained to decipher, but could not. I did, however, recognize the figure of One Death, smoking a cigar, surrounded by a number of women of noble birth, who appeared to be taking very good care of him. A strange bird, part owl, part macaw, perched on the throne above him.

One Death looked toward a sacrificial scene, with two ax-wielding figures, and the victim identified by Akbal, the sign of darkness.

"Do you see it?" Valesquez asked excitedly, gesturing to a small figure below the throne.

I looked again. At the base of the temple platform sat a bewhiskered, jowly creature with big ears, a workman's belt containing the tools of his trade around his waist. He, or it, was writing on what appeared to be a stack of paper with a rigid top and bottom cover, bound in a spotted material I assumed to be jaguar pelt. It was indeed a rabbit that writes.

I stood back and nodded.

"After you left the other day, I kept thinking about your writing rabbit," Valesquez said.

"It was a rather unusual request after all. And if it was

for Don Hernan, well, I'd do just about anything, I think," he said simply.

"There was something in the back of my mind. Then I remembered that one of our conservators had asked me, a couple of months ago, to do some research for him. He was trying to reconstruct a painted pot from a pile of fragments found in a tomb in a temple near the border with Guatemala, and was sure he'd seen something similar somewhere—possibly in an exhibition of Maya art, or in a book on the subject.

"It depicted, he thought, a scene from the Popol Vuh in which a reluctant victim is sacrificed by the Hero Twins, then brought back to life as part of a clever trick on the Lords of Xibalba.

"I knew if I could find it, it would make his task of reconstruction much easier. I often do this kind of research for museum staff. Anyway, I looked for days, every moment I could.

"Finally I found it. The pot he was thinking of is in the collection of a U.S. university, and I found a photograph of it, in color, in an exhibition catalog.

"I didn't look at the photograph that closely, frankly. I have so much work to do, I just brought it down here right away. But something must have stuck in my memory.

"See, here it is—the catalog."

The book was propped up against the base of a work lamp on the table so that the conservator could look at it while he worked.

"You can see the two pots are not identical, but

similar," Valesquez continued. "The conservator commented to me how much this has helped him."

I did see the similarity. The workmanship was different, certainly, and there were differences in detail, but both appeared to depict the same event.

I absentmindedly turned the pages of the catalog. There was an inscription in the front. *To our colleague and friend, Dr. Hernan Castillo, on the occasion of his visit to the United States, June 1989.* The signature was illegible.

"Don Hernan's book?" I queried.

"Quite likely," Valesquez replied. "He often gave items from his personal collection to the library, particularly when they were expensive or out of print.

"My collection budget is so very small," he said, almost apologetically.

"I think you must be right about this," I said. "Particularly since this book belonged to Don Hernan. And he must have been familiar with the work being done here. But what does it mean?"

"I have no idea. But you're right. Don Hernan did spend a good deal of the time he was in the *museo*, which is not as much time as he did when he was executive director, of course, down here.

"In fact I think the last time I saw him, he was in what we call the fragments room. It's just across the hall. I remember I startled him. Either that or he was quite excited about something. He barely had time to talk to me that day."

"I don't suppose I could see that, too. The fragments room, I mean," I said.

"Why not?" Valesquez sighed. "You're not supposed to be here at all. Given that you are, why should we restrict your movements in any way?"

I looked to see if he was actually making a joke. But he appeared, as usual, to be terribly serious. He carefully locked the door to the lab, then opened another across the hall.

Three walls of a very large room were lined with cabinets of what I would call map drawers, long and wide, but shallow filing drawers. Valesquez took a key from the drawer of a desk in the middle of the room and unlocked one of the cabinets.

"Pick a drawer," he said, gesturing toward a cabinet.

I pulled out one of the drawers. In it were carefully numbered pottery shards that would eventually be pieced together like the one I had just seen in the lab.

I pulled out another. Fragments of tools, I would venture to guess.

At one end of the room were pieces too large to be filed, and I turned my attention to these. Large chunks of stone, fragments of a temple frieze, perhaps, leaned against the walls. There were broken stelae and large broken masks and figures.

I smiled at Valesquez. "Wonderful place. Thank you for showing it to me."

"It is," he said, then looked toward the desk with evident distaste.

I followed the direction of his gaze, and my eyes came to rest on the computer on the desk.

I understood. "Building a collection database, are they?" I asked.

"Yes," he said. "I cannot believe the collection records will be safe in that thing. What if the power goes off? It often does, you know. All the records could be lost. It would be a catastrophe!"

I thought to tell him about backing up files on disk and so on. But there seemed no point. At some time in the future, the computer age would reach as far as his library.

Antonio Valesquez, no doubt, would either retire or, if he stayed on, continue to maintain his own set of records on his beloved little cards.

I thought of my neighbor, Alex, Valesquez's senior by at least a decade or so, and wondered what it was that allowed some to embrace the future and others to cling helplessly to the past.

Be that as it may, Valesquez had been most helpful. I offered to buy him a coffee, perhaps a spot of lunch. He looked suspiciously at his watch.

"Make that *almuerzo*," I said, remembering that the idea of an early meal is anathema to Mexicans. Better to make it a late breakfast than an early lunch.

Protesting that it was not necessary, he nonetheless agreed, and soon we were sitting in a little café nearby, enjoying vegetarian quesadillas and beer with lime. Some breakfast!

"You've found me a writing rabbit, Señor Valesquez," I began after the food arrived.

"Antonio, please, señora."

"Then it's Lara, Antonio." I smiled.

"An interesting name, I think. Reminds me of *Dr. Zhivago*," he said.

"Absolutely correct. I was born during my mother's Russian-literature phase," I replied.

"A mother who loves literature. How extraordinary!" he said. Clearly, his mother did not.

I told him a little about my family, then returned to the subject at hand.

"What do you think the writing rabbit means, Antonio?" I asked.

He paused. "Well, I'm a librarian. Naturally I think it's about a book."

"Do people kill over books? I've heard of academics destroying each other's reputations over books, maybe, but not literally killing each other over one."

"Well, I don't know. I mean what would a Gutenberg Bible be worth, for example?" he mused. "Millions of pesos, surely. Would some people kill to have one of those, I wonder?

"Or one of the Dead Sea Scrolls. An early version of the Tibetan Book of the Dead. Would people think these worth a human life? I would, I think.

"Not to actually kill someone, of course," he added quickly, "but do you understand what I am saying?"

"I think I do," I agreed. "Is there a Maya equivalent of the Gutenberg Bible?"

"There might be, I suppose. We never value our own culture, perhaps. But the Books of the Chilam Balam, for example. These are books in the Roman alphabet that are considered to have ritualistic importance for the Maya. One of the them, the Chilam Balam of Tusik—they're named after the places they are located in—vanished in the 1970s. The owner/guardian is said to have died under circumstances some consider to be suspicious."

"Interesting idea," I said. "I'd like to research this with your help."

He smiled. "You know our hours. I'll help all I can."

He suddenly looked at his watch and exclaimed, "My goodness. It's so late. I have to attend the reading of Don Hernan's will this afternoon!"

"So do I," I said. "Shall we go together?"

I paid the bill, and we shared a companionable cab to the solicitor's office. As we went we were both deep in our own thoughts. I was thinking how comfortable I felt with this nervous little man, how I'd told him things I had told no one else. Not Isa. Not even Jonathan, with whom I was reasonably sure I was heading for bed.

What did this say about my relationships? I wondered. It was a thought I was not prepared to pursue with any diligence at that moment.

We arrived at the offices of Rudolfo Alvarez a little late. The Ortiz family was already there, as was, to my surprise, Sheila Stratton Gomez. I found I was glad to see her. There were also a few people I didn't know. Antonio whispered that one of them, a tall distinguished gentleman, was the treasurer of the *museo*.

Alvarez, a dry stick of a man, began to read the will the minute Antonio and I were seated.

There was the usual stuff about being of sound mind and so on, and then we got to the heart of the matter.

Which was, if I may summarize, that the artifacts that the *museo* had on loan from Don Hernan were to become part of its permanent collection. This caused the shoulders of the treasurer to relax. He'd obviously been worrying about losing a good part of the museum's collection.

There were to be exceptions. The shoulders of the treasurer rose again. Don Hernan's collection of first editions was to become the property of Santiago Ortiz Menendez and, after his death, of Norberto Ortiz.

There was an exception to that one, too. The first editions of John Lloyd Stephens's *Incidents of Travel*, some of my favorite books, were to go to *Lara McClintoch, my friend and colleague, whose love of the civilization of the Maya may yet equal my own*. I was quite overwhelmed by this, and even more determined to see that justice be done.

Next to the personal effects. Francesca, Isa, and Manuela Ortiz were all left lovely old pieces of jewelry that belonged to Don Hernan's family. Sheila Gomez was left the watch that was with Don Hernan's remains. Doña Josefina, semiconscious in the hospital, was to receive his mother's wedding ring, a sapphire-and-diamond piece that his wife had also worn.

The bulk of the money in Don Hernan's estate was to go to a local hospital run by the nuns, where in a sad coincidence Doña Josefina now lay. An annual stipend, however, was to go to Antonio Valesquez. Antonio looked close to tears.

One item was left. Alvarez intoned, "To my young friend Alejandro Ortiz, I leave one of my most treasured possessions, a statue of a Maya ballplayer. To play the game well is to ensure that the cycles of the earth will continue. I pray this knowledge will set his feet on the right path, and give him the peace he craves and deserves."

Alejandro burst into tears and fled the room, leaving his family sitting in bewilderment.

That ended the reading of the last will and testament of Señor Dr. Hernan Castillo Rivas. Alvarez invited everyone for a glass of port, and then we all filed out of his office, deep in our own thoughts.

This did not appear to be a will to kill over. The bulk of the estate went to institutions, the *museo* and the hospital. The jewelry and books had some commercial value, certainly, but their worth, to this group at least, would be primarily sentimental. The money Antonio Valesquez was to receive would help him, but he hadn't needed to kill to get it. Don Hernan had been helping him financially all along.

I remained totally in the dark.

I WAIT FOR NIGHT TO fall, so that once again I am at ease with the light, or rather its absence. My senses, carefully tamped down by day to protect my ragged psyche, can now expand, and every action, sight, and sound has a clarity that is almost frightening. I feel as if I am in a dream, but know that I am not. Instead everything has such an immediacy that I feel compelled to do now what I have been dreading.

I leave the others at the inn, and head for the hospital where Doña Josefina lies.

I move quietly down dark and silent whitewashed corridors, the only sounds the soft whirring of fans and the distant murmurs of a late service in the chapel. Built like a Spanish cloister, the hospital has crucifixes every-where. I wonder if Doña Josephina is religious, or if she gave up on God a long time ago.

I find her room, directed by a placid sister. I wonder if the sisters know that Doña Josefina was once a courtesan and whether or not it matters in their eyes, if not God's.

The room is dimly lit, but I see her very well. She lies there, one eye closed, the other drooping half-shut. A useless hand is curled up in a spasm, the other clenches and unclenches, clutching at the sheet in what I imagine to be intense frustration and despair.

I go to the bedside. In a low whisper, I begin to talk to her. I tell her that I am the fair-haired woman who is a friend of the Ortiz family, and that I sat at the table next to her in the hotel several nights ago.

I tell her I am sorry we did not have a chance to speak, that I have heard something of her story from Francesca Ortiz, and that I wish we could talk about her life and mine.

I tell her how I came to Mérida on the strength of a phone call from Hernan Castillo, and that now that he is dead, I am obsessed with finding what he was looking for, and for bringing to justice the evil person who killed him.

I tell her that I know there is no reason on earth that she should believe what I say, but that nonetheless I need her help.

"I don't know whether you can hear me, or understand me, but if you can," I say, taking her good hand, "will you try to tell me? Press one for yes, two for no."

I feel her squeeze my hand very faintly.

One for yes.

"Did he really tell you what he was looking for?" I ask.

One for yes.

"I know you can't tell me what it is. But is it a book?" I ask again.

One for yes.

"Is it a rare book?"

One for yes.

"One of the Chilam Balam books?" I ask, thinking of Antonio's comments.

Two for no.

"But a book of the Maya."

One for yes.

"Gracias," I tell her.

The sister comes to the door.

"You must leave her," she says. "She must rest."

I turn to go, then turn back again.

"Don Hernan's will was read today. He left his mother's wedding ring to you," I tell the almost lifeless form.

As I leave I watch a tear form in the corner of her one good eye and run slowly down her cheek. I pat her hand.

"I promise to come back," is all I can think to say.

It is so little.

CHUEN

T HE EMBOSSED VELLUM ENVELOPE AND its contents informed me that the pleasure of my company at dinner that evening was requested by Señor Diego Maria Gomez Arias, and Sheila Stratton Gomez.

Obviously invitations to the Gomez residence were in such demand that no one minded being invited at the last minute. To be fair, I suppose, I should point out that had I left and entered the hotel by the front door like everyone else, I would have seen the invitation when it arrived the night before—delivered, I was informed, by limo and driver.

As it was, I had gone on one of my nocturnal journeys through Mérida, to Doña Josefina's bedside, and some-one had therefore slid the invitation under my door during the night.

Late invitation or not, I had nothing planned for the evening, and I still wanted to meet Don Diego and have a conversation with him about Don Hernan. And anyway, it was Chuen, day of the monkey, the creature who in Maya mythology is the artist, and therefore an appropriate one on which to meet Don Diego, collector and patron of the arts that he was.

It is also supposed to be a good day, a day of knowledge, and I fervently hoped that it would be. The Maya calendar was, I hoped, unfolding as it should. I accepted the invitation with alacrity.

There was one worrisome item in the invitation, however, the words in its lower left-hand corner. Black tie, it said. I had not brought anything with me that would come close to being fancy enough for a black tie event.

I made haste to find Isa, who smiled when she saw the invitation. "Leave it with me," she said. That sounded like a good idea to me.

I had lots of other things to do. This was Eulalia Gonzalez's day back at the morgue, and then there was much research to do. I could, of course, do it the hard way, which was to go to the *museo* library, and plow through rows of neat little index cards and piles of books.

But I had a better idea.

First I headed for the Café Escobar. I scanned the room for Alejandro, but he was not there. Isa had told me that he had taken to his room after the reading of the will and could not be enticed down for dinner. Francesca had left a tray of food outside his door, and while he had had something, much of it had remained uneaten. He might still be there for all I knew.

I went to the back hall again, and placed a call to Alex. I'd called Alex from the hotel a couple of times in the last few days, to tell him what was happening down here. I told him about murders and morgues, he told me about the latest antics of my cat. It wasn't that he wasn't interested in all that I was involved in, but I think he probably thought I needed to hear about everyday activities to counteract the events I was encountering.

For this call, though, I didn't want to use the hotel phone. These were strange times, and I certainly would not put it past Major Martinez to find some way to tap the lines. A pay phone, albeit in a public hallway, felt safer.

"Would you consider doing a little surfing in cyberspace on my behalf, Alex?" I began. "I need a little help with some research."

"Of course!" he replied, as I knew he would. There was virtually nothing Alex liked better than a cruise on the information superhighway. "What might I be researching?"

"Books. To be specific, rare books. Books of the Maya. You can skip the Chilam Balam books. That's not what we're looking for," I said, remembering the information I had gleaned from Doña Josefina. "Something really rare. The equivalent of a Gutenberg Bible, one of the Dead Sea Scrolls, that sort of thing."

"I'll get right on it," he said. He meant it, too. I could hear the clicking of the computer keys over the telephone. He was logging on to the Internet even as we spoke.

"Anything else?"

"Yes. I don't know if this is possible or not, but I'd like to check some credentials."

"Names?"

"Lucas May, Diego Maria Gomez Arias, Major Ignacio Martinez, and"—here I paused for a second or two—"Jonathan Hamelin. The first one, Lucas May, is

an archaeologist, Mexican, don't know much more than
that. Gomez Arias is a wealthy eccentric here in Mérida—
hotels, water, that sort of stuff, owns a shipping company,
collects art—"

"You seem to know a fair amount about him right
now," Alex interrupted. "Anything specific you want on
him?"

"I don't know really. Just see if there is anything out of
the ordinary. Martinez is with the federal police, and
that's about all I know, except that I don't like him."

"And the last one?"

"Jonathan Hamelin. Archaeologist. British. Cambridge
University. Specializes in Mesoamerican studies. Isa thinks
he's to the manor born, as it were."

I wasn't sure whether I was asking about Jonathan for
personal reasons, or as part of the research on Don
Hernan's death. I fervently hoped it would turn out to be
the former.

"Got it," Alex said. "For some of this I may need to go
into one of the news services. Unlike the Internet, these
aren't free. How badly do you need to know?"

"Badly. I'll pay any charges, Alex, don't worry. Take
it out of the house money, and I'll send some more." I'd
left some money to take care of any problems with my
house that might arise while I was away.

"Thanks. How will I reach you?"

"Telephone me at the hotel. If I'm there, tell me there's
a leak in the basement of my house or something. I'll get
the idea. I'll call you back within the hour from another
phone.

"If I'm not there, just leave a message that you've

called about some minor problem with my house. I'll get back to you as soon as I can."

"Right. I'm on this," he said.

"And Alex," I said, "be careful. You are searching for information on something that people may be prepared to kill for. So please don't do anything that would draw attention to yourself. No speeding on the Internet, okay?"

"There are no radar traps on the electronic highway, Lara," he said. "But I get your point. I'll try to be subtle."

With that we signed off, and I headed for the morgue.

I was getting to be an expert at finding my way around the hallways of this austere institution, and soon once again found myself at the little window. He of the greasy fingers was there, eating again. I asked for Eulalia Gonzalez.

"Who may I tell her is asking for her?" he said rather formally for a man talking with his mouth full.

I gave my name. It would mean nothing to her, but what else could I do?

He called someone, then pressed the button that unlatched the door and waved me in the general direction of two vinyl-covered chairs that would have looked more suitable in someone's kitchen. I waited.

Shortly thereafter, Eulalia arrived. "I thought it would be you," she said when she saw me. "How can I help you?"

I wanted to ask her questions about Don Hernan, but there was something in her manner, a stiffness perhaps, a worried glance in the direction of the glutton, that stopped me.

"I just came to thank you for your kindness the other

day. We were all so stunned, we felt afterward that we had not acted appropriately. . . ." My voice trailed off.

"Quite all right," she said. "Not many people thank morgue staff anyway," she added.

"Well, I was wondering whether it might be possible to buy you a coffee or something?"

A pause. "Sure, why not?" she said. I get a break between one and three. Meet me at the Café Pirámide," she said, naming a little café in the market area.

"About one-thirty, okay?"

"Great, see you there."

I had about an hour to kill, so I wandered over to the *museo* to look for Antonio Valesquez. A handwritten note taped to the library door said he would return shortly, but I waited fifteen minutes or so and he did not return. I headed for the café.

I got a little lost in the market, and while I still arrived about five minutes early, I came in through an entrance off the side street rather than from the front patio.

There were virtually no patrons in the restaurant proper. The café was obviously very popular, though. Everyone was seated outside in the sunshine or under the awning.

I scanned the crowd outside from the relative darkness of the restaurant. It took me a minute to recognize Eulalia.

At the morgue, she'd worn a lab coat and those white nurse-type shoes, her hair pulled severely back and no makeup. Here she wore her long dark hair down, and she was dressed in a black miniskirt, a fuchsia blouse, and black flats.

She was sitting facing in my general direction, talking in an animated fashion to a man seated opposite her, with his back to me. I hesitated, wondering whether to interrupt when the man leaned forward and squeezed her hand, then stood up and half turned in my direction.

It was Lucas. He bent over and kissed her, and she patted his cheek. Then looking up and down the street, perhaps for me, he disappeared into the crowded market.

I was completely taken aback. I'd hoped to get information from Eulalia, but now I wasn't sure how far I could take this.

I thought for a few minutes. I suppose this could be a coincidence. They were obviously friends. And why not? So much in common, after all. She worked with the recently dead, he with those who had been deceased for centuries. How romantic!

Even under these circumstances I had to smile at the thought of their dinner-table conversations. This was assuming that he talked more to her than he did to me.

I decided to push ahead with my plan.

"Hi," I said as I approached the table. "Thanks for agreeing to this." She looked a little startled at the direction I had arrived from, and I was betting she was wondering how long I'd been there.

"You were at the morgue a few days ago," she said. "Maria said you were asking for me. She said she didn't give you my name, though."

"Flextime," I said. "I figured it out from the time chart."

She nodded.

"My turn. How did you know it was me, and how did you know I'd be back?"

"Maria described you. We don't get that many *gringas* at the morgue, and you were the only one that day.

"As for returning—you asked a lot of questions, and you didn't appear to be satisfied by the answers. No more than I was, really. I saw you touching the shoes. What did you deduce from them?" she asked.

"They were covered in dust. So were the cuffs of his trousers. You couldn't see that very well, because of the color of the shoes, but you could feel it on them. I didn't much figure you'd get that sitting in an office."

She smiled. "Did you also notice one of them had been wet recently? Still felt a little clammy?"

I shook my head.

"That doesn't happen much in an office, either."

"So where and when was he murdered, do you think?"

"Well, I'm not the pathologist, only the assistant. I assist with the autopsy and write up the reports for the pathologist's signature. But not in the *museo,* surely. There was evidence he had been dragged some distance. Hence the dust on the cuffs and backs of his trousers.

"The dust looks to me to be limestone. Could be anywhere out in the country. But there was also evidence of sand. There was no salt in the sand or on the shoes, so it wasn't a beach he was walking on. He'd also done some walking in the forest. Traces of foliage you wouldn't expect in the city.

"As to time, I'd say he was killed very early in the morning, say between three and five A.M. of the day he was found, although it is difficult to estimate this with pinpoint accuracy, no matter what you read in books. He was found about eight P.M. by the cleaning staff, and rigor mortis was already starting to pass off. The method is obvious. He was stabbed several times, and not with your average kitchen knife. Blade sharp enough, but uneven."

The waiter arrived with our coffees and some snacks. We both waited until he was out of earshot before continuing.

"Tell me about the jade bead."

"Well, as I think I said the other day, it was put into his mouth after he died. There is evidence someone had to pry his mouth open to get it in."

"But why?"

"I'd say it's part of an ancient ritual. According to a friend of mine"—(Lucas? I wondered)—"jade beads were placed in the mouths of the deceased to provide sustenance on the journey through the underworld."

I pondered that for a moment. "But why would you murder someone, then later do something like that? Isn't it a rather odd gesture for a murderer to worry about the soul of his victim? Perhaps it's meant to be a sign to link the death to some Maya cause."

"No idea." She shrugged. "But maybe someone else did it, someone who liked Dr. Castillo Rivas, and for whom such things matter."

It was an interesting thought, and the first time she had referred to the deceased by name.

I thanked her for her help, and then asked one more question.

"Why are you telling me all this?"

"I guess it is because I don't like Martinez very much.

He is one of the old breed of policemen. We have a problem with the police here in Mexico. The pay is so low that it does not always attract the kind of people one would prefer. I mean, you can make more driving a cab.

"And some of those who do sign up have been known to resort to other ways of augmenting their incomes, ways that are not always totally beneficial to society, if you get what I am trying to say."

I nodded. I assumed she meant that they were either on the take, or into something even more serious.

"A lot of work is being done to change this. They're screening the applicants now, insisting they take courses, and so on. But it is very difficult to create an ethical police department under such circumstances, and the government has a long way to go. Unfortunately, there are still people like Martinez around. Bullies, really."

We talked awhile longer, about other things. She seemed to be a nice person. When it was time for her to go, I thanked her again, and she left as I paid the bill. There was much to ponder from this conversation.

I decided to return to the hotel for a rest. The afternoon sun and heat were getting to be oppressive, and with all my nocturnal wanderings, I was short on sleep. An afternoon nap seemed to be called for so I could be scintillating that evening at the Gomez dinner party.

I checked at the hotel on my return. No messages from Alex.

I went up to my room. It was filled with sunlight, and so I went immediately to the window to close the shutters.

As I turned back to the room I saw a large box on the

bed. Opening it and pressing back the tissue, I found a beautifully embroidered dress, one of Isa's designs. It really was spectacular—aqua-colored silk, with embroidery of white, deeper turquoise, and silver, a low neck, and an off-the-shoulder cut. A pair of silver sandals, my size, and a small evening bag were also in the box. It was perfect!

With it was a little notecard that read, *For my dear friend, Lara. May it help to brighten your days!*

I felt a lump in my throat. Although I'd tried to keep my depression over the failure of my marriage and the loss of my business to myself, to say nothing of the malaise caused by the murder and mayhem in Mérida, Isa had obviously recognized the symptoms, and was trying her best to cheer me up.

No matter the events of the last few days and the nasty year or so I'd been through, I knew how lucky I was to have friends like Isa.

Santiago had said he would have someone from the hotel drive me over to the Gomez residence, and I'd told him I'd take a cab home since I expected it would be late.

Just before eight-thirty I descended the stairs of the lobby. Isa and Santiago were waiting at the front desk. Isa smiled when she saw the dress.

"I love it, Isa. Thank you," I said.

"You look wonderful," she said, ignoring the bags under my eyes. "I thought the color would be good with your fair hair. You'll be a great advertisement for me. I should give you cards to hand out tonight at the party," she joked.

I gave her a hug.

Norberto had volunteered to drive me over, and he insisted I sit in the backseat so he could look like a real chauffeur.

There was no waiting at the little box at the gate this evening. A uniformed person with white gloves stood at the gate and ticked guests' names off as they arrived. We swept up to the front door, where yet another staff person sporting white gloves opened the door for me. Norberto said he had been hoping to make a big show of doing this for me himself, but clearly the establishment was over-staffed! He also said there must have been a sale on white gloves, and he was sorry to have missed it.

He made me laugh, something it was getting harder to do, and by the time I had been ushered into the "salon"—the name apparently given to the room in which I had shared a drink with the lady of the house several nights ago—I was feeling much better. It occurred to me that there had been a time, predating the last year or two with Clive, when I could have been said to have a sense of humor.

Sheila and her husband were both standing near the doorway of the salon, ready to greet each of their guests. They were an unusual pair—she, tall, blond, blue-eyed, and patrician; he, a couple of inches shorter, dark, but more attractive than he had seemed at a distance. He was also very charming.

He greeted me first. "You must be my wife's new friend. I'm delighted to meet you. And a colleague of Dr. Castillo Rivas, too. We were both much saddened by his death."

I murmured something polite and then smiled at

Sheila. She really did look lovely, in an off-white sequined dress. The center of attention in the room, however, at least as far as the men were concerned, was Montserrat. She really was stunning in a red dress that fit like a glove, very high heels, also red. Her dark hair was piled up on her head, and she was sporting diamond-and-ruby earrings and necklace, a present from Daddy, no doubt. Most of the men in the room were drawn to her like bees to honey. And one of the bees was Jonathan.

I think many, if not most, men look good in a tuxedo. Few of them, however, look comfortable in one. Jonathan was born to wear a tuxedo. In part, it was the air of confidence he was always able to maintain. It was also, if Isa's musing was correct, practice. You probably get to wear a tux a lot if you're a regular at Buckingham Palace.

He caught sight of me and pulled away from Montserrat's cozy cadre. I noticed that her eyes followed him as he crossed the room and brushed my cheek with his lips.

"What a pleasant surprise." He smiled.

"For me, too." I smiled back.

"You look absolutely smashing!" he murmured, then: "Let me introduce you to some people."

By this time there must have been about thirty people in the room. I spent the next hour or so sipping champagne and chatting with elite Meridanos—head of a bank, various political personages, the chair of the board of the *museo*, and a couple of board members.

Dinner was served about ten in the dining room. All thirty of us sat down at one table, if you can imagine one that size, under the chandelier I had seen on my first visit.

Don Diego Maria and Doña Sheila, as hosts, sat at

opposite ends of the table, but Montserrat sat immediately to her father's right. I imagined the seating arrangement reflected the dynamics of that household perfectly, Diego and Montserrat inseparable, Sheila a chasm apart.

I was seated on the same side of the table as Montserrat, but opposite Jonathan. Both Montserrat and he were being charming and witty. My built-in radar system, honed by a few years of marriage to a man with wandering eyes and a penchant for young women about Montserrat's age, told me that some of this at least was for the benefit of each other, and I felt a momentary pang.

Get a grip, Lara, I told myself, and turned brightly to the dinner companion on my right, a Dr. Rivera, who specialized in conditions of the rich: liver disease, tummy tucks, liposuction, and the like.

The food was sumptuous, several courses too many in my opinion. Cream soup, salad, fish course, quail, beef, a cheese course, and a choice of desserts. A selection of suitable wines accompanied each, and flowed freely. A steady diet of this would make Dr. Rivera very rich indeed.

Then Don Diego announced that the men would retire to the drawing room for a cigar and some port. The ladies would return to the salon for a *digestif*.

"How quaint," I mouthed at Jonathan across the table. He had trouble keeping a straight face.

I spent a polite half hour with the ladies, and as we went to rejoin the men in the dying hours of the party, I made for the powder room. It was occupied, but a server directed me upstairs to another bathroom. As I left I paused in the upper hallway to admire some of the paintings. They really were quite exceptional.

"So you enjoy art," a voice behind me said. It was the host, Don Diego Maria himself, glass of port in one hand, cigar in the other. He must have seen me studying his paintings and broken away for a few moments from the rest of his guests.

"Who could not enjoy this? A Matisse, isn't it?" I asked, gesturing toward the painting in front of me.

"It is," he replied. "One of my favorites. May I tell you a little bit about it?"

I nodded, and he sat his cigar and drink down on a small side table and began to describe the painting in some detail.

There was no question that he was very knowledgeable. But what was truly extraordinary was the passion the man brought to his subject. As he spoke, his voice became a whisper. He may even have forgotten that I was there.

For him, I am convinced, the lines of the painting were like the contours of a lover's body, the colors those of a beloved's eyes, lips, and hair, the painter, the godlike being who had brought her to life. As he spoke he moved his hand across the surface of the painting, almost, but not quite, touching it, almost as if he was caressing it. For him to describe the painting was, in some very deep sense, to make love to it.

When he had finished he stood silent for a moment, then turned to me with an embarrassed smile. "As you can see, I'm a slave to art." He laughed.

I smiled back. "You have an equally impressive pre-Columbian collection, I understand," I said.

He nodded. "I like to think so. It's one or two short, however."

No one had dared mention the subject of the theft of his statue of Itzamná during the dinner, but here he was talking about it quite openly.

"Most unfortunate. I was there actually, that night, at the Ek Balam."

"Were you? And what do you think of our Children of the Talking Cross?"

"I'm baffled, actually, as to motive. I understand no one has ever heard of this group before, and they haven't done anything since, at least nothing they will publicly acknowledge."

"My thoughts, exactly. That is why I am taking the theft so personally."

"And why, presumably, you suggested to the police that Dr. Castillo was responsible."

He looked surprised at my comment rather than annoyed. "Actually it was my daughter, Montserrat, who told the police about our quarrel. I merely corroborated what she had said.

"Frankly, if she hadn't mentioned it, I don't think I would have. Dr. Castillo and I had our disagreements over these works of art. But I do not delude myself. I know that people think he was on the side of the angels in these arguments, not I. It is, they think, a failing on my part that I wish to possess these things.

"You know, despite the fact that I'm on the board of directors of a museum, I often have trouble with some of the philosophy behind them. Almost eighty percent of any museum's collection languishes in storage. At least mine gets seen by the public. You can argue that only a select group of people get to see these works of art in my home or my hotel, but it's more than a couple of curators!"

"What about the research the museum does on these artifacts?" I interjected.

"If they want to do research on mine, they have only to ask," he countered. "As to the idea of giving the artifacts to original peoples," he went on, "do we actually think the Children of the Talking Cross are going to share their newly acquired piece of pre-Columbian art with their people? What nonsense! They will sell it on the black market to the highest bidder, a collector who, because it is stolen, will keep it hidden somewhere where only he can see it."

I wanted to tell him the idea that Don Hernan espoused was a shared responsibility for an artifact between the Indígenas and the museum for the mutual benefit of all, but I knew there was no point. This was an obsession for him.

"You mentioned that you were one or two short. Have you lost another one?"

"Yes, about a year ago. A beautiful sculpture of a couple embracing. It was stolen from the house when I was away on business. Insurance covered it, of course, as it will the Itzamná. But in my heart"—he paused for a moment—"these things are irreplaceable for me."

I believed him.

By this time it was very late. I told him that I would be

leaving shortly, and that I had enjoyed the evening and his hospitality immensely.

"I hope you will visit again before you return to Canada," he said. "My wife does not have many friends here, and it is good for her to have company."

At that moment the object of his words came into view. She had appeared to me to be drinking moderately throughout dinner, but had clearly made up for it since. Montserrat was leading, almost pulling her across the foyer. "Get upstairs," she hissed. "You are a disgrace to my father and to me!"

Sheila moved past us on the stairs, tears in her eyes. Diego looked at his daughter, then the retreating back of his wife, and sighed. He descended the stairs to say good-bye to his guests, who were now beginning to leave.

Jonathan was at the door. "Do you have a car? Can I give you a lift?" he asked.

"I can just take a taxi," I said.

"I won't hear of it. I've called for my car and it will be here in a minute."

Just then Montserrat reappeared. "Would you like to stay for a nightcap, Jonathan?" she asked.

"Not this evening, my dear," he said. "I'm giving Señora McClintoch a lift back to her hotel."

Montserrat did not look pleased. She was obviously accustomed to getting everything she wanted, including people. This was quite the family.

The car arrived, and we got in. Jonathan drove partway down the driveway, then pulled over to the side.

"How about moving our date up an evening or two?" he said. "My place?"

"Why not?" I replied. No one was waiting up for me, and despite a sense that I was still stepping out on my husband somehow, I could think of no real reason to say no.

Jonathan brought the same confidence and assurance to lovemaking that he brought to everything else, and I began to feel as if a part of my psyche I'd shut down was beginning to come to life again.

Later, though, as I lay in his bed, watching him sleep, pale in the moonlight streaming through the slats in the shutters, one arm slung proprietarially across my stomach, I wondered why I did not feel content.

EB

I AWOKE TO THE SOUND of rain, and an empty bed. A tropical downpour, stunning in intensity but mercifully brief, was passing through, appropriate enough for Eb, a rain day. Ten minutes later the skies had cleared, but my personal gloom had not.

I wandered to the kitchen to find a note on the counter. *Called away. Problem at the site. Help yourself to anything you want,* I read. *Lucas will be by about eleven-thirty to take you back to Mérida.* Then ending on a slightly more positive note: *Tonight?*

It was not quite ten, so I decided to take a dip in the pool, lack of bathing suit notwithstanding. The pool was still in the shade, quiet and pleasant, and well protected from curious onlookers by a thick hedge.

Climbing out, however, I found myself face-to-face with a tiny Maya woman dressed in the traditional embroidered *huipil*. We were both very surprised to see each other, but she had a considerable advantage over me. She had clothes on.

She regarded me with deep suspicion, and possibly

curiosity, as I clutched my towel and dashed to the bedroom. I showered and dressed, and as I did so I could hear her moving about the house.

I had nothing to wear except my silk dress from the evening before, a tad overdone for ten-thirty in the morning. I was inclined to stay holed up in the bedroom until rescued by Lucas, but I realized this was foolish, so I went into the kitchen.

We regarded each other once again across the kitchen counter. She was under five feet tall, with dark hair streaked with gray, pulled back into a bun. Her eyes, surveying me, sparkled with good humor, I thought, and intelligence.

Finally she smiled, and gestured toward a coffeepot on the stove. It smelled delicious and so I nodded, and she poured me a cup.

She spoke no English, and a heavily accented Spanish. Her native tongue, she told me, was Yucatecan. We exchanged names; hers was Esperanza, and she was, she informed me, Señor Hamelin's housekeeper. She came in every day to clean, and to prepare something for his supper.

Her interest in my dress was apparent, so I told her about my friend Isa. Soon we were chattering away. I said I was from Canada, visiting my friends in Mérida. Like so many who have never been there, many of them with considerably more formal education than Esperanza, I might add, she assumed Toronto was under several feet of snowdrifts all year round, and was eager to hear how we managed to get around, and what snow was really like.

"I have heard that every snowflake is different," she said. When I nodded, she added, "Our world is filled with wonders, is it not?"

She asked me about my family, where I had grown up, gone to school. Her curiosity was boundless. She told me about her village, not far away.

"It was much bigger when I was growing up," she said. "Now many of the young people leave. They go to the cities in search of a better life, but I do not think it improves life for them. So many have lost their center, their grounding, somehow.

"They have begun to think of Maya civilization as something in the past, something which has been superseded by another—European—civilization. And as young people do, they want to be part of the new."

"Would you have them go back to the old ways? Cut themselves off from European civilization?" I asked, thinking that was what she meant.

"Obviously that is not possible," she said. "But it is also not possible for us to embrace European civilization in its entirety, without losing an important part of ourselves.

"The young people must come to understand that European civilization has not superseded ours. Rather, the two civilizations now run parallel. Only that way can they be successful participants in contemporary life."

"We have a saying that goes something like those who forget their past are doomed to repeat it. Not quite the same idea, but the basic notion is the same," I said.

"I like that." She smiled.

"So what do you think of the Children of the Talking Cross?" I asked her.

"If you're asking me if I personally approve of stealing, even for a just cause, then the answer is, I do not.

"But if you are asking me if I understand the frustration that makes my people resort to such activities, then of course I do. My people have been subjected to centuries of oppression, some of it violent, some of it merely political and much more subtle.

"Think of our Maya brothers and sisters in Guatemala who have been driven from their land, and who live in terror of government-sanctioned death squads. At least one hundred and fifty thousand Maya have been killed there in the last twenty years; tens of thousands more have disappeared!

"Let's just say that I understand there are many ways to survive oppression. One is simply acceptance, perhaps acquiescence is a better word. Another is accommodation, a denial of what you are—becoming more European than your oppressors—there are many of us who have done that. Yet another is resistance, armed and violent if necessary."

At this point in the discussion, Lucas joined us, giving Esperanza a hug before sitting down between us at the kitchen counter.

"My godmother," he said, smiling at her, but speaking for my benefit.

If Lucas had an opinion on the new status of my relationship with Jonathan, he kept it to himself. It did not escape my notice, however, that he was avoiding looking directly at me when we were talking. When our eyes met inadvertently, his quickly moved away.

Not so his godmother, whose eyes seemed to see right to my core. If there was an X-ray machine for the soul, she was it. When Lucas went to bring the car to the door and I was making ready to leave, she suddenly grasped my hand.

"My people have an image of the sun that I like very much," she said. "In the Maya cosmos, the sun is in our world by day, but must pass through the dark underworld at night. I think sometimes that is a metaphor for our souls. Sometimes we must pass through the darkness before we can truly appreciate the light."

With that, she said good-bye and turned back to her work in the kitchen.

I climbed into the Jeep for the trip back to Mérida. I knew it would be a long and silent one unless I could get Lucas to speak.

"I like Esperanza very much," I said as a conversational gambit. "Is she really your godmother?"

"Yes," he replied. Silence. This was going to be tough.

"She seems kind of young for that, not all that much older than you are."

"Yes." Another silence.

"Not very wordy, are you?"

"No."

We sat in silence for a while.

"She is a cousin of my father's," he said finally. "Life can be hard here. People mature early. Even though she would only have been in her mid-teens when I was born,

it was considered appropriate for her to be my godmother."

"I suspect she was wise beyond her years even then,"
I said.

He glanced suspiciously at me to see if I was making
fun of her in some way, but saw that I was not. "You
noticed that, did you?" he said.

"She is an important person in my family. Her brother,
my father's cousin, is the patrilineal head of the family,
what some Maya people would call the mother-father,
the daykeeper."

I knew from my studies that daykeepers were the
diviners, the interpreters of omens and the sacred texts.

"Esperanza has status because of her relationship to
the mother-father, but she also has it in her own right.
She is considered a person of great wisdom." He laughed
a little. "Some even say she can foretell the future. I think
it is because she understands people and the world
around us so well."

"I can see how that would be so." I thought of her
comment about the darkness of the soul. "You are Maya,
then?"

"Mestizo. My grandparents were pure Maya. My
mother is Spanish." Mestizo, I knew, was more a cultural
than a racial term. Those of mixed Indian and Spanish
blood who so defined themselves tended to consider
themselves more allied with Hispanic culture.

"Your name—May—is famous in Maya history, is it
not?"

He glanced at me again. "Infamous, you mean. I
assume you are referring to a distant relative, General

Francisco May, who sold out to the Spanish. May is a very common name here in the Yucatán."

There was something in his voice that told me this was not a subject to pursue, so I left it at that.

We sat in a rather more companionable silence for a while, then I tried another tack.

"I believe I have met a friend of yours," I said.

He looked surprised. "Who might that be?"

"Eulalia Gonzalez. I met her at the morgue. She seems very nice, so we had a coffee together yesterday."

"My cousin," he said. Kissing cousin, I thought maliciously.

"Did she mention me to you?" he asked.

"No. I saw you, actually, as I came to the restaurant." That gave him pause.

"Yes, she is very nice," was all he said on that subject, too.

I tried another approach.

"Jonathan mentioned there was a problem at the site," I said.

"Yes," he replied. Another silence.

"Oh, come on, Lucas. Talk to me!" I said, my exasperation evident, I'm sure. "I've seen you engaged in what appears to be animated conversation with other people. Why won't you talk to me?"

We sat in stony silence now, watching the pavement ahead.

"There's a work stoppage at the site," he said at last. "The workers all walked out."

"A mutiny!" I said. "Whatever for? Not that it can be

fun working away down there. Both painstaking and backbreaking work, I'd say."

"It is," he agreed. "But that's not the reason they've . . . mutinied." He smiled for a moment at the term.

"They say the Lords of Darkness are angry that we're working there. That horrible things will happen—are happening—because of our work."

"What kind of bad things?"

"Just little things. One of the workmen cut himself quite badly on one of the flint blades you saw. Another found marks in the sand in the cave that he says are the work of the Lords of Death. That sort of thing.

"These are not well-educated people, you understand," he said in an apologetic tone.

"Well, that might explain it, I suppose. Either that or there really are bad things happening. My experience here to date would say that it was so."

"Yes, you've had a bad time," he agreed. "Anyway, when I get back, I'll be negotiating the conditions of their return to work." He smiled.

We'd arrived at the hotel. I thanked him for the ride and went inside.

Isa and Santiago were at the desk. He looked at me sternly, no doubt feeling that he was my parents' representative while I was here, no matter how old I was. Isa, however, smiled when she saw me. "I guess my dress was a big success," she said. I made a face.

There were two messages, one from Margaret Semple, my contact at the Canadian embassy in Mexico City, the other from Alex, informing me that there was a small leak in my basement, nothing to worry about, but would I please call him.

I called Margaret Semple first, from the hotel. After expressing her sympathy at the passing of Dr. Castillo, she got down to business.

"This is one nasty policeman you've got yourself tied up with," she began.

"Couldn't agree more," I said. "But what specifically are you referring to?"

"While I couldn't pin down anything—which doesn't surprise me, I assure you, the military and the police here are not subject to the same controls we've come to expect at home—I get the impression your Major Martinez is not above a little illegal activity himself. I'd try to stay on his good side, if I were you."

Too late for that, I thought, but thanked her for the warning.

"We're still working on the passport, although I gather you are cleared to leave the hotel. I wouldn't go out of town without checking in with the major, though. Don't give him any excuse to go after you."

I thanked her and went to hang up when she said, "Call me every couple of days, will you, so that I know you are okay?"

I guess she really was concerned. I wondered what it took to worry someone like Margaret Semple. More than it took to worry me, no doubt. And she was the second person after Eulalia Gonzalez to comment on Martinez's dishonesty.

I then slipped out of the hotel and headed for my

favorite public phone in the dark hallway of the Café Escobar.

Alex answered right away.

"I'm glad it's you. I was beginning to get a little worried," he said. I decided not to mention where I'd spent the last fifteen hours.

"What have you got for me, Alex?" I asked.

"Lots of stuff. Fascinating stuff, I must say. Where would you like me to start?"

"The books."

"Okay. You may know this already, but it won't take that long, because quite frankly, books of the Maya are fundamentally very rare. The most important, in terms of our knowledge of it, is the Popol Vuh. This is the book of Maya mythology, kind of the *Iliad* and *Odyssey* of Mesoamerica. It contains what are essentially fragments of myth—the story of creation, exploits of very witty gods called Hero Twins, and an account of the origins and history of the Quiché Maya, who, I gather, were one of the more important groups of Maya at the time of the Conquest.

"We have the benefit of this book only because in the middle of the sixteenth century, it was transcribed into the Roman alphabet by a young Quiché nobleman, and a copy has survived.

"The other post-Conquest books we know about are those of the Chilam Balam, which are, I gather, books of the jaguar prophet. I didn't do much research on these, since you told me to skip them, so I'll mention only that these are also probably fragments of earlier pre-Conquest stories, they, too, are in European script, and they are named after the places they are kept."

"What about even earlier books than these, Alex?"

"Now this is where it gets really interesting. There are only four Maya books in the world today in the original hieroglyphics.

"I was surprised how few there were—imagine judging our civilization on just four books!—until I read about the infamous friar Diego de Landa, who, with some of his colleagues in Christ, took it upon themselves to systematically wipe out all the Maya hieroglyphic books. He wrote to the King of Spain at the time saying something to the effect that since the books contained superstitions and falsehoods of the devil, they had burned them all. Any Maya caught with one of these texts risked torture and death.

"The four hieroglyphic books, called codices, are named for the places they were first exhibited. Three are in Europe: the Dresden Codex, the Paris Codex, which you can see under glass in the Bibliothèque Nationale in Paris, and the Madrid Codex. They all contain information on gods and rituals and all are in a very fragile state."

"And the fourth?"

"The Grolier Codex. In some ways it is the most fascinating. It turned up recently, very recently, in codex terms—1971, actually. There is a story that it was found in a wooden box in a cave in Chiapas by looters, and was held by a private collector in Mexico for at least three decades before it surfaced at the Grolier Club.

"These codices are made of paper of some sort. How

long do you figure something made of paper would last in the humidity of that climate? And yet the Grolier Codex has been dated to the early thirteenth century, thereby making it the oldest of the four! Many thought it would not be possible for it to have survived so many centuries outside the controlled environment of a museum, but the texts I've researched give the impression that its age has been established through carbon dating, and that it is authentic. It is in very bad shape, though."

"So what would these books look like?"

"They were written on long strips of paper folded like screens, kind of accordion-pleated, with a cover of wood or fur. You read through the stack from top to bottom, I think."

I thought of the rabbit scribe on the piece of pottery at the museum. He had appeared to be writing on a stack of folded paper, and there was a spotted material that covered it top and bottom.

"So one of these books would be exceptionally rare."

"Absolutely! Imagine a literate civilization reduced to only four books! What would ours be? A volume of Shakespeare, a book on physics by Stephen Hawking, the Bible, a book of poetry or philosophy?

"Anyway, that discussion is for another day. Let me tell you what I've found out about the people you asked me about. Gomez Arias. Pretty much what you told me yourself. Born in Mérida, lived much of his childhood in Panama. After his father died when he was in his early teens, he ran away from home, or his mother kicked him out, depending on which account of his life you believe.

Worked at various menial jobs, until he made a lot of money, a fortune I'd say, in water systems.

"Owns a number of companies. He seems to like naming them after himself and his daughter. There's the Hotel Monscrrat, Monserrat Shipping Lines, and something called DMGA Investments, which I gather invests the profits from his other enterprises.

"Three marriages, one to Innocentia, one child, the aforementioned Monserrat; the second to an English-woman, Sharon, ended in divorce after a year and a half. No children. Currently married to Sheila Stratton, wealthy American socialite. They've been married five years, also no children. He likes art and blondes, I'm not sure in which order.

"Jonathan Hamelin. Cambridge-educated archaeologist. Has published some papers in various scholarly journals. Worked in the Yucatán for the last six years. Credited with some interesting archaeological discoveries, the most recent in a site near Tulum. Seems to have had some bad luck with some of his finds, though. Grave robbers always seem to be a few steps ahead of him. One of the objects he was looking for, a jade mask, turned up in a private collection in Europe not long ago.

"Good family, apparently. Seat in the House of Lords. Although they don't appear to be wealthy. Family home has been given to the National Trust. His parents have the use of it until they die, then it becomes the exclusive property of the trust. More family status than cash, I would say. Probably broke, but in an aristocratic British sort of way.

"Lucas May. Now this one is a cipher. Studied

archaeology both in Mexico and at the University of
Texas. Interned at the Museo National de Antropologia in
Mexico City ten years ago. After that, absolutely nothing.
No papers, no attendance at conferences, no archaeologi-
cal discoveries.

"Major Martinez. Strange. Up until about five years
ago he appeared to have a distinguished career with the
federal police. Much-decorated hero, in fact. He was a
member of an unofficial antiterrorism squad that captured one of the leaders of a group of Indian rebels.

"Then he got involved in a nasty little affair at one of
the archaeological sites. Seems there was this lovely little
local market in the shadow of the ruins. The government
went and built another marketplace about half a mile
away. The local people didn't like it—it sounds like a
concrete bunker to me, so I can sympathize.

"Anyway, the locals refused to move. I gather nothing
happened for a while. But then one day the bulldozers
arrived, accompanied by the federal police, Major Martinez
in command, machine guns at the ready. The locals were
given forty minutes to vacate the marketplace . . . one
can only imagine the hysteria.

"Martinez took his assignment very seriously. One
could say way too seriously. By the·end of the day, the
old marketplace was gone, absolutely flattened. I'm sure
the authorities regarded it as a job well done, but a couple
of people got hurt, badly hurt—a really brutal affair—
and there was a public outcry. The government went
looking for someone to blame, and Martinez ended up
the villain.

"He kept his job, but seems to have been assigned to

lesser cases from that moment on, like the theft of a statue from a bar, cases you would think would have been beneath him. He's a bitter man, no doubt.

"That's about it!"

"Thanks, Alex You are a wonder. This is really helpful."

"If you need any more, call me. My computer stands at the ready!"

Later Jonathan called to say he'd have to be in Mérida in the late afternoon, and could we meet for dinner. He treated me to the dining room of the Hotel Montserrat, a rather extravagant affair that must have set him back a bit and something of a surprise considering how annoyed the young woman after whom the hotel was named had been when he had refused a nightcap the previous evening.

At some point during the meal, our conversation turned to his work at the site.

"Someone was telling me that you've had some problems with grave robbers on your digs," I said, recalling what Alex had told me earlier in the day.

"Rather!" he said. Then, losing his air of British detachment: "Bloody pigs! Sorry for the language."

"Tell me about it."

"You don't want to know. Do you, really?"

"Sure. I'm fascinated by this stuff."

"Well, I spend the rainy season, when fieldwork is impossible, doing research and writing papers on the various rulers of this region.

"A couple of years ago I was reasonably sure I could find the tomb of a prominent Maya *ahau*—a nobleman—

dating from the late classical period. I'd found a fragment of stone that indicated he'd been buried with a jade mask.

"Anyway, I could hardly wait until the rain stopped so I could go back looking for it. I found the tomb, all right, underneath a pyramid in the forests of the southern Yucatán, but there was no mask.

"What there was, however, was evidence of very recent entry into the tomb. The footprints were very new.

"About a year and a half later, six months ago, a jade mask appeared at auction in Europe. I couldn't afford it, of course. Tens of thousands of pounds sterling. Now that there are export controls on pre-Columbian artifacts, they're very scarce in Europe, and very pricey. Quite beyond my means.

"I can't prove it, but I'm sure it is the mask I was looking for.

"What really burns my butt about this, if you will excuse the expression," he said heatedly, "is that this is the second time this has happened to me here.

"The first season I was here, I was lucky enough to find another tomb, and this one, too, had recently been plundered. I have no way of knowing what treasures were taken from that one.

"It's almost as if someone's looking over my shoulder as I do my research, then he gets there first and profits from it. Irritating as hell, I must say," he concluded.

"Are you looking for something special at this site?" I asked.

"Not really. It's just a ripping great site, that's all."

"What made you choose archaeology as a career in the first place?" I asked.

"Exactly the question my parents asked me when I told them my choice of studies many years ago." He laughed, then added soberly, "We've been rather politely estranged since, actually. They thought the life of a Harley Street physician more suitable for their offspring, you see.

"But I grew up reading about the great British explorers and archaeologists. While my friends dreamed of being soldiers and statesmen, I devoured the stories of Howard Carter and Lord Carnarvon's discovery of King Tut's tomb, Sir Leonard Woolley in Mesopotamia, Sir Arthur Evans at Knossos on Crete. As long as I can remember, an archaeologist was what I wanted to be."

"Any regrets?"

"Of course. I dreamed of fame and fortune, but in reality, the big discoveries are few and far between. And I haven't found my own Lord Carnarvon to bankroll my work. But perhaps life never works out exactly the way we want, and no occupation is as exciting as it appears when we first choose it.

"To be perfectly honest, the life of a Harley Street physician has never had any appeal for me, nor has the family's seat in the House of Lords. That will go to my older brother when our elderly father dies, and he's welcome to it."

We were both silent for a few moments. I thought a little of the disappointments in my life—how I'd developed my business from scratch, nurtured it, suffered through the first tenuous years. I'd only made one mistake: I'd married my first employee, a designer by the name of Clive Swain, and given him a half interest in the business as a wedding present.

Suddenly Jonathan reached across the table and took my hand. "My only real regret is that I haven't been able to find a woman prepared to share my peripatetic and occasionally frustrating lifestyle. . . .

"At least not, perhaps, until now," he said, squeezing my hand.

We went back to the hotel, and when no one was at the hotel desk for a moment, I rushed him up the staircase. Staying with friends of your parents can have its drawbacks.

At some point in the night, while we were companionably curled up together, Jonathan said, "I've been thinking about what you said the other day at the morgue, about the police investigation of Don Hernan's murder."

"Ummm."

"I think maybe you're right. Martinez is a bit of a weird duck, isn't he? Maybe there is something strange about this investigation."

"Uh-huh."

"Did you go back to the morgue?"

"Yes."

"And?"

"Don Hernan was probably killed outside the city. He had dust on his shoes and trousers, and there were traces of forest vegetation on them."

"Maybe you and I could do a little research on this ourselves?"

"Like what?" I said cautiously.

"Well, Don Hernan called you down here on a project. Maybe we should try to figure out what the project was."

"I guess," I said noncommittally.

We drifted off to sleep.

Sometime later, in the very, very early morning, he got up to leave. We were both a little embarrassed at the thought of his going out the front door, so I showed him how to exit through the bathroom window. He said it made him feel like a teenager all over again.

BEN

In one of those extraordinary coincidences that divert, if not entirely change, the course of history, Hernando Cortés managed to arrive in the New World in the year 1 Ben, which also happened to be the year that the Aztecs had prophesied that Queztalcoatl would return from the eastern sea.

Presumably the pale and bearded Spaniards, attired in their suits of armor and plumed helmets, bore some passing resemblance to the locals' idea of a pale-skinned serpent god. One thing is certain: they came from the right direction.

The Mesoamerican equivalent of a year was eighteen times the twenty-day Tzolkin, or 360 days, plus five very unlucky days at the end to make their calendar square with their knowledge of the solar year. Solar years were named for the day on which they began. Without going into the intricacies of it all, the Tzolkin and the year, in this case 1 Ben, arrived at that same combination once every fifty-two years. Cortés was a lucky man.

The result of this convergence was that Cortés and his

army were, for a time at least, considered gods and treated with the appropriate respect and fear. Cortés was able to press the psychological advantage and by 1521, just two years after his arrival, had conquered the Aztecs.

In 1697, the Itzá fell to the Spaniards, the last of the Mesoamerican groups to do so, notably at the start of Katun 8 Ahau, a Katun, or twenty-year cycle, that always signaled trouble for the Itzá. The Spanish generals may or may not have understood the Maya calendar by this time, but they invariably profited from it.

What armies, the prophecies of the Maya calendar, and superior weapons could not do, smallpox, influenza, measles, and the Spanish liquor *aguardiente* did. The diseases alone wiped out ninety percent of the native population within a century of the Europeans' arrival.

But the principal agent of European culture was the church. The Spaniards brought with them their rituals, their images, and of course, their priests. The Franciscans were given an exclusive in the territory: they were the only order allowed into the Yucatán.

Knowing the power of a language, both written and spoken, many of these friars strove systematically to wipe out any traces of it. To do that they made the performance of Maya rituals and the ownership of Maya books punishable by torture and death. Maya children, when they were educated at all, were educated in Spanish and Latin only.

Diego de Landa, a Franciscan friar who later became bishop of Yucatán, was one of the worst. In the 1560s in Mani, a site near Uxmal, one of the most beautiful Maya cities, Landa held a full-blown auto-da-fé. Huge bonfires were built, onto which all the books Landa could find were thrown. Thousands of Maya were tortured, hundreds died.

To add insult to injury, one of the few eyewitness accounts we have of Maya life at the time is Landa's own *Relación de las cosas de Yucatán* of 1566. The book, which loosely translates as a report on things of the Yucatán, was written to the King of Spain in the defense of the friar's outrageous behavior. It is a second-rate account, and basically chronicles a lifestyle he tried desperately to stamp out.

But the Maya are a resilient people. Denied their language and their books, they wrote down their history in secret, using the only alphabet they knew by that time, the alphabet of their conquerors. Without that stubborn tradition, the Popol Vuh of the Quiché Maya and the books of Chilam Balam of the Yucatecan Maya would not exist, and the ancient culture would be virtually lost in the mists of time.

What was lost for centuries, in fact until very recently, was glyphic literacy, the ability to read the old hieroglyphic language and many of the stories and history that went with it.

It was an unbelievable tragedy. The Maya were not as technically advanced as some civilizations. They did not use the wheel, for example, nor did they work with metals. They were no more or less warlike than their neighbors, no greater custodians of the environment.

Instead, their great achievements were those of the intellect. They invented zero and place-system numerals, something the cultures of ancient Greece and Rome never did. They had an intricate way of measuring and recording the passage of time. They measured the visible cycles of the heavens and had the ability to understand them mathematically.

But perhaps their greatest achievement was their literacy. The Inca of Peru, despite their artistic and architectural achievements, had no written language. There were other written languages in Mesoamerica certainly and the Maya were not the first to develop a writing system.

What the Maya had that many other groups did not was a fully functional written language that represented the spoken word and could be used to convey complex ideas, something that made them the most literate of all Mesoamerican civilizations.

Scribes were valued and honored members of the society, and their work recognized through glyphs that named them. Writing, whether in the folded bark-paper books now called codices, or in stone on monuments, was treasured. And while it is highly unlikely that everyone in classic Maya times could read and write, there is evidence to suggest that the elite could.

All that is left of this language, which the Maya themselves nurtured and preserved for centuries before the arrival of the Spaniards, are fragments from ruined cities, and four codices, each one a tattered window into the past.

The question for me was, was it possible there were five? And if so, where would the fifth be?

The question of whether or not there could be another was a pretty basic one. While, as Alex had told me, one

codex, the Grolier, had surfaced in 1971, found somewhere in the region maybe thirty years earlier, it was in
extremely bad condition. As time went on it became less
and less likely that another could be found.

Under what conditions, I wondered, would one of
these survive at least five centuries?

Jonathan had said we should work together on Don
Hernan's murder. And he would know the answers to my
questions if anyone would. But I was afraid to ask. It
required a level of trust in him and our relationship that
I could not yet summon.

Who else? Lucas? That would require even more of a
stretch than Jonathan.

Antonio Valesquez.

I returned to the *museo* and his dusty little library. He
actually looked mildly pleased to see me.

"Antonio," I said, "I'm exploring your idea about a
book. But I keep wondering how a book would survive
these many years. Even the first-edition Stephens that
Don Hernan left me in his will is not in great condition.
The leather is worn, the pages damaged in some cases by
the damp. And it dates from 1841.

"How could something made of paper survive from
before the Conquest?"

"Certainly I can find you some books on conservation,
piles of them actually, since this is a museum. I think,
however, there may be a faster way," he said. "I think I
owe you what you call lunch. Meet me at the Café
Pirámide. It's in the market area."

"I know where it is," I said.

"I'll be there with a colleague of mine. One-thirty all right with you?"

"See you there." I nodded.

I had no trouble finding the café this time around, and was waiting at a table when Antonio approached with a young man, early twenties I would say, in white slacks and T-shirt, his ears well decorated with pierced earrings and studs. The most surprising thing about him was his hair, cut very short, and very blond, bleached to within an inch of its life, and by an amateur at that. It was quite the fashion statement.

"Meet Ernesto Diaz, one of our more talented conservators. The one who was working on the vase I was telling you about the other day."

"Nice to meet you," I said.

"Same here," he said.

We ordered our meal. In Mexico, the food at this time of day is often taken from what is called the corn kitchen, a cuisine that dates back to Aztec times. In those times, corn had to be dried, then boiled with lime, then ground. Now, of course, you can buy the flour, *masa harina,* in any grocery store. Sort of takes the romance out of it, though.

We ordered an assortment of green enchiladas with coriander and green *tomatillos,* enchiladas with *mole* sauce, and tamales, Yucatán style, with spicy peppers and chicken, and a pitcher of beer to wash it all down.

We were well into the food before we finally got around to the subject at hand.

"Señora McClintoch has an interesting question for you, Ernesto, for a paper she is writing for her graduate degree in Mesoamerican studies," Antonio began. He could lie with almost the same facility as I.

"It's Lara, please, Ernesto," I said as the young man turned to me with some interest.

He smiled. "And the problem?"

"I'm researching Maya codices," I began. "The background, the provenance, of the last one, the Grolier, is rather . . ."

"Vague?" he offered.

"Vague," I agreed. "I know that carbon dating has made it the oldest of the four—"

"Early 1200s," he agreed.

"But surely that is not possible! How could something as old as that, and that kind of material survive, even in terrible condition for that long?"

"Interesting question," he said. "Not our field, you know. Terra-cotta is what we do. We would have to think about that, wouldn't we?"

We waited.

"They're made of fig-bark paper, we believe. Organic. Cellulosic. But coated in gesso or something, probably mineral in origin. The worst thing in this climate is the dampness, the relative humidity. Encourages mold. That's the real killer. That's one of the reasons the codices in Europe are in such bad shape. Even if they were cared for once they arrived, which they probably weren't, there was only one way to get there in those days—by ship. Nasty, damp journey!

"At least one kept here would not have to survive a sea journey. And the good news is that bark often contains a natural fungicide. That would protect it for a while. But it would still have to be somewhere where it could be kept relatively dry.

"Lots of other things to worry about; secondary, though. Paper is very susceptible to acids. But the soil here is alkaline—limestone. That's one good thing. And paper is relatively unaffected by light, although we're not so sure about whatever they used for inks. Colors might easily fade. Probably not a problem, though, since the fact that the Grolier only surfaced recently would indicate it was kept well hidden, presumably in a dark place. Bugs, though. Insects and bacteria. Thrive in the warm damp climate," he mused.

"That is what we're trying to find out, isn't it? Where the Grolier might have been?" he observed.

I nodded. If Antonio was prepared to lie to this man, so was I.

"That would be an interesting area of study. There are lots of rumors, of course."

"For example?"

"The most likely one is that it was found in a cave near Tayasol, by grave robbers."

"Where's that?"

"Tayasol, or Tah Itzá, was the last stronghold of the Itzá before they were subdued by the Spanish in the late 1600s. It was located where the town of Flores in Guatemala is now."

"So if it were in a cave, wouldn't that take care of a lot of the problems—light, for example? The Dead Sea Scrolls were found in caves," I said.

"Yes, but not the bugs, and certainly not the mold. The

Dead Sea Scrolls were found in caves in a desert climate."

"What about tombs? You'd think sealing them in tombs would do it, wouldn't you?" I said, growing slightly impatient with all these musings.

"We might think so, but that has not proven to be the case. Books were very special to the Maya, so we would expect they were put in the tombs all right. Something to pass the time in eternity." He laughed. "But they haven't been found in tombs."

"Tomb robbers?"

"Maybe, in some cases. But really, tombs are not that well sealed, and even if they are, there is a lot of air in them when they're closed up. Damp air, at that. So the air and the pests just work away at the books in the tomb."

He paused for a while, munching an enchilada.

"What we would be looking for would be an environment in equilibrium. Away from energy sources like light, heat, vibration, and other materials that would react with the book."

He paused for a few seconds. "Ideally, we'd want our book sealed in a container, something waterproof and resistant to the alkaline environment."

"What would that be?" I asked.

"Well, limestone itself, although it's pretty porous. Most siliceous materials—ceramics, glass, and stone—would do. Jade survives nicely, as does flint, obsidian. Terra-cotta, too, although that may be too porous.

"It should be a small container. Not too much air. If it could be sealed, well, all the better. The idea here is for the environment in the box to come to equilibrium quickly and stay that way.

"So we'd say a box. A stone box. With only the codex in it. We've never heard of them making stone boxes, but why not? Maya scribes worked in stone all the time—the Maya built whole cities. So why not carve out a box of some kind?

"If we remember correctly, these codices had wooden or jaguar-fur covers. It would be better if they were not in the box with the paper. Too complicated when there are greater numbers of materials. They react differently and can affect each other detrimentally.

"What we'd really like would be to seal the box in plastic wrap. Won't do, of course." He laughed.

"So what would *we* seal it in, then?" I asked, falling into his particular speech affectation.

"We'd have to think about that for a minute. We wonder if the Maya had raincoats of any sort at that time. Cloth—they had cotton, I'm sure—coated in some substance to repel water. We used to think the Maya didn't know about rubber, but recently there has been evidence that suggests they might have. Don't know much about natural rubbers myself, what the long-term survival of natural rubber would be, so couldn't say much about that. Maybe some kind of gum."

He chewed on his enchilada some more.

"Waxes!" he exclaimed triumphantly. "Of course! Much more waterproof than gums. The Maya were great beekeepers. How about beeswax? Gum elemi? It's found in the Yucatán. Or candelilla wax. It's from a weed native to Mexico. Even bitumen. It's a natural asphaltic material we bet they knew about. Any of these could be used."

"So are we saying that it is possible one might have survived, in reasonable condition, all this time?" I asked.

"Depends on our definition of reasonable. The Grolier is in terrible condition. Theoretically, though, it should be possible for one to survive in better shape than that. But we were researching the Grolier, were we not? Or perhaps we are looking for another!" he said slowly, excitement in his eyes.

"Only in theory," I said, wondering if this conversation had gone too far.

I thanked him for his help and changed the subject as quickly as I could without looking too obvious. I could see I had not been that successful, so I excused myself and went looking for the washroom.

It was at the back of the restaurant, and on my return, I once again found myself witnessing, from the relative darkness of the restaurant proper, a scene between friends. As I watched, Ernesto reached out and put his hand on Antonio's knee, and then quickly kissed him on the cheek. The Café Pirámide was quite a romantic spot.

By the time I got back to the table, everything was back to a businesslike atmosphere. Both were discussing some research that was needed. But I understood a little better why Antonio had spent so much time helping the conservator find the picture of the vase with the rabbit scribe, and why Ernesto had been so helpful on first meeting.

I told them it was time for me to go, thanking Ernesto for his help and Antonio for lunch, and headed back to the inn. I made a slight detour, however, to the hospital where Doña Josefina still lay paralyzed. There was little or no improvement, the sister told me.

I sat by her bedside once again, holding her hand. I asked her if I should be looking for a fifth Mayan hieroglyphic codex, and she pressed one for yes.

I asked her if she knew where it was. She pressed two for no.

I wanted to sit with her a little longer, so I told her I had been to a spectacular party, and all about the house, the food, the guests, my new dress. But when I told her that it was at the Gomez Arias residence, she became agitated, so much so that I called the nursing sister to the bedside.

Sister Maria told me that she would take care of her, but that it would be better if I left. I did, much agitated myself. I did not wish to cause Doña Josefina grief, but I thought I needed to know what upset her about Gomez Arias.

All of this was forgotten, however, when I got back to the hotel. The Ortiz family was in considerable distress, to an extent that it took me a while to figure out what happened.

Major Martinez had arrived at the hotel with a warrant for Alejandro's arrest, not just for the robbery of the statue of Itzamná, but for the murder of Don Hernan.

Ricardo Vallespino, Luis's brother had also been charged, as were a couple of other students at the university. The police said these were the ringleaders of the Children of the Talking Cross. Luis, though dead, was named as a participant.

Alejandro had been led away in handcuffs. Once again I was confined to the hotel, as an important witness to some of these events.

OUR CHAMPIONS, THE HERO TWINS, after entering the realm of Xibalba by climbing down into a deep abyss and crossing a river of blood, are set a series of tests by the Lords of Darkness, any one of which would appear to mean certain death.

The first night they must spend in the Dark House, given one lit torch and a lighted cigar each, and told that the torch and the cigars must be returned in this same condition when the night is over. The crafty twins substitute a bright macaw feather for the torch flame, and fireflies for the cigar tips, and are able to return the objects as requested.

Next they enter the Razor House, but are able to persuade the knives not to cut them by promising them the flesh of animals. As a little added joke, they send an army of ants to take the flowers of One and Seven Death, two of the nastiest Lords of them all.

The next night's trial is the Cold House, with freezing drafts and falling hail. With their powers, they simply shut out the cold.

Next is the Jaguar House, where ferocious animals are diverted by a pile of bones the twins give them to fight over.

The last, and worst of all, is Bat House, where monstrous snatch bats are sent to kill them. They survive by sleeping inside their blowguns. Hunahpu, however, sticks his head out a little too soon, and loses it to a nasty bat, his body still inside the blowgun. This will call for real ingenuity on the part of his brother, Xbalanque, but once again our twins win the day.

The test the twins never had to endure was trial by media.

Major Martinez's face was much in evidence on the front page of every newspaper and relentlessly, every hour, it seemed, on television.

The way Martinez told it, Alejandro Ortiz and Ricardo Vallespino were key members of a terrorist group that stole works of art to support its nefarious activities. This group had its headquarters at the university, a place, Martinez noted often, that was always known for its subversive activities.

Three professors had also been arrested and charged as ringleaders of the terrorist group. The bewildered expressions on their faces, as they were shown being herded into police vans, spoke volumes.

Luis Vallespino, apparently, had also been one of the terrorists, but he had broken from the group and had tried to warn Dr. Hernan Castillo that "he had been marked for death", Martinez said, because Don Hernan had, through his connections in the art community, figured out who the robbers were. Luis had been intercepted at the *museo* and had been murdered, possibly by his own brother, his body left on the roof.

The terrorists had then waited in ambush for Dr. Castillo and had murdered him, too. More arrests, Martinez hinted, were imminent.

It was all very neat, except for the fact that Don Hernan—as I knew and Eulalia Gonzalez could confirm—had not been murdered in the *museo*. I tried calling her at the morgue, but was told she had asked for, and been granted, an extended leave of absence from her job. I wondered if she had done this voluntarily and if she was okay.

Equally outrageous was the media coverage of the event. This was big news. The Children of the Talking Cross had captured the imagination of the public immediately following the theft of Itzamná from the bar. Many local pundits had voiced their opinions on the subject, many of them supporting the cause, if not the theft itself.

With the latest developments in the case—the allegations of murder of the young Luis Vallespino and one of Mérida's most distinguished citizens—these champions of the downtrodden were distancing themselves very quickly from their former protégés.

To ensure maximum coverage of the event, the local television station had set up a mobile unit right outside the Casa de las Buganvillas, the van, the satellite dish, and the cables making it almost impossible for vehicular traffic to get down the little street.

Every time anyone was audacious enough to leave or enter the hotel, the lights came on and cameras rolled. Not to be outdone, the local newspapers and radio stations also had reporters on the spot. Food carts moved in to supply them.

No effort was spared to plumb the depths of human misfortune. Reporters, in the absence of any real facts, desperately sought out details of Ortiz family life. Santiago's diplomatic career was dissected, as was Isa's business. Shots of her little factory in Mérida were prominently featured.

Neighbors willing to parade themselves in front of the cameras were asked about the hotel, the Ortiz family, and most particularly Alejandro. One neighbor, a blousy woman by the name of Carmelita Chavez, was shown saying she had known Alejandro would come to no good ever since he had stolen an orange off a tree in her garden when he was eight.

The absolute depths were reached, I thought, when a prominent local psychologist was interviewed on a daytime talk show. Alejandro, he said, was suffering the effects of being the youngest son of a very successful man. He was probably the victim of paternal neglect, since his father was undoubtedly never home and therefore never gave his son the discipline and care he needed.

It was appalling.

We held a council of war about noon. Jean Pierre, Isa's partner, flew down from Mexico City to be with the family. I called Jonathan. Both men ran the gauntlet of reporters and curious passersby to get into the inn.

Acting on the assumption that action was better than waiting, we assigned ourselves tasks. First we hired a security company to maintain order outside the inn, and to keep the reporters off the property. There was nothing we could do to keep them off the street.

Next we polled all the guests at the hotel to ascertain their wishes. For the temporary guests we found accommodation at nearby hotels. Some of the permanent residents chose to stay; others were able to lodge with relatives and friends. By late afternoon, all who wished to leave had done so.

Santiago's condition, always exacerbated by stress, worsened. A doctor was called, but there was little he could do except tell him to rest.

Jonathan, I have to admit, was terrific in this situation. It was he, along with Jean Pierre, who got us all mobilized, and he was tireless in carrying guests' bags to the end of the street, since it was almost impossible for taxis to make their way down the little street to the inn.

At one point in the afternoon, he pulled me into the empty drawing room for a hug and a little conference.

"Look, Lara," he said. "We have to do something here. You must know more about all this than you are telling me. Why did Don Hernan call you down here anyway?"

"I really don't know for sure, Jonathan," I replied. "I've been trying to piece it all together myself, but really, he never told me anything, except that he was seeking what the rabbit writes."

Jonathan looked at me as if I had lost my senses, of course.

"As I've been able to piece it together so far, I think what the rabbit writes must be a hieroglyphic codex, but where it is, I have absolutely no idea."

"Interesting idea. Maybe Doña Josefina knows," he said.

"I don't think so. I've been to see her, and we've tried to communicate by a sign language of sorts."

"Have you indeed?"

"Yes. She was able to confirm it is a codex Don Hernan was looking for, but not where it is located. I don't even know if Don Hernan knew where it is."

"Interesting," was all he said.

Twilight arrived soon enough, and with it the relief I felt every day now when the sun went down. During the brightest hours of the day I found myself seeking out the shade and the darkened rooms of the inn, just waiting for the darkness.

Jonathan left after a light supper, and we all retired early, exhausted from the ordeal. Francesca, I knew, would not sleep until Alejandro was back at home, but she was persuaded to try to get some rest.

I had hidden Don Hernan's diary in a plastic bag behind a panel in the bathroom that allowed access to the pipes. I took it out now and, climbing into bed, started to read through it.

Other than several references to meetings with Gomez Arias, the most recent a week before my arrival in the Yucatán and Don Hernan's subsequent disappearance, there was little of any note. He'd missed a dentist appointment and a meeting with his banker. My arrival date was also noted. Nothing very unusual here.

Don Hernan was a doodler, and the margins of every page were covered with his scratchings. Most were just geometric designs, the kind lots of people do while sitting in boring meetings or talking on the telephone. On the last page, however, Don Hernan had made three very detailed and intricate drawings.

One was of a woman in a mantilla holding a child. The second was of a Maya warrior wearing a costume complete with feather tail and a large ballooning headdress topped by a bird with elaborate tail feathers. The warrior carried a spearthrower and a club. Above the warrior was a Mayan hieroglyph that I took to be the warrior's name.

The third was even more elaborate. It looked like two serpent or dragon figures joined at the tail, rather like a great gaping jaw hinged at the bottom to form a *U*.

I believed I could identify both of these drawings, given a chance, either from the books in Don Hernan's office or in Antonio's library. I wondered whether the *museo* key I had would get me into the library, since it was not possible for me to go during normal business hours.

I took a piece of hotel notepaper, which was of the airmail variety and therefore perfect for my purposes, and traced the last two drawings carefully. I then put the diary back into its hiding place and tried to sleep.

I must have fallen asleep almost immediately, but awoke about two A.M., as I had begun to do almost every night. I lay in the darkness for a while, and then once again felt the impulse to go out in the dark.

I dressed, then slipped down the stairs to the front and looked outside. The television van was still there, but all the lights were out, and I could see two people in the front seat of the van, silhouetted against the streetlights.

Both appeared to be sound asleep. The other reporters seemed to have left for the night, although I had no doubt they would be back in the morning. There was, however, a police car on the street, and its occupants were very much awake, reading newspapers by the car light.

I returned to my room, and went out again through the bathroom window. I waited for several minutes, hidden in the tree, until the security officer we had hired completed his patrol of the perimeter of the property and disappeared around the corner.

Then I was off and running away from the hotel, down the darkened residential streets toward the *museo*. Once again I waited in the darkness of the little garden at the back, and then went in through the back door. This time I went down to the basement, trying in the darkness to retrace the route I had taken with Antonio Valesquez a few days earlier.

Even the emergency lighting was not on down here at night. I switched on my flashlight and made my way past the storage shelves that lined all the hallways. As I turned the corners grotesque faces and figures of Maya gods seemed to leap out at me, caught in the beam of my flashlight.

I remembered that this was Ix, day of the night sun, the Jaguar God, that passed through the underworld each night. It felt as if the *museo* came alive at night, and these statues really were the gods of the underworld, waiting for their human victims. I'll admit I was terrified, but I pressed on.

Antonio had said that the last time he had seen Don Hernan, he had been greatly excited or agitated about something, and he had been leaving the fragments room. It was there that I headed, although I had no idea what to look for.

I let myself in, and found the little desk in the middle of the room where, I knew, in the daylight, someone was cataloging the collection on the computer.

I pulled down the blind that covered the glass in the doorway and taped it into place, then I turned on the little desk light. I was reasonably sure that the security guard would do little more than take the elevator to this floor and shine his light around from there. It was too creepy a place for him to do much more than that.

It is amazing what you can learn about people from their desks. The owner of this desk was a woman by the name of Maria Benitez. That much was easy to ascertain: there was a nameplate on the desk. Señora Benitez had four lovely children, three boys and a daughter, their photographs all lined up where she could see them while she worked. She doted on her youngest, the little girl. A crayoned stick drawing of a house, a mother, and child—the tree in the yard, the people, and the house all exactly the same scale, in the style of children everywhere—was given a prominent place on the desk. *For Mommy, love, Frida,* it said.

Maria Benitez was a very neat and organized person, and the orderly desk reflected that. I turned on the computer and logged on using her name. Then there came the prompt I was dreading: *password.* I tried the usual stuff, first name spelled backward, Mérida, the name of the *museo. Incorrect password,* the screen flashed. *Try again.* I wondered how many tries you got before you got locked out entirely.

I looked around the desk again. My eyes fell on the child's drawing. *Frida,* I typed.

I was in.

It took me a while to figure out how the collection was being cataloged. In time I realized that objects were coded by type, but also by location. I kept running back and forth between the computer and the drawers that I had opened by taking the key from the desk drawer as I had seen Antonio do when we were last here. I found I could list by type of object—tools, weapons, pottery fragments, etc.—but also by drawer. I could, I found, punch in a drawer number, and a list of its contents would appear. This would be useful in assisting someone doing research who wanted to know what a particular object in a particular drawer was, I guessed.

I opened one drawer, checked the contents, then went back to the computer and typed in the number. There were twelve objects in the drawer, I counted, and twelve items appeared on the screen.

I tried another drawer number. Ten objects, ten names on the list. I scanned the list to see if anything looked unusual.

I then tried the objects themselves. *Terra-cotta,* I typed, and several drawer numbers showed up on the screen. I ran to the drawers, and indeed, the drawers listed did contain pottery fragments. A couple of pieces were marked out on loan.

I kept looking. I had no idea what I was looking for.

Something out of the ordinary. I tried typing *codex*. Nothing.

I tried *stela*. Several drawers held fragments of stone stelae.

I tried typing *weapons*. Two drawers contained weapons. I looked at the first. There were bits of flint spear points. Fifteen items listed, fifteen in the drawer.

I checked the second drawer's listing. Nineteen items. I checked the drawer. I counted, then counted again. Twenty items. Maria Benitez had made a mistake.

I looked at the contents. They were various fragments of flint and obsidian blades.

Hardly breathing, I tried to reference the descriptions to see what had been missed. I printed off a copy of that drawer's list and went to the drawer to check it item by item.

But I knew which one was extra. It was the beautifully carved blade at the back. There will be nine, Lucas had said. Nine blades for the nine Lords of Darkness. Only eight had been found in the cave. This had to be the ninth.

What did this mean? Perhaps someone exploring the cave a long time ago had found it and had given it to the *museo*, not realizing there were more treasures to be found at the site. Maybe it was from a different place entirely, which I couldn't know because it had not been cataloged properly.

At first I could not bring myself to pull the thought that was forming in my unconscious and examine it carefully. Señora Benitez was a meticulous cataloger, and it would be unthinkable for her to miss the biggest and most beautiful object in the drawer.

I lifted the blade from the drawer and looked at it very carefully. When you have spent so much time in the darkness, color vision is not good, and eyes need time to adjust to the light from a flashlight, but in my imagination I saw the blade drenched in blood.

I knew, as well as I would know if I had examined the blade under a microscope, that this was the weapon that had killed Don Hernan. Someone had hidden it in plain sight. Someone who had access to the *museo* and the curatorial and storage spaces. Someone so ruthless that they could kill a man, bring his body to the *museo,* and place it in his office, and then calmly hide the murder weapon in the fragments room.

This could have been anyone who worked at the *museo,* Ernesto and Antonio among them. It could be anyone with research privileges. I wondered if there was a logbook of visitors, other than staff, who had been in this room.

I searched the desk, and found it. The visitors' book. I scanned the names of people who had been there in the days surrounding the time that Don Hernan's body had been found. Most of the names meant nothing. Two of them I knew.

Jonathan Hamelin and Lucas May.

TEARS IN MY EYES, I close the drawers and the cabinet, log off the computer, and turn off the desk lamp. Stumbling in the darkness, I find the door, remove the tape, and roll up the blind, then make my way back to the main floor and the street.

Now even the darkness is dangerous. I believe I can find sanctuary with Doña Josefina, amid the whiteness and the silence and the calm of the hospital. But when I get there, a police car is outside, its blue light flashing directly in my eyes.

I run back to the hotel, shadows lunging at me as I go. I do not know who the enemy is, only that there is one, and he is close to me.

As I near the hotel the shadows take human form and grab me from behind. I am choking. The world becomes very, very dark and I fall. I hear a whirring sound, a shout, and the shadows move away.

I sit, my back to the stone wall of the inn, and fight for breath. Don Santiago, also gasping from exertion, sits in his wheelchair. Unable to sleep, and seeing that the reporters are all gone, he has chosen this time for some solitude on the street outside the hotel.

He has saved my life.

I find I am still holding the knife. I am very frightened.

MEN

I SPENT THE NEXT DAY jumping at shadows and trying to pull together the tatters of my self-confidence so that I would be able to do what I knew I must.

Santiago had wanted to call the police, of course, but both of us soon realized that since I was not supposed to be out of the hotel at all, this would not be helpful for me.

He was unable to tell me anything about my attacker, other than that he wore a cape, black gloves, and a black mask, hardly unusual for Carnaval. Santiago promised me he would not tell the rest of the family about the attack. They had enough to worry about as it was.

I returned to my room and tried with limited success to get some more sleep. I had my recurring dream again, chasing the rabbit, this time through the streets of Mérida, then falling through space, watched by a black-hooded creature with the face of an owl, the death bird. Once again the voices of the Lords of Xibalba surrounded me as I fell. It was not a restful night.

Late in the morning Isa brought me coffee and toast, plus, as a special treat, she said, the *International Herald*

Tribune and one of the large Mexico City newspapers. Jean Pierre had apparently braved the crowds of reporters outside to get these for me.

The *Herald Tribune* was a gloomy edition. The main feature was about the sorry state of the world economy. Falling oil prices, unstable currencies, and plummeting stock markets seemed to be the order of the day.

There was a special feature about Mexico that talked about the efforts, so far unsuccessful, to prop up the nose-diving peso and restore confidence in the Mexican economy and its political leaders. One of the factors contributing to the lack of confidence in Mexico was more guerrilla activity in Chiapas and the government's inability to reach an agreement with the rebels that would end the fighting. Much was made of the fact that the rebel forces appeared to enjoy the support of the church, an interesting reversal from earlier times, I thought.

The Mexico City paper contained coverage of the Children of the Talking Cross affair, as it had come to be known, but not, mercifully, as much as the local media, which is probably why Jean Pierre had picked it instead of the local rag. The article, which I read despite my growing aversion to this kind of coverage, also referenced the trouble in Chiapas, speculating that there might be a link between the Children and the Zapatistas, an idea I found quite ludicrous, considering that it was probably just Alejandro and his friends playing at being rebels.

The Mexico City paper also carried very gloomy economic news. The stock market in Mexico City was extremely volatile, but the trend was by and large down, and hysteria reigned as fortunes were being lost almost daily.

I began to think about Gomez Arias, and wondered how all this would affect him. An unstable currency wouldn't help any of his businesses, which seemed to be exclusively Mexico-based. Maybe an increase in tourism due to the low peso would make his hotel the big moneymaker of his portfolio, although I had never heard of the hotel business being the sure way to financial security. Hotels seemed to be changing hands and closing all the time. He was certainly still giving extravagant dinner parties.

Francesca and Isa, in an effort to keep busy while they waited for news of Alejandro, undertook the sad task of packing up the belongings of Don Hernan, and I elected to join them to keep my mind off my own situation. The knife was stashed in the bathroom wall with the diary, but its presence was burning a hole in my psyche and I could hardly wait to unburden myself of it.

The police had returned the suit Don Hernan had been found in, and that as well as his other belongings were being packed up to send to a charitable organization.

Once again I felt the cuffs of the trousers. Traces of dust still remained. Then, when Isa and her mother were occupied clearing out the closet and bathroom, I searched through the pockets.

I could only find one item. Stuck in the bottom of an inside pocket was a stub of a ticket of some kind. It didn't look like a ticket to a film or an attraction. Bus or train ticket, I would guess, although I wasn't sure. The last

letters—*o-l-i-d*—were all that was left of the destination, if a transport ticket it was.

"Did Don Hernan travel much, outside of Mérida, I
mean?" I asked the Ortiz women in what I hoped was a
casual tone of voice.

"Not much lately, I don't think," Francesca replied.
"He used to, of course, all over the world. He was always
disappearing on us. But when I think of it, the only trips
I can recall his taking in the last couple of years are
buying trips with you, and a trip to Mexico City a month
or two ago to receive some kind of award from the
university there.

"Otherwise, he stuck fairly close to home. He occasionally stayed overnight at the museum. He'd fall asleep
in his office, and when he woke up in the middle of the
night, he would sleep on the couch in the staff room
rather than come back here in the dark."

Digesting this information, I stuck the stub in the
pocket of my jeans and went on helping clear out the
room. It was a very sad task for Francesca, who broke
down often while we worked.

Later that day Isa came to me and said, "We're
thinking of getting this all over with at once. Are you up
for helping us clear out Doña Josefina's room, too? The
hospital has said it is unlikely she will ever return here."

I said I thought I was. Still, Doña Josefina's room was
a shock. First off, it was very dark. The shutters were
closed. Isa said they always were. It also seemed like a
little museum, somehow, a room from a different era.
Doña Josefina had brought a few items of her own to

furnish the room, a small chair with embroidered cushions, a lady's writing desk.

What was truly bizarre was the chest of drawers at one end of the room. This had been set up like a little shrine. The top of it was covered with a length of black velvet. A very old sepia-toned photograph of a young boy, presumably her lost son, rested in a silver frame on the velvet, along with a small silver baby spoon, a silver cup, and a bronzed baby shoe. The photograph was draped in black crepe. The remains of votive candles were stuck in a candelabra to one side of the photograph.

In the top drawer of the dresser wrapped in tissue was a yellowing christening dress and bonnet and some old wooden toys. It was as if the child had died, and perhaps he had, for all I knew. It was very, very sad.

While we were working Isa asked me if I had heard that there had been an intruder at the hospital where Doña Josefina lay. I remembered the police car from the night before but said nothing.

"Apparently someone was prowling the halls, looking in patients' rooms," Isa said. "The sisters didn't like the look of him, so they chased him away. Or rather the mother superior did. I imagine being chased by her would be quite the experience!"

The thought of this brought a hint of a smile to Francesca's face.

Isa cleared out the rest of the chest of drawers, which contained no more children's items, but Doña Josefina's black mantillas, fans and gloves, and what Isa described as some very extravagant black silk underwear.

I was assigned the task of clearing out the closet. Doña

Josefina's taste in clothing was fairly consistent. The closet was filled with black dresses, several long black skirts, and blouses in an old-fashioned Spanish style.

There were two boxes on the closet shelf. One contained a couple of very beautiful antique lace mantillas, both white, and some beautiful white lace gloves. And a gorgeous black lace mask, perfect for a masquerade ball.

The other held a scrapbook.

"Does anyone think Doña Josefina would mind if I looked at her scrapbook?" I asked as we finished packing up the room, this time for storage in the hotel, since Francesca said she had a feeling in her bones that Josefina would be back.

"I can't imagine that she could care now," Francesca said, so I took the book with me to the sitting room downstairs.

The first pages held a few cherished photographs of Josefina and her son. In these she was wearing white, as was her son. The black attire must have coincided with the disappearance of her son, not what everyone assumed was her so-called widowhood.

In addition to these photographs, Doña Josefina had kept clippings and photographs of people who had meant something to her. The more recent clippings were articles about Isa and her fashion business, or reviews of the hotel and Francesca's cooking.

Somewhat earlier clippings alluded to Santiago's distinguished diplomatic career. There was a small article from a local paper that told how the local high-school soccer team had made the play-offs, thanks to a winning performance by none other than Norberto Ortiz.

There were articles about Don Hernan and his museum, and a long feature on his work with indigenous communities to preserve Maya culture.

There were old dance cards, invitations to what looked to be elaborate parties and gala balls, to theater and gallery openings. Doña Josefina appeared to have enjoyed the good life in Mérida, and I was happy for her.

There were several references in the papers to a masked mystery lady who attended a number of social events in the city, and I was reasonably sure I had discovered the use to which the elegant mask in the closet had been put.

Along with these mementos were several articles documenting the successes of a number of businessmen of Mérida, many of whom would no doubt be embarrassed to know their financial and social exploits were being documented by what I guessed to be their current or former paramour.

One of the businessmen singled out for attention was Diego Gomez Arias, described in the early clippings as a young man on the way up. The earliest article talked a lot about his windfall in windmills, so to speak. He had apparently licensed the design to a large European and a North American manufacturer.

There were announcements of his various marriages, the birth of his daughter, the champagne launching of his first ship, the opening of his splendid hotel. There were a number of articles about the lavish coming-out party he had thrown for Montserrat, apparently the social event of the season.

Doña Josefina had been keeping close tabs on this man over the years, and I had to wonder why. She had to be at least twenty or thirty years older than he. Maybe she had been responsible for his sexual awakening, I speculated with some amusement. He certainly had a penchant for blondes.

Or maybe it was something else. I remembered her agitation when I had mentioned his name at the hospital. At the time I had thought that it was because she had known he was involved in some way in Don Hernan's death. Maybe he was.

I thought of my earlier speculation as to his current financial status. I had thought at the time that even if the oil business were in the Dumpster, his other businesses would still be bringing in the cash. But now I wasn't so sure. Maybe he was just keeping up appearances, as they say. And presumably his wife was well-off.

I would have to check into that in some way. He was one of my prime suspects, and I knew money was a very powerful motivator, although why killing Don Hernan would fix his financial situation, I could not hazard a guess.

I returned the scrapbook to its box, and put it with the rest of Doña Josefina's things. I fervently hoped that Francesca was right in thinking she would be back to enjoy them.

For the rest of the day I made preparations for my escape. I borrowed a large shoulder bag from Isa and filled it with small necessities, toiletries, a change of underwear, my jeans and T-shirts, and a couple of things I thought I might need: a photograph of Don Hernan and a flashlight.

When no one was looking, I went into the boxes of Doña Josefina's belongings and took out a long black skirt, a mantilla, gloves and fan, and finally the mask. In my room, I tried on my newly acquired Carnaval costume.

The skirt, which would have been floor-length on the diminutive Josefina, was well above the ankle on me. The skirt was full over the hips, thankfully, and the waist, way too small for me, had to be held together with a large safety pin. I planned to wear a black long-sleeved shirt on top.

I tried again to rest late in the afternoon, the shutters in my room closed tight against the sun. Major Martinez arrived at the hotel and insisted on seeing me personally to assure himself I was still there.

Darkness fell at last. I waited until the inn was totally silent, then leaving a note for Isa telling her not to worry, and asking her if there was any chance she could cajole Jean Pierre into using his banking connections to find out about Gomez Arias's financial status, I climbed out the bathroom window one last time.

It was considerably more difficult in a skirt and carrying a large tote bag, but eventually I managed it. I waited until a couple of revelers went by, then climbed the wall and ran as fast as I could for the Paseo de Montejo, where I pulled on the mask and mantilla and tried to blend into the partying crowd.

While I had been fairly systematic pulling together my

costume, I really hadn't thought through a plan in any realistic way. I knew I had to rid myself of this knife before I lost my sanity, so I followed the crowds on the *paseo* until we were near the museum, then moved quickly through the side streets and then once again into the garden.

When I was sure no one was looking, I went back into the *museo,* filled with real dread. I went down to the basement as quickly as I could, into the fragments room, into Maria Benitez's desk, and then her computer, to find the drawer I needed. Soon the knife—wiped clean, I hoped, of my fingerprints—was back in the drawer.

Like some modern-day Lady MacBeth, I felt as if my hands were covered in blood. As indeed they were. In my fervent cleaning of the blade, I had cut one hand quite badly. This was not a good start.

I looked for a public washroom, and found one several long blocks away in the bus station. I washed my hand, telling the attendant that I was suffering from too much Carnaval, a lie she found amusing. She was kind enough to find me some iodine and a length of gauze, and soon I was on my way again.

As I passed the ticket window I thought of the ticket stub I had found among Don Hernan's belongings, and I watched as people picked up their tickets. They seemed to match the stub in appearance.

I went to the board that listed departures, looking for somewhere that ended in *olid,* and found one that seemed to fit the bill. There was a bus leaving almost hourly, every two hours during the night, for Valladolid, some one hundred miles to the east of Mérida. I bought a ticket, then melded back into the Carnaval crowds while I waited for the appointed hour of two A.M.

I had very little cash left, only traveler's checks, but I found an all-night exchange that demanded an exorbitant surcharge, but was not picky about things like identification, a good thing since Major Martinez still had my passport.

When the hour came, I waited until the last possible minute, then boarded the bus. No one seemed to think a tall woman dressed all in black with mantilla and mask out of place here. Perhaps they assumed I had gone to Mérida for the evening to enjoy Carnaval and was now returning home.

I moved to an empty seat at the back of the bus and hoped the driver would be turning the lights out as soon as we departed. He did, and I hunkered down in the darkness.

I was very tired and soon drifted off. The bus stopped once at Pisté, but soon enough it arrived in Valladolid. Valladolid is much smaller than Mérida, and not quite the Carnaval town that Mérida is, so I quickly removed my mask and mantilla, and hiked the skirt up as best I could.

I didn't think I could check in at a decent hotel, with so little luggage and not wanting to use credit cards with my name on them, so just as dawn was breaking, I found a fleabag hotel not far from the bus station where once again they were not too picky about things like proper identification. I paid cash for a two-night stay.

It was a walk-up, a dingy little place. There was only a sink in the room, the bathroom was down the hall, and the bed creaked horribly. I was afraid to take my clothes off, so pulled back the bedspread, a very nasty green color, checked carefully for bugs, and lay fully clothed on top of the sheets. Not since my student days, and maybe not even then, had I stayed in such a place.

I had only a hazy notion of why I had come here, perhaps because Don Hernan had done so, but even then I didn't know if it had been a recent trip. I was operating on automatic pilot right now, just going on instinct. Two things I knew for certain: that I had to get away from Martinez, and, more importantly, whoever it was who had tried to choke me the night before; and that all of these events, the robbery, the murders, the disappearances of all these pre-Columbian masterpieces, the jade bead in Don Hernan's mouth, even Doña Josefina, were all linked in some way I could not yet understand.

I knew I needed to rest, and while I did not think I could sleep in such surroundings, I soon found myself dozing off. As I did I thought that in the Maya calendar this very long day had been Men, a day associated with the eagle, a day that was supposed to be one of wisdom.

If I was any wiser at the end of this day than I had been the day before, it was not immediately apparent to me.

CIB

In 1846, YUCATÁN SECEDED FROM Mexico, and wealthy hacienda owners, fearful of attack from Mexico or from the United States, armed their Maya laborers, virtual slaves on their henequen and sugar estates, thinking the laborers would protect them.

In 1847, however, the Maya used their masters' arms to sack Valladolid, killing every European they could find, thereby avenging the destruction of their sacred city of Zaci, and the subjugation of its inhabitants by Francisco de Montejo almost exactly three centuries before.

It was the first strike in what came to be known as the War of the Castes.

Valladolid, pronounced Bay-ah-doh-*leed,* should you ever get there, is now a sleepy little agricultural market town, built around a central square, like Mérida its bloody past well hidden by its colonial ambience.

I was forced from a heavy sleep by a slamming door and voices out in the hallway. I opened one eye just in time to see a very large cockroach scuttle for cover in the darkness under the bed.

The room was hot, and I felt as if I had been drugged. My watch showed it to be after noon, which I found hard to believe, even considering the late hour I had arrived in this horrible place.

I had not intended to sleep this long. I assumed Major Martinez would show up at the hotel in Mérida at some point during the day, later rather than earlier, I hoped, and the search would be on. I had much to do before that.

I had a sponge bath of sorts from the sink in the room, casting a wary eye out for the cockroach and any other insects that happened to be about, then pulled on jeans and a shirt and went out into the heat and sunshine of the early afternoon.

I reasoned that if Martinez was already looking for me, he'd be looking in Mérida. Or perhaps thinking I would be trying somehow to get out of the country, which I might be if I had my passport, he'd be watching the airport. I didn't want to take any chances, though.

The central square where I headed is not far from the area around the bus station, and feeling like a fugitive, which I guess I was, I kept my head down and walked in the shadows wherever I could.

In the central square, I looked longingly at the pleasant hotels and then found my way to the Bazar Municipal, an arcade on the main square where food vendors put out tables and chairs at mealtimes. It was now about two P.M., time for *comida,* the main meal of the Mexican day, which can be taken anywhere between two and 5 P.M. The little tables were filled with businesspeople and workers on their afternoon break.

There were few menus to be had, none in English. One

simply looked at the food as it was being prepared and pointed at something that looked appealing. I tried to blend into the crowd, and sitting under an awning, facing the square so no one could come up behind me, I ordered a *sopa de elote con pimientos,* a corn soup with sweet red peppers, and a rice dish with the hot sausages for which Valladolid is famous.

Normally one is expected to order a meat or fish dish after this, and then have dessert, but I wasn't that hungry, nor was I keen on staying in one place too long. Besides, I had work to do.

I made my way back to the bus terminal by another route, trying to ensure that I had a good idea of the lay of the land in case I needed to make a run for it again.

I had brought the picture of Don Hernan with me. He had been a distinctive-looking man, and I was hopeful that someone would have seen him. I asked anyone who looked to be a permanent fixture about the place—the boy in the newsstand, the man who shined shoes on the corner, bus-line personnel. No luck.

A woman selling flowers about a block from the station thought she remembered selling him a carnation for his lapel. That sounded like the dapper Don Hernan to me, but she had no idea what direction he had come from, nor which direction he had headed to. All she did was give me the slight hope that I was on the right track.

I went into a couple of hotels not far from the bus station. No luck there, either. I hadn't thought to inquire at mine, but it was unlikely Don Hernan would have stooped so low even on his worst day.

I knew Don Hernan did not drive. He could not have

rented a car. If he went anywhere, he would surely have taken a taxi. Near the bus station was a taxi stand where drivers sat together, drank coffee, and gossiped while they waited for fares. From time to time I went there to show the photograph to the various taxi drivers who came and went.

Finally, when I was about to despair, a young taxi driver said he recognized the photograph. I was elated.

"Can you remember where you took him?" I asked.

The young man scratched his chin, a rather grizzled affair, and looked thoughtful. Suddenly I caught on. I handed him fifty pesos.

"American dollars?" he queried.

I obliged, exchanging the pesos for a ten-dollar bill. It appeared to be enough.

"I think I can remember," he said obligingly. "I could take you there. But it is very far, very expensive." He named a figure that was close to two hundred dollars.

I was running out of cash, and was not sure I could manage this, but he was obstinate. In his mind, he knew something I didn't, and I was going to pay for it.

The other cabdrivers were watching this with interest. One of them broke away from the crowd, came over, and literally boxed the ears of the younger man. The young man slunk away.

"My younger brother," he said. "I apologize on his behalf. I know where he took your friend, and I will take you there, for one hundred dollars. But I cannot take you now, because tonight is the last night of Carnaval, and I must accompany my family to the festivities.

"Be here tomorrow at noon, and I will take you."

I surmised that as frustrating as this might be, it was the best that could be done at this point, so we shook hands to seal the arrangement. As I left I could hear the two brothers, if indeed that was what they were, arguing. They were speaking very quickly and from a distance I couldn't follow the conversation, but I thought I heard something that sounded like "Huaca de Chac."

It was late afternoon by this time. I went back to my hotel to wait until dark when I could put on my Carnaval attire and blend into the crowds.

Curtains drawn tight, I sat cross-legged on the bed, afraid to put my bare feet on the floor lest the huge cockroach return with friends and relatives.

It occurred to me, in my tired, and in retrospect, morose state, that I should perhaps feel a sense of kinship with the creature sharing this room with me, always hiding, and with so strong an affinity for the dark. I wondered what on earth I was doing, and what I had ever thought I could accomplish by coming here.

About nine, I put on Doña Josefina's clothes and headed out again. I watched in the crowds as the Carnaval parade began. It consisted essentially of two floats, one of them a six-foot conch shell constructed of wire and canvas, painted a bilious pink, mounted on the back of a blue pickup truck.

The other float was a farm wagon pulled by another pickup. On it, several people dressed up as Maya Indians were pantomiming a ritual sacrifice of some sort. In an anachronism of immense proportions, a speaker on the top of the truck was blasting disco music.

Many of the spectators were in costume themselves.

Little girls were dressed up in shimmery dresses with aluminum-foil crowns on their heads, their faces all made up with lots of their mothers' rouge and lipstick. They were having a wonderful time.

There were clowns on bicycles, their young children in the carrier baskets, balloons, people in fantastic headgear of all kinds. People were literally dancing in the streets. I looked on enviously, wishing this were another time or place where I could feel free to join in.

Suddenly there was a hush, then some nervous laughter. Out of a side street came someone dressed up as a priest, followed by a number of men dressed in army camouflage, carrying play rifles cut from plywood, their faces shrouded in black masks.

"Children of the Talking Cross," people whispered, and soon there was a smattering of applause from the crowds. The men raised their rifles in a salute and joined the end of the parade.

Shortly thereafter, the federal police arrived, and I hastily pulled back into one of the dark side streets to stay well out of their view. As I did so I saw them hurrying to catch up with the revelers dressed as rebels. A few people, presumably the same ones that applauded the "Children," hissed as the police went by. I didn't hang around to see what happened, but I felt sorry for anyone audacious enough even to pretend they were rebels right now. The federal police did not appear to have a sense of humor.

Trying to put some distance between me and the police, I went down one of the back streets in the less salubrious part of town. I wasn't sure exactly where I was, but I rounded a corner and found myself in a little square with a lovely tree and wooden bench in the center.

At one end of the square was a café with large barbecues set up out front. Smoke from the cooking filled the square and it smelled delicious. I realized I was hungry, and headed in that direction.

The café, open to the square with a palapa-style roof of interwoven palm fronds, was called Pajaros—Birds— for no apparent reason that I could see. The patrons of the place were predominantly white, Europeans and Americans, the Americans immediately recognizable by their baseball caps and cowboy boots. The women tended to fringed vests, short skirts, and cowboy boots of their own. There was an old-fashioned juke box at the back: Waylon Jennings wailed from the loudspeakers.

I sat at a small table in the corner and listened to a group of men at the next table talk about their adventures in 'Nam. I had obviously found the place the ex-patriots in the area liked to hang out in the evening. At least being white here was not going to call attention to my presence.

The waitress brought me a beer, almost without my asking for it, and then told me to go and help myself to food. I went up to the barbecue grills, where a tall American, probably the owner, also dressed in cowboy gear which seemed to be de rigueur here, and a pair of mirrored sunglasses despite the dark, served me something wrapped in a banana leaf, a warm tortilla, and some refried beans.

Inside the green wrapper was chicken in a spicy red sauce, chicken *pibil*. I devoured it, using my fingers to finish the last of it off. The waitress smiled as she saw me. "It's all you can eat," she said. "Get some more."

I thanked her, but I had an appointment, arranged in the note left for Isa, so I told her I'd just sit and finish my beer, and asked directions to a public telephone. She gestured to a dark corner. "The light's out," she said. "You'll have to kind of feel your way. But the phone works."

Since finding a phone that worked could be a challenge, I headed for the dark corner and fumbled around for some change, getting through to the Casa de las Buganvillas with some difficulty.

Santiago answered the phone.

"It's me," I said.

"Theresa!" he said. "How nice of you to call. Isa is right here."

Theresa?

Isa came on the line immediately, "Hi, Theresa," she said. "Glad to hear from you."

"Is someone there—Martinez maybe?"

"Yes. We're all terribly concerned about your recent illness. Are you okay?"

"Yes," I said. "How's Alejandro?"

"Mother has been to see him, and he's having a rough time."

"I'm sorry."

"Thanks. Anyway, you'll be wanting to know about those investments you were thinking of making. Jean Pierre is right here."

Jean Pierre came on the line.

"Hello, Theresa. I checked on those companies you

were thinking of investing in, and you were right to be concerned. I would advise you against investing in them because their value has plummeted in the last year or two. The company has been resting on its laurels, as it were. The major shareholder and his family will have taken quite a substantial loss, I'm sure, and I wouldn't want you to risk your money with them."

"The major shareholder is Gomez Arias, I take it," I said.

"That is correct."

"Are you telling me someone has come up with a better windmill?"

"Not only better, but cheaper, if the rumors are to be believed. And frankly there is only so much call for the product these days. The market, quite frankly, is a diminishing one. On top of that, some of the other investments are being adversely affected, to say the least, by the volatile peso. The companies are rumored to be in serious trouble. And whether the rumors are true or not, the stock market believes them!"

"I see. Did you happen to have a look at the boards of directors of the three companies?"

"Yes, I did. Other than the major shareholder and his daughter, there are only a couple of names in common. No one whose name means anything to me, though."

"Company executives?"

"Same again."

"You're terrific, Jean Pierre. Thank you."

"My pleasure. Isa would like to talk to you again."

Isa came on the line. I could hear Santiago in the background talking to someone, probably Martinez. The conversation was an unpleasant one. I guess Martinez had discovered I wasn't there, and Santiago was bearing the brunt of his anger.

"Take care of yourself, Theresa," she said. "Call me again as soon as you can."

"I will. And thank you, Isa, and your whole family. I hope I'm not causing you real grief with that horrible man."

"Nothing we can't manage," she said, and we hung up.

I made my way back to my table and sat there finishing my beer, listening as the country-and-western music blasted from the speakers. The waitress came around with a pot of coffee, and I had some of that, too.

As I sat there another baseball-cap type arrived and pulled up a chair at the table next to me. He began to excitedly tell his companions about the parade and the arrival of the federal police.

"You shoulda seen it. Guys in the parade all dressed like Indie rebels. Cops arrive. Obviously they think these guys are for real.

"Maybe they are, too. Just when I think the feds are gonna smoke 'em, they disappear, vanish more like, into the backstreets, like the VC in the rice paddies. It was somethin' else!"

The others at the table were impressed. One of them said, "You know, I've been hearing that there really are guerrilla groups out in the woods here, training for a big revolution. Called Children of the Talking Cross. Tied in with the Zapatistas, you know."

All nodded wisely. I thought of Alejandro training in

the jungle. Too much of a stretch for me. But I was glad the rebel revelers got away.

One of my neighbors headed for the jukebox, and some more hurtin' music came on.

I'm not a particular fan of country music. Normally I can take it or leave it. But tonight it made me homesick for my little house, my family, Alex, my friends, my cat.

I ordered a Xtabentun, the local liqueur, then another. If I wasn't careful, I was going to be one unhappy drunk tonight. Nobody talked to me. This seemed to be the kind of place inhabited by regulars. Strangers like me were viewed with curiosity, but left alone.

I thought about the Ortiz family. They were risking much talking to me with Martinez standing right there, but they had obviously planned what they would say, and carried it off with great panache. They were wonderful friends to have.

I thought of the Gomez family, enjoying the good life, but for how long? Perhaps they were living off the Stratton family fortune. If that were the case, Montserrat might try being a little nicer to her stepmother.

Perhaps the thefts of the Maya pieces from the family collection were an insurance fraud. But why? It would be tough on Gomez Arias to give up any of his art collection, no doubt about that, but if times were tough, why not just sell a Matisse or two? That would provide enough to keep most of us going for quite a while!

But none of this was getting me any closer to finding what the rabbit wrote, only maybe a little closer to a motive for Don Hernan's death.

Finally, about three A.M., I headed back to my horrible

hotel, awash in self-pity. It had not been one of my better days. It had been Cib, a bad day in the Maya calendar, day of the owl, birds associated with the Lords of Darkness. The Lords obviously had had the upper hand today.

CABAN

I BARELY SLEPT. WHEN I did, I dreamed of enormous cockroaches heading my way. That's what too much Xtabentun will do for you.

I got up early, and after another sponge bath in the sink in the room, the bathtub down the hall being absolutely unspeakable, I packed up my meager belongings and checked out. The clerk at the desk did not look at me as I handed over the key. Perhaps people who work in places like this learn not to scrutinize the clientele.

The streets were quiet, except for a few hardy souls out sweeping away the debris from the previous night's celebrations. Most others would be sleeping off the night's activities for several more hours.

As I stood on a corner a van pulled up, and a young man hurled a stack of newspapers in the general direction of a kiosk, then the van moved on.

It was the Mérida paper, and while the kiosk was not yet open, I pulled off the top copy and left a few coins on the pile. I took the paper over to a little café where it appeared there might be someone prepared to get me some coffee, and opened it up while I waited.

The front-page story was still about the Children of the Talking Cross, but to my dismay, a lot of it was about me. A material witness had escaped custody, it said, and police were on the lookout for her. They even had my picture, a sad reproduction of my passport photo. Fortunately, I'd never thought my passport picture bore more than a passing resemblance, so I didn't think I'd be recognized from that.

There was, however, a rather good description of me from the washroom attendant at the bus station, who told in graphic detail how she had found me in the washroom covered in blood. She told how she had helped clean me up, never once realizing I was a criminal on the run. The reporter implied I had acquired this in some unspecified, but clearly horrific activity, and there were some questions as to whose blood I might have on my hands.

If it had been someone else's blood, I wouldn't have required the iodine and Band-Aid, of course, but that thought had either not crossed the reporter's mind, or it was a fact that interfered with a ripping good story.

In any event, I was described as the mysterious lady in black, and my attire was described in minute detail. If any of the guys at Pajaros read Spanish, I would be the topic of discussion at their table for weeks to come!

I still had a few hours to kill until the appointed time at the taxi stand, and while I didn't know whether Major Martinez had figured out I was in Valladolid, I certainly couldn't assume that he hadn't.

I headed for the market area, usually a good place to

get lost. The farmers, not influenced at all by Carnaval, were already at work selling their produce, and I just kept moving between the stalls as fast as I could.

I bought a straw hat with a large brim and pulled it down over my eyes. I was in jeans and a denim shirt, so I didn't think I looked at all like a mysterious lady in black, just an ordinary tourist.

From time to time I could see police in the market area, but I just kept on moving, staying out of the bright sunlight, and trying not to call attention to myself.

About eleven A.M. I started to make my way back to the taxi stand, taking a roundabout route, and being careful not to rush around corners into the arms of the law.

When I got near the taxi stand, I stood in a darkened doorway and surveyed the scene. My driver was already there, still arguing with his younger brother. All looked reasonably normal.

I was about to step out of the darkness and make a dash for the taxi when I heard sirens, and a police car pulled up to the main door of the bus station, just a few yards from the taxi stand. Major Martinez himself jumped out of the cruiser. It would seem that he was a good investigator when he chose to be.

I quickly reversed direction, away from the taxi stand, but I could see a figure I recognized coming up the street from the opposite direction.

I ducked back into the doorway and pressed myself back as far as I could into the shadows. Within a minute or so, Lucas May passed my position, apparently without seeing me. I waited until he rounded the corner, then went as fast as I could in the opposite direction.

I passed through the little square where I had been the night before, past Pajaros, now locked up tight. I headed down another little lane, uncertain as to which direction I was going.

Eventually I came out to a main road, hailed a taxicab, and directed the driver to the only place I could think to go.

Almost an hour later the taxi pulled up at Jonathan's little house and I made a dash for the door. It was opened by Esperanza, who looked genuinely pleased to see me. She led me to the little study off the bedroom where Jonathan was working. "I'm so glad you've come to me, my dear," he said. "I was hoping you would."

In short order my clothes were all handed to Esperanza for washing, and I found myself in a hot bath, bubbles almost overflowing the tub. Jonathan brought me a cognac—"It's never too early in the day for Rémy Martin," he said—and sat on the side of the tub while I soaked.

Later, all squeaky clean, and wearing a white terry-cloth robe of Jonathan's, I sat with him in the living room, the midafternoon sun streaming through the window.

Suddenly he crossed the space between us, knelt beside the sofa on which I sat, and took my hand.

"Lara, I really would like to help you. But you must confide in me. I don't know what I am fighting here, and I must if I am to be of any use whatsoever."

"Jonathan, I'll tell you everything, I promise. But I really don't know where to start."

"Why not from the beginning?" he said.

"I guess the beginning is the call I received from Don Hernan to come here to help him find something—something he told me over the telephone was written by a rabbit.

"I've been trying to figure out what that is ever since. But as I told you a day or two ago, I think it is a hieroglyphic codex. I have no idea where it is, or how to find it. All I know is that two people have been killed—at least one of them on account of it."

"Any idea who would have killed Don Hernan?"

"All trails seem to lead to Diego Maria Gomez Arias. He and Don Hernan had a fight over ownership of Maya artifacts; from what I can tell he is in grave financial difficulty and there is no question a Maya codex would be worth whatever the possessor asked, at least in some circles; and frankly he seems to be the kind of person who could manage to do this kind of thing."

"All by himself, you mean?"

"No, I guess not. He doesn't seem the type to do his dirty work himself. If I had to point a finger at an accomplice, I guess I'd say Major Martinez, but maybe that's just because I don't like him. Or maybe someone close to you, Jonathan," I said, thinking of Lucas.

He looked surprised. "Perhaps the best thing then would be to try to find the codex," he said slowly.

"That's what I'm trying to do. I found the stub of what I think is a bus ticket to Valladolid in Don Hernan's personal effects, so I went there. . . ."

"And then?"

"And then . . . and then . . . Jonathan," I said, "I am unbelievably weary. I really want to talk to you about all this. But first I need to sleep."

"I'm sorry, my dear. I really am. How thoughtless of me!" he exclaimed, getting up and pulling me up off the sofa. "Come, get some rest. We'll talk later."

Just then he noticed the cut on my hand. "How did you do that?" he asked.

"Later, Jonathan," was all I could manage.

And so with that, he led me to the bedroom and tucked me into bed. It was so soft and white and clean, I could have wept with sheer gratitude, and I soon felt myself slipping into sleep.

"Don't tell anyone I'm here," I murmured. "Especially not Lucas."

"You can be absolutely sure I won't," he said.

The last thing I remember was the brush of his lips against my cheek and the thought that, with time, I really could love this man.

I awoke in the very late afternoon, the western sky already turning pink. The house was absolutely silent. I went out to the kitchen and found my clothes all neatly washed and ironed, on a chair. There was also a note on the counter from Jonathan.

Another crisis at the site, it said. *I'll be back in time for supper. We'll talk some more then. Love, Jonathan.*

I checked the refrigerator. There was cold chicken and a bottle of very nice white wine. I had a shower, just on principle, and changed into my clean clothes.

I supposed that while I waited for Jonathan's return, I

might as well continue my search. I went into Jonathan's study, which I noticed had a nice collection of books on the Maya, and retrieving the scrap of paper on which I had traced Don Hernan's jottings, began to try to find the two glyphs.

There was a book of Maya hieroglyphs I was familiar with from my studies that I began to work my way through. It did not take me long to find that the glyph associated with the Maya warrior was the glyph for Smoking Frog, an *ahau,* or nobleman, of Tikal, who had waged war on the rival city of Uaxactún on behalf of the king of Tikal, Great-Jaguar-Paw.

It was a new kind of warfare for the Maya, one in which the stakes were very high. For the first time, rather than simply humiliating rivals and taking captives, the winner took the kingdom of the loser. Tikal conquered Uaxactún on January 16, 378, and Smoking Frog was installed on its throne. Tikal became one of the most powerful and prosperous cities of the early classic period of Maya history, and its influence on the arts, architecture, and perhaps more importantly, on Maya ritual was enormous. I suppose in some ways, it signaled the beginning of the great Maya civilization as we know it.

The second glyph took a little longer. But when I found it, it made me sit back and ponder for some time. The glyph that had reminded me of two upraised arms, sort of like two dragons hinged at the bottom, was the symbol for the Maw of Xibalba. It is supposed to be a gaping head of some skeletal creature, marking the point at which our world and the world of Xibalba meet. Presumably to pass through a portal on which this symbol appears is to enter the realm of the Lords of Darkness.

I opened the desk drawer to find some paper and a pen on which to make notes, and found, wrapped in cotton and tissue, part of a terra-cotta vessel with a hieroglyphic inscription. Much to my surprise, the Smoking Frog glyph and the symbol for the Maw of Xibalba both appeared on the fragment. Holding the Maya hieroglyphic dictionary in one hand and the pottery shard in the other, I tried to decipher the inscription on the fragment.

I cannot say that I got it exactly right. But I was able to figure out that the fragment had been etched by a scribe by the name of Smoking Frog, not the warrior of Tikal, but someone living at the time of the Spanish Conquest.

This second Smoking Frog was trying to protect what he called the Ancient Word, probably the history, mythology, or ritual of the Maya people, by hiding it in what he referred to as the caves of the Itzá, at the entrance to Xibalba.

I sat in the study for a long time, watching the shadows grow longer as the sun set.

I heard a car approaching. Jonathan, I assumed. I went to the study window and watched as the Jeep parked. It was not Jonathan who got out, but Lucas.

My heart pounding, I grabbed my shoulder bag and let myself out by the glass doors at the back, running past the swimming pool, through a hole in the hedge, and then onto a dirt road. I didn't stop running until I was completely out of breath, then I ducked into the brush at the side of the road and waited, almost paralyzed with fear, to see if Lucas was following me.

When it was completely dark, and there was no sign of anyone coming after me, I crept back on to the road and walked out to the old highway, where I flagged down a car. I told the driver, a very pleasant man by the name of Renaldo Salinas that I needed to get to La Huaca de Chac, the name I'd heard at the taxi stand. He told me it was not far, and he obligingly took a slight detour down a road marked NO EXIT to drop me off.

I found myself in a little town not far from Jonathan's archaeological site. The town was marked with a bright pole light, and was made up of only a few buildings, including a general store, not open, and a little café.

I went into the café where the wife of the proprietor, who told me her name was Guadelupe, offered me a home-cooked meal of *panuchos* with a glass of cold beer. I showed her Don Hernan's photograph, and she recognized him at once.

"He had a meal here, a week or so ago," she said. "He was a very kind man. He gave Arturo—my little boy—a few pesos and was very nice to him. He sat out on the veranda for quite a long time. I did not see him leave."

"I need a place to stay, Guadelupe. I'm tired, and I'm kind of desperate. Can you think of anywhere I could stay that is not expensive?"

She gestured toward the back, and I followed her through the kitchen. We crossed a little yard—I could smell oranges—and she showed me into a little *na*, or wood hut with a palapa roof. In it was a hammock, a

245

washbasin, and some towels. Everything was scrupulously clean.

The price, she said, was twenty pesos, just a few dollars, which would include a light breakfast the next morning. The bathroom was across the yard in the main building, next to the kitchen. I nodded and she left me there with a candle or two and some matches.

I lay in the hammock staring up at the palapa roof. I felt that all the information there was to know, maybe I knew already. That somewhere in my mind I knew where the codex was, and that if only I thought hard enough, the idea would surface. Today being Caban, a very powerful day in the Maya calendar, one associated with earthquakes and thought, the idea should come to me soon.

I lay there waiting for inspiration, convinced that I would be unable to sleep in a hammock, but sleep—and dream—I did.

I AM RUNNING THROUGH THE forest chasing a giant rabbit once again. This time I see that he carries a codex with Smoking Frog's glyph on the cover.

As I am about to catch him we come upon a portal marked with the sign of the Maw of Xibalba. It looks odd, a doorway in the middle of a path in the forest, but the rabbit and I step through it.

Then I am falling through utter darkness, a babble of voices I cannot understand around me. The wind whistles in my ears.

Watching me from way above are two hooded figures. One has the face and the bright tail feathers of a macaw, a bird often part of the headgear of the Lords of Xibalba.

The other has the face of an owl, a death bird, and one of the few creatures left to worship the dark Lords after their defeat.

I fall farther and farther into the darkness until this time I hit bottom. I am in inky darkness, barely able to tell which way is up.

I know there is another presence here, but for some reason I am not afraid. The smallest glimmer of light reveals a black jaguar watching me, and I realize that his eyes are providing the light by which I can see him.

The jaguar makes a gesture with his head that I take to mean "follow me," and I step into the darkness.

I AWOKE AND NEEDED A moment to get my bearings. I had been awakened by the arrival of a pickup truck, its muffler in serious need of replacing.

I crept to the door of the little hut and looked back toward the café. It was closed now, only one light illuminating the back door.

Guadelupe had told me that her husband had taken a second job to help make ends meet and that she was expecting him very late. I saw a light in the café come on briefly, then go out, then another go on in the bathroom just off the restaurant. I assumed the proprietor was home for the night.

It was a while before I returned to my hammock and was able to sleep again. For a long time I sat in the doorway, looking up at the millions of stars of the southern sky, which seemed to me to be suspended only a few feet above my head.

I was not entirely sure what my dream meant, all those strange creatures, and the fall into darkness. But one thing it had made clear to me was that what I sought was right under my nose, and had been all the time.

ETZ'NAB

AND HOW, AND BY WHOM, are the Lords of Darkness defeated? Is it by someone pure of heart and spirit who overcomes all temptations to win the day? Or by a great warrior who kills the monster and saves the world? Or someone who gives up his life so that the rest may be saved?

Not at all. The Lords of Darkness are defeated by a pair of ragtag dancers and magicians, through nothing more lofty than trickery.

The Xibalbans, convinced their enemies the Hero Twins have been utterly defeated, are interested to hear of two vagabonds who are said to perform amazing feats of magic.

Looking for some entertainment, the Xibalbans command the two to come and perform for them. The two vagabonds protest that they are not adequate enough entertainers to perform for the Lords, but they come anyway. They will not reveal their names.

So they appear before the Lords of Darkness. They

dance the dance of the poorwill, the dance of the weasel, the dance of the armadillo.

They set fire to a house and restore it. They kill a dog and bring it back to life. The Xibalbans thirst for more and demand a human sacrifice. A man is chosen, his heart ripped out, and then he, too, is brought back to life. Needless to say, he is very happy to be alive.

Even that is not enough to satisfy the Lords, who demand that the vagabonds sacrifice themselves. So Xbalanque (because of course the vagabonds are the Hero Twins still—or is once again?—alive) sacrifices Hunahpu and brings him back to life as well.

The Lords of Darkness then ask to be part of the performance. They want to be sacrificed and brought back to life, too. One Death, head Lord of Xibalba, and Seven Death step forward.

One Death goes first. He is sacrificed. The vagabonds do not bring him back to life. Seven Death pleads for mercy, but he, too, is sacrificed. The rest of the Lords cower before the magicians, and the Hero Twins reveal themselves. The defeat of the Lords of Xibalba is complete.

I AWOKE TO A VERY strange sensation. I felt as if the room were swaying, and I could feel hot breath on my face. It was a baffling experience, but when I opened my eyes, all became clear. There was little Arturo peering at me from very close up. He was also rocking the hammock. It was the first time I had felt like laughing in days, and I did, a hearty laugh that sent him scurrying for safety.

Guadelupe was looking for him, and she was displeased to find her son bothering me. I told her it was okay, and that I would be over to the café shortly for a cup of coffee.

It didn't take me long to get there. I'd slept in my clothes, of course. I had nothing else. I was counting on the general store for a lot of things.

I was too nervous about being seen to sit on the veranda, so I had my coffee and some biscuits in the bar area, then went out back to get the lay of the land.

The village was really tiny, but quite attractive. While the little houses were really only huts, they seemed well kept, and the colors were wonderful. The general store was painted an astonishingly bright purple with hot-pink trim. The café itself was a brilliant aqua, also with pink trim.

The rest of the houses were whitewashed, like my little hut out back of the café. Bougainvilleas climbed everywhere, and almost all the houses had window boxes filled with scarlet blooms.

Out back there was a communal well where the women of the village seemed to congregate. The object of their attention this morning was undoubtedly me.

There was also a play area. The older village boys were playing volleyball in a desultory way until I came along, and then with an audience, the game became rather more competitive.

One of the boys, Carlos by name, he told me, came over. Obviously the leader of the group, he was the logical one to inquire what the *gringa* was doing here.

I told him I was just a tourist, but that I really wanted to see the countryside. He looked suitably dubious.

I asked him about the name of the town—La Huaca de Chac.

"That's a mixture of Spanish and Maya," he said shyly. "*Huaca* in Spanish is a sacred place and Chac—well, Chac is the Maya rain god, a very powerful god.

"No one knew why our town was called that until very recently. Not very far from here, archaeologists have found a cave with huge carvings of Chacs. My father works there, and he's told me about it.

"My father says that our people, the Maya, were a great civilization at one time, with huge cities and everything. He says the more we learn about them, the more proud of being Maya we can be."

I told him I agreed with him, and I thought back to my earlier conversation with Esperanza about how Maya youth are turning their backs on their heritage.

But Carlos was right. The more we learned about Maya civilization, the more impressive it became. All the more reason to find Smoking Frog's codex. But I wanted to hear more about the cave.

"What you are telling me about the cave, the sacred place, is amazing," I said. "Is it possible for tourists to see this cave? Is it open to the public?"

"No, it isn't. And maybe it never will be," he said, lowering his voice. "My dad says the gods are angry that we are working there."

"What makes him say that?" I asked.

"Things," he replied. "Just things." And with that, he turned back to his volleyball game.

Just about then the general store opened for business. I went in and was greeted by a woman by the name of

Maria, who, like Guadelupe, was minding the family business while her husband worked elsewhere to add to the family's meager earnings.

I spent a long time in the store. First I attended to personal necessities. The store had a small section in the back that sold toiletries, so I was able to get a toothbrush and toothpaste and shampoo.

Next I stocked up for the expedition I was planning to take. I found a couple of tarpaulins, an army camouflage color, some rope, and flashlight batteries. I also found a little compass, but it looked as if it had come from a cereal box, so I was hesitant to rely on it.

In a dusty old corner filled with various secondhand and broken things, I found an old pair of army binoculars in a brown leather case. One lens was scratched, and the covers for both lenses were missing. The strap for the case was long gone, too. But all things considered, it was perfect, particularly the price, which was about five dollars. I then found a backpack, also used, but still serviceable, to put everything in. I felt pleased with my purchases.

Next I went back to the café and asked Guadelupe if I could stay another night, and if she could make me up a sandwich, a *torta,* to go. She agreed.

Soon I was hiking into the forest in the general direction of the cave. I was not entirely sure how to reach it, and I certainly did not wish to blunder in, so I moved cautiously through the forest.

I smelled smoke before I actually heard the voices, and was able to take cover, then move forward very cautiously toward a small clearing in the forest.

Four men were sitting in a semicircle under an overhang of rock. One of the men, an older man, was tending to something, which, when I trained my binoculars on it, appeared to be an altar of some kind with some candles and a pottery brazier in which something, probably copal incense, was burning. The older man chanted quietly while the others spoke to each other.

Because of their position, I could see only three of the men, the old man who appeared to be functioning as a priest or shaman, a young man, and another older man. The fourth man had his back to me, and had a black windbreaker pulled up high, so that I could not see him.

They spoke in low voices, presumably so that they would not interrupt the ceremony, whatever it might be. The young man appeared agitated, and his voice carried better than the others.

"I don't care what you say," the young man said. "There is something really funny going on in that place. It gives me the creeps."

If he was talking about the cave, that opinion was beginning to sound universal.

The older man made a dismissive gesture, and made some sort of joke at the expense of the younger man that I could not hear, but that made the other two laugh.

"It was blood," the young man said. "Not water, not mud, not someone's lunch. Blood!"

One of the men said something I couldn't hear again.

"It was before Gustavo cut his hand, not after, so don't give me that one!

"And anyway, how do you explain the moving crates?"

"The artifacts are still there. That's all that counts."

"Crates don't move by themselves," the young man said.

"And who do you think is moving them?" the older man asked. "The Lords of Darkness?"

All of them laughed at that.

"Maybe it's the Children of the Talking Cross," the older man went on. "Hiding out in the cave during the night when we're not there, stealing artifacts to add to their growing collection."

The group really found that hilarious. The older man was rocking with laughter.

"The Children of the Talking Cross are a figment of someone's imagination," the third man said. "Just like all this stuff about vanishing crates and pools of mystery blood are figments of yours," he said, gesturing in the direction of the young man.

The young man looked sullen. "Maybe then the real guerrillas should do something."

"Maybe they are," the older man said.

Suddenly the fourth man, who up until this moment had said nothing, leaned forward and began to speak very softly. All three leaned forward to hear him. I could not.

After a few minutes the three nodded, and then got up and shook hands.

"I'll take the watch tonight," the third man said. "You are on duty tomorrow," he said, gesturing toward the mystery man, who nodded.

I pulled back into the forest as the four left, walking away from my position. I kept my binoculars trained on the fourth man, who, obligingly, paused at the edge of the clearing and looked back.

Lucas May again! He appeared to be looking directly at me and I held my breath. But of course I was using binoculars and he was not. I wondered if he had caught a flash from the lens or something. But after a few seconds he turned back and followed the others.

I sat back on my tarpaulin, my back against a tree, and thought about all this.

Who were these people? Guerrillas? Zapatistas? And were they, too, on the trail of Smoking Frog's codex? Certainly such a find would be a powerful tool to increase nationalistic feelings among the indigenous peoples, and as such would be a potent weapon for the guerrilla groups.

If the group, whoever they were, was intending to guard the cave at night, then this would definitely throw a wrench into my plans. I would have to find some way of luring the watchman away, or distracting him in some way.

I found a place in the forest where I could see the cave opening clearly. Workmen came and went, and I was able to pick out the three men who had been with Lucas in the clearing in the forest.

About one, I munched on the sandwich Guadelupe had given me, and sipped at the bottled water she had included with my lunch. I had told her that I was going to be exploring the countryside on foot, and she gave me a big lunch so I could keep up my strength, I guess. Sitting there in the woods, it was difficult after this big lunch to stay awake, and it is possible that I dozed off from time to time.

At about five the Jeep pulled up and Jonathan got out.

I watched him carefully as he went into the cave. About an hour later he and Lucas came out at the same time, got into their vehicles—Jonathan the Jeep, Lucas one of the pickup trucks—and pulled away. I wondered where Jonathan thought I was, and whether or not he was worried about me.

Shortly after that a whistle sounded, and the workmen trudged wearily out of the cave. The last man out turned off the generator.

Several of them crowded into the back of another truck, which was driven by one of the men from the forest. A couple of others waved and headed off cross country, presumably for another village. One of them was the man who had volunteered for tonight's watch, if I was not mistaken about the intent of that conversation in the woods.

The site was absolutely silent. Darkness came quickly, and the forest itself seemed very dark. Still, I didn't move, but kept scanning for some signs of movement near the site.

I waited for more than an hour before I saw it. Just a quick burst of light, a match struck, then quickly extinguished. Perhaps he was lighting a cigarette, or perhaps checking his watch. But it was enough for me to locate the position of the watchman.

He was fairly close to the cave entrance, and I knew it would not be possible to get into the cave that night.

Tomorrow, however, Lucas was on watch, and that presented some interesting possibilities.

When I returned to the village, I found the boys playing at volleyball by the light of a bright pole lamp. I called my young friend Carlos, and he and I talked awhile. After a few minutes he and I had a deal. If trickery was what it took to defeat the Lords of Darkness, then trickery it would have to be.

Today was Etz'nab, the day associated with sacrifice, with the obsidian blade used for that purpose. If anything was going to be sacrificed, I suppose it was the truth.

CAUAC

THE STORM BEGAN JUST AFTER dawn with surprising ferocity. Just before the first light, the air became very heavy and still, the calm before the storm. Then the first large drops of rain fell, forming little craters in the dry soil. But these soon vanished before the onslaught. Sheets of water, driven by heavy winds, blasted the roads, making them muddy tracks in a matter of minutes.

Thunder rumbled almost constantly, and lightning cracked with elemental force, sending the little dogs in the village whimpering for favorite hiding places.

The storm's intensity, together with its arrival several weeks ahead of the rainy season, surprised everyone. Anyone unfortunate enough to be out and about that early was caught largely unawares, and scurried quickly for cover.

By noon the storm was the number-one topic of discussion and debate in the village, where theories ranged from clouds of dust in the stratosphere, caused by volcanic eruptions in the South Pacific, to holes in the ozone, to destruction of the rain forest, to my personal favorite, the rain gods' anger with the current political shenanigans in Mexico City.

From my perspective, the last theory was closest to the truth. The storm was here because this was Cauac, a day of thunder and lightning. The Tzolkin was unfolding as it should.

By midafternoon, I had ensconced myself in a little lean-to in the forest, one tarpaulin under me to keep me out of the mud, the other strung from three branches over my head to provide some shelter. Fortunately the storm was abating.

My binoculars were trained on the entrance to the cave, several hundred yards away. I wasn't sure what I was looking for, but I watched with a concentration that surprised me, brushing the droplets of rain off the lenses as I waited.

Siesta time over, a number of the workmen returned to the cave and made a dash for the entrance, newspapers or paper bags, or whatever was at hand, held over their heads for protection from the rain.

About five once again, a pickup truck arrived, and Lucas got out and made the dash for cover. A few minutes later Jonathan arrived and did the same. From what I knew of activities of the dig, both had arrived to check the day's work, and to assist with the recording of any of the archaeological finds.

Darkness came soon enough, and I could see little except shadows emerging from the cave, running for the trucks and departing for the evening. A dark figure that I assumed to be Jonathan got into the Jeep and pulled onto the road, or what was left of it after the torrents of water, turning in the direction of his house.

A few minutes later another figure followed, presumably Lucas, the generator at the entrance was turned off, and a truck pulled away, leaving the site in silence and darkness.

I waited, my binoculars trained on the spot where the sentry had stationed himself the previous night. If I had calculated correctly, Lucas would be doubling back to the spot. Soon I saw some movement in that general area, but I couldn't be sure. Lucas, if there, was stealthier than last night's sentry.

Right on time, Carlos, my young and unwitting co-conspirator, showed up, his flashlight announcing his arrival long before he actually got there. By the time he reached the cave entrance, Lucas was down there to meet him. Carlos handed him a letter and Lucas read it by the light from Carlos's flashlight.

Carlos left, and shortly after that I could see some movement in the darkness down by the entrance. A few minutes later I heard an engine start up somewhere down the road, and soon Lucas's pickup went by the site, heading out to the main road.

I did not have to ask what the note said. It was from me, telling him I had news about the murder of Don Hernan and asking him to meet me at the *museo* at ten P.M. I figured that would mean he would have to leave right away for Mérida, and it would keep him fully occupied for the evening. I believed that unless he found someone else to stand his watch—and I didn't think I had allowed him enough time to do so—I now had the place to myself.

I very carefully checked my watch in a short burst from my flashlight, concealed as best I could. It was now about eight P.M. I decided to wait another couple of hours before proceeding. I unwrapped the *torta* Guadelupe had given me and sat munching it, taking swigs from my water bottle. A rather soggy dinner, but it would have to do.

The time passed extremely slowly, and I was beginning to lose my concentration. Suddenly I had the sense of another presence. I froze in my place and peered in the direction of the cave.

I thought I saw some movement near the cave entrance, but in the darkness, and without benefit of the moon on such a stormy night, I couldn't be sure. The generator was certainly not turned on, and I had not seen a flashlight.

I waited another hour, however, just in case. I neither heard nor saw anything else except the sound of the wind in the trees, and the rain, and in the distance, thunder. Even the creatures of the forest, the owls, the night insects, had all taken shelter from the storm.

Just before midnight, I decided to make my move. Leaving my tarpaulin behind, I moved as quietly and carefully as I could to the cave entrance. I remembered that the entranceway was fairly steep, but was unprepared for the slippery slope it had become because of the storm. I slipped in the mud and slid down the first slope on the seat of my pants, making a fair amount of noise as I did so. I moved cautiously after that, holding on to the line from the generator to find my way, until I felt I was a safe distance inside.

Then I switched on my flashlight, certain that it could not be seen from the entranceway, and proceeded toward the cavern, stopping at intervals to listen for any sounds that would indicate someone else was still there in the dark.

The passage seemed much more menacing than when I had first visited it with my friends, or at least people I thought were my friends. It was sobering to think that one of them might be a murderer.

I reached the cavern at last, and shone my flashlight around the area, trying not to be frightened by the awful visages of the Chacs on either side. I took a quick look at the faint carving over the tunnel, which dropped off into the cenote, and was both gratified, and terrified, that it seemed to match the drawing in Don Hernan's diary and the pottery shard I had found in Jonathan's desk.

Everything in the cavern was much as I remembered it. The large crates containing the artifacts, all cataloged and ready for shipment to the *museo* for safekeeping were still there, although there were fewer. I remembered the crates I had seen in the basement of the *museo*. Presumably they had come from here.

The beam of my flashlight swooped over the pile of unnamed artifacts—what had Jonathan called it?—the GOK pile, for God Only Knows. It had grown considerably, I noted, and smiled as I thought of its name.

I passed by it on my way to examine the carving around the tunnel leading to the cenote, to see if in fact it was the symbol for the Maw of Xibalba, the place where Smoking Frog's codex might wait.

As I did so I stepped over a dark rivulet that meandered between me and the tunnel opening. A leak from the storm above, I thought, but then I looked again.

It was not water. It was blood. I followed its winding course with the beam of my flashlight. It appeared to emanate from the GOK pile just a few feet away from the tunnel entrance.

I didn't want to look, but I knew I had to. I moved woodenly to the pile of dirt and artifacts and, setting the flashlight down with its beam aimed to assist me, used a stick lying nearby to scrape away the layers of dirt. Soon the very dead face of Major Martinez stared up at me.

I backed away from the horrible sight and turned away quickly, my back to the GOK pile and facing the tunnel entrance, my hands over my face.

I heard a sound, but before I could turn I felt someone grab me from behind. I struggled as hard as I could and almost broke free. But as I did so I lost my balance, and strong hands pushed me very hard, propelling me through the tunnel opening.

It seemed a long way down before I hit the water. Unprepared, I hit it very hard, and my mouth and nose filled with water. Gagging, I flailed about in the water, trying to find first the surface, and then the side of the cenote.

My attacker, above me, had moved quickly to get a flashlight, probably mine, and soon the beam of light was swinging about searching for me. Fortunately it was a long and steep way down into inky darkness, and it would be difficult to lean far enough out to see the bottom without falling in yourself.

I pressed myself to the side of the cenote directly under the opening and tried to get my bearings. There was a small ledge or outcropping above me that afforded me some protection from the light. But otherwise the sides of the cenote seemed very smooth. It would be difficult at the best of times to climb out of this. I was not sure it could be done without ropes and some kind of assistance. In this case, even if I could, there was certainly no point with my attacker waiting up there for me.

I stayed in the water, hugging the side of the cenote, and watched the flashlight move erratically around the space above me. With one swing I could see that there was another opening, just a couple of feet above the waterline. Another tunnel perhaps, or a small cave.

It was the only chance I had, but the beam of light kept moving in a frenetic way above me. Whoever was above me was making sure I was not climbing out.

Fortunately for me, it is human nature for people's actions to fall into a pattern, whether they intend to or not. The beam of the flashlight, unpredictable at first, had, over a period of several minutes, begun to settle into a fairly consistent rhythm.

By and large I found I could count slowly to about fourteen or fifteen before the next round of light came by, and the beam now invariably swung from right to left.

I waited for the beam to swing by, then very carefully, trying not to let my arms or legs break the surface of the water, swam toward where I remembered the opening in the side of the cenote wall to be. When I reached the far side of the cenote, I reached up in the darkness to try to find the ledge below it.

By my count I was now at thirteen, and sure enough the light began to swing around the perimeter, right to left, and I felt very exposed. I took a breath and sank below the water's surface. With my eyes open under the water, and looking up, I could see the distorted beam of light pass overhead.

When the light vanished, I surfaced carefully, then felt once again for the ledge. It took to the count of ten to find it, so I waited in the water and once again ducked below the surface as the beam went by.

I knew I would have to move fast, because it would not be possible to haul myself out of the water and into the cave without making some sounds as I left the water. Once again I waited for the beam, ducked under the water, and then pulled myself up as quickly and quietly as I could.

As I had expected, there was what seemed to be a thunderous splash as my body left the water. The light reappeared quickly, but my attacker must have moved back from the edge after the last swing by, and by the time the light had reappeared, I had pulled myself back far enough into the opening that I was reasonably sure I could not be seen.

I sat with my back to the side wall of the cave to try to get my breath. I could hear voices now, and sounds of activity from the cave. I had an idea that I could outlast them, maybe wait for the staff to come to work in the morning. But I was not sure that I could climb out of the cenote, and I was afraid that whoever was up there must have heard the splashing as I moved into the cave. Either he would find some way to come after me, or would wait long enough that he was sure I was drowned.

So I sat there for what seemed to be a long time, watching from the darkness of the cave as the beam of light flashed around the sides of the cenote from time to time.

I wondered who would be up there. Had those shadows I thought I had seen while I waited outside the cave been Martinez and his killer, or had he been killed during the day? The last person to leave had been Lucas, that much I remembered, but I had not seen Martinez enter in the daylight. I found it difficult to think the body had been there all day unnoticed by the workmen. No wonder they went on strike! But maybe they were all in on this. I'd heard more than one voice above me, but could not recognize them, perhaps because of sound distortion in the cenote.

And why was Martinez here at all? Still looking for me?

Despite the dank, humid air, I began to get very cold. I was wet, and I was frightened, and my teeth were chattering. I tried to huddle up to keep warm. It was some time before I realized that I could feel a definite draft on the right side of my face, the side away from the cenote. Air was coming from the darkness on my right.

That had to mean that there was another way in, or more importantly in this case, out. I turned my face toward the darkness. I could see nothing at all. But I could feel the cool air on my face.

Turning my back on the menacing light, I began to edge my way into the inky darkness. The walls of the tunnel were very damp and the floor very rough. Many times I lost my footing, a couple of times I banged my head on protrusions. I could taste the saltiness of the sweat and probably blood that was running down my face.

From time to time I was wading through water as deep as my thighs. Other times I had to crawl on my hands and knees to clear overhangs.

Another time I felt something brush past me, and it was all I could do not to scream. I could hear a loud squeaking from off to one side, perhaps a side tunnel of some sort, and a stench assailed my nostrils. Bats!

As one swooped past me I lost my balance and fell, lying breathless for a few minutes, the wind knocked out of me by the fall.

But always I felt the draft, the breath of hope, on my face. I picked myself up and kept going.

At some point in my long journey, I began to feel that this was what the last several days had been leading up to; that I had been destined to make my journey through the dark and watery realm of Xibalba from the moment my feet had touched Maya soil. That the darkness I had sought, my almost nightly nocturnal journeys, had been but a preview of this night and this journey.

I began to realize that my obsession with the dark, the pain the light had caused me, had been a symptom of a dark depression of the soul that had begun to show its face during the last few months of my marriage, divorce, and the loss of my precious business, and had become a pervasive and powerful force with my discovery of Luis Vallespino's body and the death of my friend Don Hernan.

I began to see this journey, the crossing of the river of blood, the fall into the dark chasm, and the struggle through this house of darkness and bats as my own personal life test.

I wondered what creatures could live in this darkness so far from the light of life. I remembered having read about fish in the waters of underground cave systems that, in a stroke of Darwinian logic, are born with no eyes. I thought how strong the life force must be for there to be fish with no eyes in these waters.

I had no idea how far I had come, or how far I had yet to go. But I knew that I wanted to live, to see the light again, to regain the zest for life that I knew I had once felt and whose loss was a terrible ache. I knew that I wanted to love again, no matter what the risks.

I felt, or imagined I did, that the breeze was becoming stronger, fresher, every step I took. That the path was angling upward, to safety.

And then I hit the wall. Literally. I was up to my waist in water when I came upon a wall of solid rock.

But the breeze was still there. I could even hear the air whistling. This had to be the way out. I felt the rock like a blind man, trying to fathom what was ahead of me.

And then I realized where the breeze was coming

from. It was through a crevice only about six inches wide and maybe fifteen inches high. On the other side might be freedom, life, and love. But I could go no farther.

I pulled myself out of the water onto a narrow ledge, leaned my forehead against the opening, and cried.

AHAU

I AWOKE, COLD AND CRAMPED, the breeze still on my
face. But now I could see a hint of light through the
slit in the rock, a tantalizing glimpse of a world I could
not reach.

It was very clear that I could not get through the hole
in the rock. I watched, like a prisoner on death row, as the
light I might not live to see again, only a few feet away,
grew brighter with the dawn. I clawed at the rock face in
frustration until my fingers bled.

The light outside began to illuminate my little prison
more and more.

I looked above me, and in the dim light it seemed there
might be a way out, a trapdoor of sorts to the outer world.
I climbed up a shaft, but there was a slab of rock across
the top of it. I pushed with all my might, but could not
budge it.

As I sat there in despair a shaft of early-morning light
shot through the crevice and shone on the rock on the
other side of the stream. I looked longingly toward the
light, then looked back again. The sun had illuminated

what seemed to be a small niche in the wall of the tunnel. I jumped across the stream to where the ray of light ended, and looked inside.

What had Ernesto said? A stone box, sealed with wax, covered with some material that would keep it dry. It was a stone box, all right, and there were remnants of some material, possibly leather or pelt on the outside.

I tried to open it, but the lid fit too tightly. Perhaps it contained Smoking Frog's precious codex, perhaps it didn't. What difference did it make? I wondered. I was trapped here. If I went back, I'd surely be murdered. If I stayed, I'd eventually starve to death, or maybe die of thirst. The water tasted slightly salty.

Didn't people go mad from thirst? Maybe I'd spend my final hours trying to pry the box open. Decades from now I would be found, a skeleton with a ghastly grin on my face, my bony arms wrapped around a stone box.

Alone, I watched as the beam of sunlight continued to bring my little prison to life. I looked more closely at the rock face at the end of the tunnel. There was a carving here, too. Similar, but not identical to the one at the other end of the tunnel in the cave. This one, if I remembered correctly, was the carving that would be seen from inside the realm of Xibalba, the one that led to the world of men.

I sat watching the light catch the water of the little stream, so very clear. I was mesmerized by the interplay of blues and greens as it rippled along. I watched as tiny little silver-gray and blue fish dodged the currents and each other, and wondered where they came from.

Then a mental light dawned, too. I rolled into the water and sank beneath the surface.

I could see the brightness ahead of me, a watery pathway through the rock. The way through was several yards long, and it narrowed menacingly in places. But it was the only hope I had. I surfaced, took a deep breath, and swam as hard and as fast as I could, pulling myself through the narrow opening and then up toward the light.

I was free.

I surfaced gasping for breath into the light. I found myself in a primeval world, a lovely cenote—the clearest water I have ever seen—surrounded by forest. Long vines tumbled down toward the water from the banks several feet above me.

Towering over the cenote was a pyramid-shaped structure, which must have been at least forty or fifty feet high, judging by the fact that I could see it while floating in the waters of the cenote.

I swam to the water's edge and pulled myself out using one of the vines, stumbled up the embankment to the forest, and looked about me.

It was not long past dawn, and the forest was still filled with mist. Faint tongues of sunlight were breaking through, breathing life into the wakening world. I looked at the azure of the cenote below me, the pinkish blue of the sky above and the fresh greens of the forest washed clean by the rains of the previous day, and I thought the world had been created again, all shiny and new, just for me.

I turned to survey the pyramid, guardian of this magic spot, custodian of the entrance to Xibalba, for that is what it must have been. It was in ruins, the steps the Maya climbed for centuries now a ramp of rubble. Two or three enormous ceiba trees, the sacred trees of the Maya, now grew out of the structure, their roots entwined about the huge stones. The temple at the top could still be distinguished, but barely, its lintels and doorway now covered in vines.

But even in this state it was magnificent, and I felt as the early explorers must have when they first set eyes upon the ruins of the great cities of the Yucatán. Even in its desolation, a sense of the magnificent civilization that once flourished here was evident, and I thought of the people who had lived here, the sculptors, warriors, and kings, the scribes and farmers, now forgotten, whose lives might yet be illuminated by the words of Smoking Frog's codex.

There seemed to be a path of sorts leading away from the pyramid and the cenote. It snaked past other heaps of stones and other ceiba trees that appeared to mark the cornerstones of a giant plaza.

I followed the narrow footpath, which became a wider path of stone, then finally a road. I just kept walking.

The day was going to be a very warm one, I could tell. Already ahead of me I could see shimmering in the pavement, and from time to time I thought I could see people in front of me. But I was too tired to catch them and they got smaller as they moved on ahead of me.

Two little figures, however, seemed to be coming my way, and I watched them get bigger and closer with a rather strange detachment.

I recognized one of them. It was Esperanza, and with

her a man dressed in the traditional guayabera of Maya men. As I approached them I could see the shock and concern on their faces, and I realized that I must look dreadful.

Trying to reassure them, I opened my mouth to speak, but my tongue felt swollen, and my voice came out a croak. "I've had a bit of an accident," I said. "But fortunately I'm all right now."

And with that my new and shiny world became much too bright, then faded to darkness once again.

I came to in the back of a pickup truck, looking up at several grizzled faces. One of the men was holding a rifle. Guerrillas, I thought. But my head was reassuringly on Esperanza's lap, her cool hands stroking my face and head.

It was very hot now. My mouth felt very dry, and I couldn't move or open my eyes. I felt strong arms lifting me from the truck and carrying me to a bed. Darkness came again.

Later I knew the Lords of Darkness were angry with me. I had found something they did not want me to find. Their voices were all around me, their hot breath on my face, their hands, rotting from disease, reached up from the underworld to pull me back to their realm beneath the heap of stones in the forest. I tried to call out, but could not; I tried to run away, but my legs would not carry me.

I felt arms around me, and a voice I knew I would recognize if I were able to pull together threads of consciousness told me I was safe. Finally I slept.

I awoke late in the afternoon, judging from the light filtering through the cracks in the walls of the room. I was in a room I did not recognize, on a simple cot. A jug of cool water and a plate of fruit, cheese, and tortillas was on a small nightstand, and I ate and drank gratefully.

I could hear no sounds outside the room, but I got up quietly and tried the door. It was locked. I seemed to have gone from one prison to another.

I was still feeling very weak, but I knew I must get away from here. These people had seemed nice enough, but I was developing a real aversion to being trapped in small places. Furthermore, I was convinced I had to retrieve the box that I felt must contain the codex. Only then would I have some bargaining power with those who pursued me.

I opened the shutters on the window, only to find another set of shutters, these latched on the outside.

There was a crack between the two outside shutters, however, and I was reasonably sure I could lift the latch clear if I could find something that I could maneuver through the crack. I looked around the room until I found a metal coat hanger, which I pulled apart and made into a long stick.

I eased it through the crack, and slowly and as quietly as possible started inching the bolt up. The shutters opened, and I climbed out.

I found myself in back of a small thatched-roof cottage on the edge of a clearing. There were chickens in the yard, and in the distance I could see smoke rising from cornfields as the farmers went back to clearing them for next year's planting. After all the rain, there was definitely more smoke than fire, but perhaps it would afford me some cover.

The pickup truck I must have arrived in was in a shed at the back of the house. There was a flashlight in the back of the truck that I thought might come in handy, so I grabbed it.

A road, or rather a muddy track after the rains, seemed to end at the house, so I moved into the brush at the side of the road and moved parallel to the track away from the cottage.

Eventually I came to a paved road. I looked toward the sun, now low in the sky, and thought very hard about the direction of its rays when I came out of the forest in the morning. I turned in what I hoped was that direction.

A couple of times I heard vehicles approaching, but with the brush at the side of the road so close to the pavement, it was relatively easy to step quickly out of sight.

After about a half hour of walking, I saw a path that veered off to the left, the direction I thought I should be going, so I followed it. The light was growing dimmer, but I was afraid to turn on the flashlight lest my captors see it.

By the time I reached the pyramid, it was almost dusk. I was certain that the shaft above my position in the cave would lead to the pyramid, perhaps a stone in the plaza in front of it. But it would take me a while to find it and I was reasonably sure that I could find the underwater passageway back into the cave. I was unsure how to protect the flashlight until I recalled the slit in the rock. If I could locate that, I could push the flashlight through, then swim in myself.

I lined up the pyramid the way I remembered it, and

carefully climbed down to the water's edge. Holding the flashlight above my head as I swam, I found the slit, and pushed the light as far as I could through it, then dove down and found, albeit with some difficulty in the fading light, the underwater route.

I surfaced once again in the cave and listened carefully. I could hear nothing except the ripple of water. The bats were not yet awake for the night.

I retrieved the flashlight and switched it on.

The box was where I had left it, next to the niche in which I had found it. I rested the flashlight where it would be most useful and, using two small stones, one as a little hammer, the other for leverage, worked away at the rim of the box, which, as Ernesto had predicted, had been sealed in some waxy substance, the remains of which were still visible in places.

The lid finally loosened, and holding my breath, I lifted it up.

I guess because of my intense concentration on getting the box open, and the tapping sounds I was making with my two little stones on the edge of the stone box, I did not hear them coming until it was too late.

Suddenly there was a very loud scraping sound almost directly over my head, and the large rock at the top of the shaft above me was moved aside. A dark figure slid down the shaft, followed closely by another. Both wore black hoods over their heads. The first one carried a gun and it was pointed at me.

"Thank you so much for leading us to the codex, my dear," the English voice said.

I could not believe my ears. My immediate reaction

was that I had been found by a friend, but the tone of voice, and the presence of the gun, were at odds with that thought.

Jonathan pulled the hood off with one hand, the other holding the gun very steadily in my direction. The figure behind him remained hidden.

"You have certainly caused us a great deal of aggravation, Lara, but I believe you may also have saved us some time. I'm not sure how long it would have taken us to find this passageway, if we had not been in hot pursuit of you."

"Who's we?"

"I'm not sure you need to know that. We'll be taking the box, if you please."

"But this is your dig, Jonathan. Of course you will be given credit for the find. I'm not one of those grave robbers you get so upset about," I said, my mind not yet grasping the significance of the gun.

"Credit? I prefer cash to credit, my dear, any day. And this should bring a significant amount of it."

Light was beginning to dawn. "So is this what you do?" I asked incredulously. "Pretend you are on a legitimate archaeological dig, anguishing in public about how grave robbers have got there ahead of you, when in fact you've taken the stuff yourself?"

He merely smiled and gestured toward the box. "Hold it up where we can see the contents," he ordered. I did so with some difficulty. The box was heavy.

The codex was there all right. For the few moments that I had had it to myself, I had seen the fragile bark paper, the beautifully rendered drawings in black and red, and the fluid hieroglyphic text. It was badly damaged, of course, but what little I could see looked legible.

At that moment I had no doubt that what I had found here were messages that would ring across the ages, that would illuminate the Maya past as never before, and ensure Maya civilization its rightful place among the truly great civilizations of the world.

And these people were going to take it, sell it for profit to someone far from Mexico, far from the people to whom it rightly belonged.

"You will be found out, you know. You can't keep something as important as this a secret."

"I think you are the last one, other than us, to know," Jonathan said. I thought about Antonio, and hoped the proverbial wild horses wouldn't drag his name out of me.

"You'll kill me, no doubt, just as you killed Don Hernan"—and then, taking a deep breath, I added—"and Luis Vallespino."

"Regrettably, yes."

The figure behind him shifted in an angry movement. Then I knew who it was.

"And Montserrat," I said. "Does she steal from her own father, or is he part of this, too?"

"Steal his beloved art? I hardly think so. Loves it too much. Prepared to go down the tubes financially, but wouldn't sell a single one of them. Wouldn't ask his fancy-pants wife for money either. His shipping company was useful, though, for getting the stuff out of the country. You might as well take off the balaclava, love, she's figured out who you are," he said, turning slightly to the figure behind him.

"Fortunately for him, and of course for me, his daughter has no such inhibitions. And she's good at math, too. Figured out that if she stole the art, her father would collect on the insurance, and she and I could keep the proceeds from the sale. Worked out well for the whole family."

Montserrat Gomez.

Under different circumstances, I would have found my own stupidity laughable. I had assumed that because so many trails led to the Gomez Arias household, it was he who was the guilty party. It had simply never occurred to me that what applied to him applied equally to her. If he was in trouble financially, then so was she. Wasn't she a director of all his enterprises, vice-president of the investment company, manager of the hotel?

"Can't she speak for herself?" I asked bitterly.

"I'm sure she can. What else would you like to know, since it's not the amount you know, only that you know anything at all about our plans that is problematic under the circumstances?"

"Why didn't you save yourselves a lot of time and trouble and just steal a Picasso or a Matisse?"

But I knew the answer even as I asked it. A Picasso or a Matisse is easily recognized, and possibly traced. And Jonathan and Montserrat would not have had the unwitting help of their erstwhile accomplices, the self-named and essentially self-deluded Children of the Talking Cross.

"How did she . . . you," I said, addressing the retiring figure in the rear, "convince Alejandro Ortiz and Ricardo and Luis Vallespino to get involved in this?"

The figure to the rear whipped off the balaclava, dark hair tumbling across her face.

"Stupid, sentimental children! They never even knew who was directing them. Spent more time deciding on the name of their organization than they did actually accomplishing anything," she said. "They thought they were stealing these art pieces for the cause, for the revolution. They saw the Zapatistas negotiating with the government and quarreling among themselves, and decided that it was they who were the true champions of the oppressed. But Luis wasn't part of this."

"So why did you kill him?"

"Ricardo was stupid enough to boast to his brother about his exploits. Luis headed right for Castillo to tell him about it. He'd heard Castillo give a lecture at the museum about how the museum and the indigenous communities could work together to preserve Maya heritage, thought this might be a better way to go. Castillo wasn't there, of course, but there was no point in waiting for Luis to come to his senses," she said very matter-of-factly.

"And Don Hernan? Figured it out, too, did he?"

"Not him. He just figured out about the codex, and was determined to get it before my father did. He was just a silly old man who got in the way. The fact that he knew there was a codex just complicated things for us. He might have figured out that too many things were disappearing from Jonathan's digs."

"So you killed him here and shipped his body back to the *museo* in the artifact crates, hid it in the museum until it closed, then dumped his body in his office."

"So clever of you to figure it out," she replied sarcastically.

I realized as she was speaking that I had made an error in thinking she was Jonathan's assistant in all this. I could tell by the way she was speaking, and the way that he deferred to her, that she was in fact the leader. The aggressive, stubborn Gomez character gone bad.

"And Martinez?"

"Just another corrupt cop on the take. Thought he saw a pattern, got himself assigned to these robberies, and figured a couple of things out. Seemed to think that entitled him to part of the proceeds. No one will miss him, I can assure you.

"I think you've covered just about everybody now, Señora McClintoch. Except that Jonathan may have to have another go at smothering that Doña Josefina person if she ever comes to. Take care of her, sweetie, and do it right this time," she said, tapping her scarlet fingernails on Jonathan's shoulder and gesturing in my direction.

I looked at this man I was wondering forty-eight hours ago if I was in love with, and said incredulously, "Do you mean to tell me you have killed three people now over a book?"

"Four," he said, turning to me and cocking the pistol.

I suppose no one knows what they will think in the split second before they die. Some, no doubt will worry about the quality of their underwear; others, more philosophical, will wonder if they hugged their kids enough.

I had this ludicrous image of my parents, Alex, Clive, and the Ortiz family gathered in a cemetery around a headstone that read: LARA MCCLINTOCH, THE WORLD'S WORST JUDGE OF MEN.

It was just too embarrassing!

In a fury I hurled the box and its priceless contents in the general direction of Jonathan and the stream just seconds before he fired. The shot was so loud in these close quarters that it almost deafened me, and I felt a spray of rock fragments as it hit the wall above me.

Time seemed to stand still for a moment, the three of us forming a horrified tableau as the box and the codex hurtled relentlessly toward the ground. It hit the stone floor of the cave with a crack that echoed the sound of the gun. But the box landed upright, its contents still intact. As the other two moved toward it I hurled myself into the water and swam frantically for the cenote outside.

I surfaced and started scrambling up the bank, but it was very slippery and they were faster than I was. They must have climbed up the shaft and made for the edge of the cenote immediately. I felt strong hands pushing my head back under the water and holding me there.

Then suddenly the pressure ceased, and I rose to the surface, gagging on the water in my throat and nose. I stumbled up the side of the cenote and saw, coming out of the forest, a semicircle of flashlights and torches, maybe twenty of them.

Jonathan and Montserrat had seen them, too, and were making a run for it. As the row of lights broke into the clearing around the pyramid, I could see the leader. It was Lucas.

He dropped his flashlight and started after Jonathan. I

went after Montserrat. I caught up with her just as she was coming to the outer edge of the giant courtyard, and we went down, slipping and sliding in the mud.

She was smaller than I, and maybe not as strong on a good day. But she was a lot younger, and after what I had been through in the last few days, I could feel myself tiring almost immediately. She also had longer finger-nails, which she used to real advantage. We sloshed around in the mud in the closest thing to women's mud wrestling I ever hope to be involved in, and she soon had me lying on my stomach, her knees in my back, pummeling me as hard as she could.

I managed to turn my head to the side, and said in as close to a conversational tone as I could muster under the circumstances, "Did I mention to you that Doña Josefina is probably your grandmother?"

She hesitated for only a second, but it was enough. I rolled to one side and swatted her as hard as I could on the side of the head. She gasped and fell back, and I was able to get back on my feet.

Then we both froze. Jonathan, framed by the lights and followed by Lucas, was scrambling up the side of the ruined pyramid. Why he chose that route, I will never know. Maybe it was the only one left to him as the lights from the forest closed in on him.

He reached the summit, Lucas about twenty feet below him. But the rain and the winds of the previous day had made the pyramid unstable. A terrible sound, an un-earthly groan, was heard as the stones of the temple on the summit gave way under his weight. Lucas scrambled quickly out of the way. Jonathan was not so lucky.

As we all watched in horror he fell, caught in the vines and stones, his body sliding down with the temple lintel and doorposts until he reached the bottom. He lay there, half-buried in mud and stone, his head at an unnatural angle.

Lucas ran to him, knelt beside him for a few seconds, then rose, shaking his head. The Lords of Xibalba had claimed one of their own.

By this time two of the other pursuers, both of whom I thought I recognized from the pickup truck earlier in the day, caught up with me, and Montserrat was led away.

I sank to my knees in the mud, too exhausted to move.

Lucas crossed the several yards between us, and also sank to his knees facing me. He put both hands on my shoulders, looked me straight in the eye, and said, "You are one tough woman to keep tabs on!"

EPILOGUE

MAYA FOLLOWERS OF THE TALKING Cross predict a coming cataclysm of mythic proportions. According to the prophecy, a new leader will arise at Chichén Itzá. Creatures of a former creation, along with a petrified feathered serpent, will come back to life and destroy all the creatures of this creation, the fourth of Maya mythology.

In the meantime, I suppose, we all soldier on as best we can.

Alejandro Ortiz spent several months in a Mexican jail awaiting trial for his part in the theft of the statue of Itzamná in the Ek Balam. In the end his sentence was reduced to time already served, and he returned to his family and his studies, a much-chastened young man.

Montserrat Gomez will probably not be so lucky. It will be interesting to see what her sentence will be under a justice system that has no presumption of innocence, and no guaranteed right to a trial by jury.

From what I've heard, her defense will be that Jonathan was the murderer, she the unwilling accomplice whose only role was to arrange the export of the pre-Columbian artifacts through her father's shipping company. I expect to be called as a witness for the prosecution, and I suppose I will do my best to see that she is convicted.

Diego Maria Gomez Arias has, to all intents and purposes, lost a daughter, but was reunited with his mother and reconciled with his wife. Sheila Stratton Gomez showed the stuff of which she is made and stood by her husband, bailing him out financially and providing the emotional support he needed through this period. She told me, last time I saw her, that she realized that Diego had married her because she resembled some subconscious image of the mother he had lost, but that she felt, in time, he would come to love her for what she is. She has not, she told me, had a drink in six months.

Told that her son wanted to see her, Doña Josefina awoke from her semicoma, and contrary to all medical predictions is back ensconced in her room at the Casa de las Buganvillas, imperious as ever. I think she must have recognized Don Diego as her long-lost son when he first returned to Mérida, but perhaps because of her colorful past, was afraid to approach him. Now she and her son have been reunited after all these years, and are slowly piecing together the past.

I did not return to my studies. Real life had intervened in a significant way. Sarah Greenhalgh, the woman who had purchased McClintoch and Swain, approached me about buying back a share of the company. She felt, she said, that she did not have the eye for the merchandise or the wanderlust necessary to make such a business succeed.

Initially I declined, telling her about the warning from my lawyer to stay away from business for a while so that Clive couldn't come after me for more money.

Then Clive did me a favor, although he may not have seen it that way. He found himself a wealthy widow, wooed her, and married her in short order. The wedding was, I am told, the social event of the season. I gave it a pass.

But the minute the union was legal, I called Sarah and asked if the offer was still open. It was. I took it. The new Greenhalgh and McClintoch sign was in place a month or two later, all traces of Clive erased. Alex comes in for a couple of hours every day to help us out.

Lucas has agreed to be our temporary agent in Mexico until I can find a replacement for Don Hernan. I'm in no hurry to do so. Every three or four months I fly to Mérida to see what Lucas has found for us. In between we meet in Miami about once a month for a long weekend together.

It was Lucas who first found Don Hernan's body at the *museo*, after days of searching for him, not knowing that Don Hernan had journeyed, as I would later on, to the very spot where Lucas was working. And it was he who put the jade bead in the dead man's mouth. He hadn't been able to save the old man, he told me, but at least he felt he was able to give him something for the journey through the next life.

In many ways my relationship with Lucas is perfect for right now. I'm not interested in marriage again, not yet anyway, and he is a gentle and considerate friend and lover.

It is an interesting question, though, isn't it, as to whether it is possible to have a truly trusting and intimate relationship with someone who keeps something very important from you.

He has not told me who the men who followed him through the forest are, or what his involvement with the guerrillas might be.

Even more important, I will never ask, nor do I expect he will ever tell me, what he did with Smoking Frog's codex. Knowing him as well as I do, I can only assume it will not be used for evil purposes.